Jason pulled out his skinning knife and placed it in Talking Owl's hand. The Indian drew the blade across his wrist, bringing blood. He handed the knife back to Jason and nodded his head toward Jason's wrist. Jason understood. He drew the blade across his own wrist and pressed it tightly against Talking Owl's wrist. "Now we are brothers, Jason Coles. You are not an enemy of the Cheyenne people. You must tell Two Moon this."

That done, Talking Owl sank back again and sighed. It had all happened so quickly. Talking Owl was quiet then and closed his eyes to sleep. Jason turned back to the meat roasting over the fire. When he turned again to Talking Owl, the Cheyenne was dead . . .

"Give me your knife."

Charles West

CHEYENNE JUSTICE

A SIGNET BOOK

SIGNET
Published by the Penguin Group
Penguin Putnam Inc., 375 Hudson Street,
New York, New York 10014, U.S.A.
Penguin Books Ltd, 27 Wrights Lane,
London W8 5TZ, England
Penguin Books Australia Ltd, Ringwood,
Victoria, Australia
Penguin Books Canada Ltd, 10 Alcorn Avenue,
Toronto, Ontario, Canada M4V 3B2
Penguin Books (N.Z.) Ltd, 182–190 Wairau Road,
Auckland 10, New Zealand

Penguin Books Ltd, Registered Offices:
Harmondsworth, Middlesex, England

First published by Signet, an imprint of Dutton NAL,
a member of Penguin Putnam Inc.

First Printing, February, 1999
10 9 8 7 6 5 4 3 2 1

Copyright © Charles West, 1999
All rights reserved

REGISTERED TRADEMARK—MARCA REGISTRADA

Printed in the United States of America

Without limiting the rights under copyright reserved above, no part of this publication may be reproduced, stored in or introduced into a retrieval system, or transmitted, in any form, or by any means (electronic, mechanical, photocopying, recording, or otherwise), without the prior written permission of both the copyright owner and the above publisher of this book.

BOOKS ARE AVAILABLE AT QUANTITY DISCOUNTS WHEN USED TO PROMOTE PRODUCTS OR SERVICES. FOR INFORMATION PLEASE WRITE TO PREMIUM MARKETING DIVISION, PENGUIN PUTNAM INC., 375 HUDSON STREET, NEW YORK, NEW YORK 10014.

If you purchased this book without a cover you should be aware that this book is stolen property. It was reported as "unsold and destroyed" to the publisher and neither the author nor the publisher has received any payment for this "stripped book."

For Ronda

Chapter I

Jason Coles was not in a happy frame of mind. His disposition was caused primarily by the fact that it was necessary for him to be flat on his belly, crawling cautiously up to the top of a low rise in the prairie, when he should be on his way to Fort Lincoln. This little delay in his journey had already cost him half a day and it might be a couple of hours more by the time he took care of the problem.

He raised his head slightly, just enough to peer over the top of the rise. It was just as he figured. Below him, on the other side of the rise, the two young bucks who had stolen his horse were busily going through his pack, taking inventory of the supplies they figured were now their property. Jason shook his head, disgusted. It didn't bother him that the two young Sioux braves had stolen his horse—that was a natural way of life for Indians and he didn't blame them for that. He also didn't really blame them for stealing the supplies he had packed on the horse. What irritated him was the mess they were now making of the pack. There was no call for that.

He backed away from the top of the hill and circled around to the west in order to have the sun at his back. Keeping low to take advantage of the cover the slope afforded, he worked his way up through the buffalo grass until he was within thirty yards of the two young Indians. They were far too engrossed in their newly gained goods to be on the alert for an attack by a white man.

Jason paused to survey the situation before moving in to recover his property. Two Sioux boys, maybe fifteen or sixteen years old, one broken-down sorrel horse for the two of them, no weapons other than bows and knives—they were a pretty scrawny-looking pair of warriors. He felt ashamed of himself for letting them sneak up to his camp and run one of his horses off. They had hit him at sunup when he was saddling his other horse. He had reacted in time to stop them, and he would have if they had been grown men. Before they had made fifty yards, his Winchester was out and he had drawn a bead on the skinny back of one of them. He was about to pull the trigger when he realized they were just boys. He had lowered his rifle, cursing himself for being too softhearted. They must have figured they could easily cover their tracks and lose the white man. Now here they were, thinking they had stolen themselves a fine Appaloosa pony.

Jason sighed as if resigning himself to take care of a bothersome chore, stood up, and started walking toward the two boys, who were still unaware of his presence. When he was within twenty yards of them, he raised the Winchester hip high and started firing in rapid succession, spraying the sand around them, the bullets flying only inches from their feet. The sudden explosion of rifle fire startled the two so severely that they both jumped up in a panic, not knowing which way to run. In their panic, they collided with each other, landing both of them on the ground. When they tried to scramble to their feet again, they were stopped cold by a bullet neatly placed on each side of them. In an instant, both pairs of hands were up in surrender.

"Boys," Jason started, speaking to them in the Lakota tongue, "you've put me to a great deal of trouble." He stood over them, calmly reloading his rifle. One of the boys, seeing this, started to get to his feet. He was stopped cold by the simple movement of Jason's hand coming to rest on the handle of the pistol in his belt. When the young Sioux settled back again, Jason resumed the loading of his rifle. "Now, what should I do with you two thieves?"

The two boys looked at each other and exchanged puzzled expressions. They had assumed that, having caught them, he was now going to shoot them. Jason studied their faces for a long moment. They were still within the reservation although a long way from the agency. From the look of them, they weren't hunting. Jason didn't have to think hard to guess where they were going. He didn't blame them.

"Going to join Sitting Bull?" He paused. They did not answer. "Crazy Horse?" Still there was no answer. "While you're sitting there, suppose you start putting that stuff back in that pack."

They did as he directed. When they finished, he took the pack and put it on his horse. He glanced at the two skinny Sioux boys and, before he tied the pack down, he pulled some jerky out and tossed it to them. Still puzzled, they backed away from it as if suspecting a trick.

Jason smiled. "You better take it. You're gonna need something to eat if you're planning to ride that broken-down nag there all the way to the Big Horn country."

Again they exchanged puzzled glances. Then one of them finally spoke. "You are not going to shoot us?" Jason shook his head no. "We will not go back to the reservation," the boy said, his jaw jutting out defiantly.

Jason shrugged. "I don't care where you go. I'm just telling you you're not going on my horse."

They stared at him in disbelief, still expecting to be shot at any moment, or tied up and dragged back to the reservation. Jason did not tell them that he would not make anyone return to the sorry life the government forced on reservation Indians.

"Now, the two of you climb up on that horse of yours and get going." He pointed his rifle toward the northwest. "Sitting Bull is that way."

Still wary, they got to their feet, collected their scant belongings, and climbed up on the sorrel. Both boys watched the tall white scout with suspicious eyes, finding it hard to believe he was going to let them go. When it appeared he was not going to stop them, one of them, the one who had remained silent until then, spoke. "You are Jason Coles, aren't you?"

Jason was surprised but answered simply, "I reckon."

He watched them until the sorrel disappeared over the second rise before leading his packhorse back to his other Appaloosa.

Jason sat easy in the saddle, even though he had ridden four hours without a break since starting out at sunup. It was time to step down for a while and stretch his stiffening muscles. The line of cottonwoods in the distance indicated a stream and he figured to reach it at a point where it cut through a low flat in the rolling plains. He would rest his horses there.

He glanced back at the Appaloosa on a line behind him. "You didn't put up much of a fight when those two young bucks ran off with you yesterday. Maybe I should have let them have you." He had named the horse White because she was predominately white, with black spots on her rump. The horse he rode was called Black for the obvious reason that he was mostly black. Jason was not a man to put a great deal of thought into the naming of an animal, although he had on occasion become especially attached to a particular horse. Both horses were Appaloosas and the last remnants of Jason's only attempt to settle down in one spot. His thought had been to breed the animals, but these two, Black and White, were all he had left of the original fourteen.

As he neared the cottonwoods on the east bank of the stream, his thoughts turned to the reason he was heading to Fort Lincoln. Once again he was responding to a summons from Colonel Holder. The telegram had mentioned nothing about the nature of the trouble and had only requested that Jason come as quickly as he could. That won't be anytime real soon, he thought. Fort Lincoln was ten days to two weeks away, depending on how hard he pushed his horses. Jason felt no real urgency, to get there as soon as possible, in spite of Colonel Holder's request. If there had been any real urgency, Holder would have told him what it was. Jason suspected the colonel was just dissatisfied with his present complement of scouts and simply wanted someone he had confidence in. *So, I reckon I'll get there when I get there,* Jason thought.

It was still June but the warm dry weather seemed more suited to July or August. Man and horses were glad to reach the shade of the trees. Jason dismounted and led his horses to the stream, which, although down to less than half its normal size, pushed enough water through to satisfy their thirst. While the horses drank, he scanned the horizon in all directions. Just because he was riding through the great Sioux reservation didn't mean any Indians he encountered would be friendly.

Most of the people in Washington thought there were only two classifications of Indians—those who had come to the reservation and those who had not. They saw the reservation Indians as "tame" Indians, while the bands still running free were regarded as "hostile." Jason knew it wasn't that simple. The reservation Indians were finding that the Great White

Father was not taking care of them like he had promised and every month more and more of them were slipping out of the reservation to join their free brothers in the Powder River and Big Horn country. Jason didn't blame them. He didn't like what he had seen at Camp Supply in Oklahoma Territory, and the Red Cloud Agency, part of which he was now crossing, wasn't much better. The Indians living on these reservations were a pathetic looking bunch of people. Once proud and fierce warriors were being turned into "Loafer Indians." He had to admit one thing—the government had been highly successful in convincing the Indian that it was a helluva lot better to die fighting than to rot away on one of their reservations. Too bad the folks in Washington failed to see that the lesson the Indians were learning was the opposite of the one the government intended to teach them.

He leaned back against the trunk of a large cottonwood and bit on a piece of hardtack. "Damn," he uttered. "I'm gonna have to hunt up some fresh meat." He'd made many a meal on the army's hardtack but he didn't like it any more than the next man. Still, it kept his belly from rumbling when there wasn't anything else. There was also a sack of jerked buffalo meat in his kit, but he was saving that back for supper. He took another large piece of hardtack from his saddlepack and broke it in two with the butt of his pistol, put half of it back in the sack, and started gnawing on the other half. He was comfortable sitting in the shade of the trees and, after another look around the horizon to make sure he was alone in this part of the world, he settled back to relax for a few minutes before getting back in the saddle. Without conscious effort, his thoughts wandered back to his early years on the frontier and where they had led him.

Still green on the vine when he first hired on as a

scout for Captain Phil Sawyer, riding out of Fort Cobb, Jason was quick to learn that he didn't care much for the Pawnee scouts assigned to the company. At that tender age it was easy for him to make a general distinction between red man and white—he worked for the army and Indians were the enemy. The army told him that the red man refused to go to the reservation where he belonged, instead raiding the settlements and killing innocent whites, attacking army patrols and mutilating prisoners. It was easy to see a clear line between the savages and civilized man. With experience and years of seasoning, however, that attitude changed until now things were not that simple. Jason no longer accepted his earlier impression that there was a clear-cut line between right and wrong. After many encounters with Indians, he had come to know the red man as an individual and had begun to see that there was another side to the conflict—the Indian side. That didn't mean there were no bad Indians—he could readily think of a few that he had personally sent to meet the Great Spirit. But he had found that the army's way was not always the right way and he was lately becoming more and more uncomfortable with his role as an invader in the Indian's homeland.

He had not been consciously aware of the changes in his attitude—they had been gradual over the years. But they had consequently transformed him into a loner. Oh, he had many friends, both in the army and among the various villages of Lakota and Cheyenne. He had even lived briefly with a young woman of the Osage tribe. But he worked best alone. He continued to scout for the army, but on his own terms. He was a free man.

After the horses were rested, he climbed on Black and splashed across the shallow stream, up through the cottonwoods on the opposite bank, and set out to the north again, keeping well west of the Red Cloud

Agency. He let Black set the pace. All that day he rode on without sighting any recent sign of Indian traffic. The trails he came upon were old and he figured them to be left by hunting parties from the agency. He had traveled this country many times before, so he set a course that would ensure a supply of water. He was to find, however, that streams that had always been dependable before were now dried beds of sand, baking under the relentless sun of the dry season. After several unsuccessful attempts to dig up water for his horses in dry stream beds, he decided to take a more westerly direction. This way he would strike the south fork of the Cheyenne River and then cross over to the Cheyenne, east of Pumpkin Buttes. It would take him a little out of his way but he knew he would at least have water.

There were two more days of riding before he struck the river and it was early afternoon when he led his horses down to the water's edge to drink. There was still enough daylight to make four or five more hours, but he decided to make camp there and rest the horses. He felt a strong hankering for something for supper other than jerky and hardtack, so he decided to hobble his horses and do a little hunting along the riverbanks. Although he had left the boundaries of the reservation some miles behind him and was now in hostile territory, he decided there was not much risk in firing his rifle. After all, he had ridden all day without finding any sign that indicated anyone had recently passed that way.

After the horses were hobbled out of sight in one of the many coulees that broke down to the river, he took his Winchester and started up the riverbank on foot. Within a hundred yards of his camp, he came upon a narrow cut in the bluffs where there were so many tracks that it was obviously a favorite watering hole for antelope. He had hoped to find something like this. *Made to order for supper,* he thought, *this is as good a spot as I'm likely to find.* Checking the breeze to make sure he was downwind of the watering hole, he settled himself in a patch of young willows and waited.

After an estimated hour had passed with no visitors to the watering hole but a few dragonflies and one thrasher, he was beginning to believe he was going to have to settle for hardtack and jerky after all. He was about to get up and hunt farther on upstream when one lone antelope appeared at the top of the bluff. The animal stood there for a few moments, looking at the water below.

"Well, come on down for your evening drink," Jason muttered under his breath. It was unusual to see one of the fleet-footed animals alone. The antelope hesitated, jerking his head around from side to side as if unsure about going down to the water. *What the hell's bothering you?* Jason thought. He knew the animal could hardly sense his presence. He was downwind and well concealed. Maybe the antelope was not a loner after all and was waiting for his friends to catch up. *Something's bothering him,* Jason concluded. At that moment, the antelope made up his mind and, after nervously stamping his front hooves a few times, descended gracefully from the bluff and made his way to the river's edge.

Jason waited to let the animal have one last drink, then slowly raised his rifle and drew down on him. Almost without realizing he was doing it, he whispered a brief Lakota prayer of thanks to the antelope for sacrificing his life for his survival. Then he dropped the animal with one shot placed neatly behind the shoulder and through the heart.

As a precaution, Jason waited a few minutes, listening and watching before he moved out of the willows to retrieve his kill. He had not taken more than a dozen steps toward the slain antelope when he stopped dead in his tracks. A sound, at first unidentifiable, caused him to drop to one knee, his rifle ready. He listened while his eyes searched the edges of the river on both sides . . . nothing! He was about to suspect his mind was playing tricks on him when he heard it again. This time he identified it as a low moan. He had killed hundreds of antelope in his time but he had damn sure never heard one moan. Yet the sound seemed to come from the dead beast, where it lay on the sandy edge of the river.

Exercising extreme caution, he advanced slowly toward the carcass. It was not until he was within a few yards of the antelope that he realized the moaning came from beyond and, at the same instant, he realized the sound he was hearing was a Cheyenne death song. His senses totally sharpened now, he immediately flattened himself behind a small rise in the bank and quickly scanned the river beyond. He could not pinpoint the source of the chant. Weak and feeble, the moaning stopped for a while, then started again. The river was skirted by a series of bluffs and gullies and the source had to be in one of the many gullies that led down to the river.

Jason decided it best to climb up the bluffs and work his way upstream so he could search the gullies from above, figuring that whoever was doing the moaning might be watching the river downstream. Working his way carefully past the numerous coulees and cuts, he came upon a narrow gully that descended to a grassy flat, hard by the water's edge. There, lying among the willows, he discovered the origin of the death song.

The man, a Cheyenne warrior from the look of him, appeared to be alone and, even from his position up on the bluff, Jason could see that he was seriously wounded. Obviously dying, the warrior was too weak to take a defensive position. Instead, he was lying on his back, seemingly indifferent to who or what might happen upon him. This was the reason the antelope was so jumpy. He had no doubt gotten scent of the Indian.

Jason remained on the bluff and watched the stricken man below him for a while. The Indian would lie still for a few minutes and then start his death song again until, exhausted, he lay quiet again. Jason looked carefully around, making sure the Indian was indeed alone. He didn't want to stumble into an ambush. Satisfied that there was no one else hiding in the gullies, Jason finally made his way down to the water, his rifle ready. A bullet from a dying Indian was just as fatal as one from a healthy one.

There was no need for caution. The wounded man made no effort to defend himself when Jason stood over him. In fact, Jason wasn't sure at first if the man was even aware of him. It took but a moment for Jason to realize there was nothing he could do for the man other than possibly ease his discomfort a bit. He was not a young man, and was respected in his village, judging by the three eagle feathers he wore. Jason surmised the warrior had been wounded in battle before, maybe once for each feather. He had been gut shot and the wound looked bad. His belly was swollen from internal bleeding and there was a smell of gangrene about him. After a moment, he opened his eyes. He registered no surprise when he saw the tall white scout standing over him.

"I can run no more; my strength is gone. You would not have caught me, but my wound is bad. I am ready to die."

Jason was surprised. "I wasn't chasing you," he replied, answering in the warrior's tongue.

"You are not with the soldiers who attacked our camp?"

"No, I'm not with the soldiers. I just happened to stumble on you." He knelt down for a closer look at the warrior's wound. "I'll help you if I can." Looking at the wound, he knew that he couldn't.

"Water," the warrior said.

Seeing an empty water skin lying beside the wounded man, Jason picked it up and went to the edge of the river to fill it. When he returned, the warrior took it eagerly but, with no strength left in his arms, he dropped the skin bag. Jason picked it up and held it to the Cheyenne's lips. Jason knew that it probably didn't do the man's wound any good to give him water but he couldn't see any sense in denying him some little comfort in his remaining moments. The warrior drank in great gulps until he started to vomit some of it back, mixed with blood.

After retching uncontrollably for a few moments, the warrior seemed to relax. "Thank you," he gasped weakly.

Jason looked into the man's face for a long moment, not knowing what to do for him. Finally he told him that he was going to fetch his horses and the antelope he had just killed. Then he would return to make camp there and do what he could for him. The warrior nodded, understanding. Jason got to his feet and walked back down the river. As he told the warrior, he would return and make camp there, but he halfway expected the man to be dead by the time he got back.

To his surprise, the Cheyenne was still alive when he returned and even appeared to be resting more comfortably. The warrior, in turn, was surprised that Jason had come back. He smiled weakly at the scout when he came to check on him.

"I'll see about building us a fire and then I'll cut up some of this meat to cook." He glanced back at the warrior. "Can you eat something?" he asked, knowing that it was not a good idea.

"Yes. I would like to taste some meat before I die." Jason hurried to skin and butcher the antelope, afraid he could not get it done before the Indian died. The Cheyenne studied his unlikely benefactor with curiosity. "How are you called?"

"My name's Jason Coles," Jason replied as he busied himself with the butchering.

"Coles," he whispered. "I have heard that name. I am Talking Owl of the Cheyenne." In weak and halting phrases, he went on to tell Jason how he happened to be there beside the Cheyenne River, dying. He and his wife were in Tall Bull's village on the Powder, visiting her relatives, when the village was attacked by soldiers. The people tried to fight but they were badly outnumbered and forced to flee for their lives. Talking Owl's wife was cut down as she ran from their tipi. He was shot in the stomach when he tried to go to her aid. After that, all the people fled into the hills. He managed to catch his pony and escape, hoping to reach Two Moon's village on the Tongue River.

Some soldiers chased him for a few miles, he said, but they gave up when they realized they were too far from their brothers. Talking Owl's wound became worse and worse, and he knew his insides were torn apart. Finally he became too weak to ride and he lay down to rest here by the river. A day passed and he found that he could not summon the strength to get to his feet. He lay there another day. His pony wandered off sometime during the second night and he resigned himself to face death. When he heard Jason's rifle, he assumed more soldiers had tracked him and he started to sing his death song.

Jason cut some strips of meat and set them over the fire to cook. While they roasted, he got some water from the river and cleaned Talking Owl's wound. There was nothing more he could do for it— the damage was all inside and, in Jason's opinion, even a doctor wouldn't have been able to do anything to save the Indian. The Cheyenne had already accepted the inevitable and seemed to be at peace with it. When the meat was done, Jason propped his saddlepack behind the wounded man so he could sit up a little, and for a little while Talking Owl almost appeared to be getting better. He ate the hot meat eagerly, even though it caused him painful spasms and he could only manage a few bites before giving up. He laid back and watched Jason while the white scout ate.

"I think you are a good man, Jason Coles. I'm sorry we could not have fought on the same side." He studied the scout's face for a long time, making up his mind before he spoke again. His decision made, he continued. "There is a bundle under me, under the robe I lie on." With a weak gesture of his hand he indicated the left side of the deer hide he had made his bed upon.

Jason reached under the edge of the robe and got the bundle. There were four arrows with stone heads, wrapped in a strip of fur. He looked at them for a moment, wondering, and then it came to him. Four arrows, wrapped in fur—from the back of a coyote, he'd bet. The shafts were expertly fashioned and decorated. These were the tribe's medicine arrows—Talking Owl was the Keeper of the Medicine Arrows and consequently a very respected man in his village. He glanced up at the Cheyenne warrior and found the Indian studying his face intently.

"You know what they are." It was a statement, for Talking Owl had read the reaction in Jason's face.

"Yes," Jason answered. "They are the medicine arrows."

Talking Owl nodded solemnly. "If you know this, then you know how sacred they are to my village." Jason nodded. "They must be carried safely to Two Moon's camp and returned to my people."

Jason could see the desperation written in Talking Owl's face. He knew the importance the Cheyenne people placed on the medicine arrows. They, along with the medicine hat, were the two most important symbols in their religion. Without the sacred arrows, they would not usually go to war. They were so sacred that the women of the tribe were not permitted to even look at them. Yes, he knew the importance of the arrows and he also knew what Talking Owl was going to ask him to do.

"I am dying, Jason Coles. For the sake of my people, will you take the arrows to Two Moon's camp?"

Jason didn't know what to say. It was no small request, asking him to ride deep into hostile territory, right into a hornet's nest of angry Cheyennes. Most likely they'd skin him alive for even having the arrows in his possession. He gazed directly into Talking Owl's eyes when he answered. "I thought it would destroy the medicine if an enemy touched the sacred arrows. I have fought the Cheyenne. Two Moon would see me as an enemy."

"The medicine cannot be destroyed as long as the arrows are returned to the people. There is no other way. I am going under. You are the only way." Talking Owl's eyes gleamed in the reflection of the campfire as he pleaded with Jason. "The arrows must not be lost!"

"I understand the importance of returning the arrows, but I don't like my chances of coming back with my scalp if I do what you ask."

"You will not be harmed for returning the arrows," Talking Owl stated.

Jason was not convinced. "How will they know I didn't steal them . . . killed you and took 'em off you?"

"They will know your heart is good because you will bring the arrows back to the people. They will also know that we are brothers. They will not harm you."

Jason began to wish he had taken another trail to

Fort Lincoln. He didn't like the odds of riding into a Cheyenne camp with the present state of hostilities between the army and the Indians. But, looking into the desperate eyes of the Keeper of the Medicine Arrows, he couldn't refuse the dying man's request. Damn, he thought, it won't be the first damn fool thing I've done. To Talking Owl he nodded and said, "All right, I'll take them back for you."

Talking Owl smiled and sank back against the saddlepack. "I knew I had read your heart correctly. Give me your knife." Jason pulled out his skinning knife and placed it in Talking Owl's hand. The Indian drew the blade across his wrist, bringing blood. He handed the knife back to Jason and nodded his head toward Jason's wrist. Jason understood. He drew the blade across his own wrist and pressed it tightly against Talking Owl's wrist. "Now we are brothers, Jason Coles. You are not an enemy of the Cheyenne people. You must tell Two Moon this."

That done, Talking Owl sank back again and sighed. It had all happened so quickly that Jason was almost stunned. He looked at his wrist in disbelief. Talking Owl was quiet then and closed his eyes to sleep. Jason turned back to the meat roasting over the fire. When he turned again to Talking Owl, the Cheyenne was dead. The awesome responsibility of the medicine arrows was the only thing that had been keeping him alive. Jason looked at the peaceful face of the dead warrior and then at the insignificant-looking bundle he had been entrusted with, then back at the face of the Indian. "Yeah, you look peaceful enough now. Your worries are over. My hind end is to the fire now."

The next morning, Jason scratched out a shallow grave for Talking Owl. There were not many rocks to be found near the river, so he dragged a dead log over the grave to discourage scavengers from digging up the Cheyenne's remains. When he had done as

CHEYENNE JUSTICE

well as he could for him, he stood over the grave for a moment. He felt like he should say something, but Jason was not a praying man. Finally he looked up toward the tops of the cottonwoods and mumbled, "Lord, here comes another one. I reckon you know whether he was good or bad."

He saddled White and loaded his pack on Black. He picked up the bundle of medicine arrows and looked at them with a curious eye. "A helluva thing," he muttered. "On my way to Fort Lincoln and here I am with the Cheyennes' big medicine." He glanced down at the cut on his wrist. "Blood brother to a dead Cheyenne," he added. "Helluva thing!" He tucked the bundle into his pack.

White protested a bit when Jason tried to step up in the saddle, causing Jason to hop around in a circle on one foot, the other in the stirrup, while he chased the reluctant horse. "Dammit, White! You're getting too damn rank. You ain't been pulling your share of the load." When he finally got a good handful of mane and pulled himself up, White took a couple of steps sideways, then settled down when she felt the solid weight of the scout in the saddle. Since Jason favored the black Appaloosa, he didn't work White as much as he should, so this routine was one he almost always went through when he decided to ride her. He glanced back at Black. The horse tossed his head up and down as if mocking him. "You know you're the favorite, don't you?"

Jason rode to the river's edge and paused. He had to decide. He didn't take lightly his promise to a dying man, unreasonable as Talking Owl's request seemed. But he was on his way to Fort Lincoln. The telegram said, "Get here as soon as you can." In all likelihood, he would be riding for the army again, maybe against Two Moon's village for all he knew. "Dammit! Why the hell did I have to come this way?" Talking Owl had said he believed Two Moon was camped on the Tongue, near the fork of the lower branch. That was a good bit deeper into hostile territory than Jason had planned to go.

The thought occurred to him that he was in possession of the sacred arrows. As a rule, the Cheyennes didn't like to go to war without the medicine arrows. It might be a devastating blow to the Indians' morale if he took the arrows to Fort Lincoln and sent word to Two Moon that the army had captured the medicine arrows. Colonel Holder would like that well enough. So would that flamboyant rakehell with the Seventh Calvary, Custer. He'd love to get his hands on them. When it all boiled down, however, there really wasn't much deciding to do. Jason had given his word. A promise was a promise—white man or red man, it was all the same. He pulled White's reins to the left and the other side of the river toward the Powder and the Wolf Mountains beyond.

Chapter II

Leaving the Little Powder, Jason pushed hard for all of that day, not permitting White to settle into a leisurely pace. Once the decision was made to take the arrows to Two Moon's camp, he wanted to get it done. Heading due west, he hoped to make the Powder that night. It would be a long day but his horses were rested and fed, and they were a strong breed. He should strike the river by nightfall.

Talking Owl said Two Moon was camped on the Tongue. Even though he had told him approximately where he was on that river, it still left a lot of territory to search in. It was hard to say how long the village would stay put before moving on to another site. And there were other concerns to keep in mind as well. When he left Fort Fetterman, scouts had reported that Crazy Horse's band of Lakotas were camped somewhere on the Little Horn, and that Sitting Bull had moved his village north, somewhere on the Yellowstone. That meant they should be nowhere near Two Moon's Cheyennes, but Jason knew that information was several weeks old. He hadn't hung on to his hair after this many years by being careless, and it was always a good idea to assume you weren't alone in Indian territory because you generally were not. Although he saw no one, there was plenty of sign so he kept a sharp eye as he encouraged his horses to keep up the pace.

A little before dark, he struck the Powder and,

after scouting up and down the river for a considerable distance, he picked his campsite on the western bank. Before making his camp, he took care of his horses. Although both horses had done a good day's work, White was still ornery enough to kick her hind legs when Jason went around behind her after pulling the pack off of Black. Jason, wary of the animal's disposition, easily avoided the hooves. It was not a vicious kick, but more a halfhearted effort, meant to register her displeasure rather than to maim.

"You don't like toting me around, do you?" Jason talked to the spotted white Appaloosa while he pulled the saddle off of her. "Well, you can carry that light pack tomorrow and I'll ride Black. He ain't so damn temperamental."

Late the next day, Jason found the place Talking Owl had described on the lower Tongue. There had been a large camp there, all right, but it was gone now. Their pony herd had just about used up the grass, and probably the game in the area too, Jason figured. From the wide trail left by the horses and travois, it was apparent they had moved farther up past the fork of the river. Jason looked around the campsite for a little while, calculating the size of the village. They had remained there for several weeks, judging by the circles left in the grass where the tipis had stood. After studying the trail north, he figured they had moved out two days before. "Well, they won't be hard to find," he mumbled and climbed aboard Black.

He followed the trail for what he estimated to be about eight miles before darkness overtook him again and he made camp in a shallow ravine that ran down to the river. The Cheyennes had held close to the river and had passed several likely looking campsites. *They must have figured they had run all the game off for quite a ways*, he thought. He was in the saddle again at sunup.

CHEYENNE JUSTICE

A little before the sun was straight overhead, he stopped near the top of a low ridge. In the valley below him, some two or three miles ahead, lay the village of Two Moon.

Well now, he thought as he dismounted to observe the village for a few minutes. *So much for the easy part. Now all I have to do is figure how to ride down there and give them the arrows and ride out again with all my parts.* With the heated situation on the frontier, he knew there was a better than even chance he would be shot on sight if he rode into the village, even if he waved a white flag. He never liked taking the short odds when it was a matter of saving his hair, so he decided what he needed was an escort. He stepped up on Black again and rode down the ridge toward the river bluffs.

He didn't have to wait long. His horses back out of sight in a narrow gully, he crouched beside a scrubby bush near the bottom of the coulee. He had picked this spot because it was an obvious trail to and from the village on the other side of the river. He waited.

He could hear their voices long before they rode into view following the winding trail through the coulee. There were six of them in the party. They were joking with each other, laughing. It must have been a good hunt, he figured. The laughing stopped abruptly when they rounded the bend in the trail and found themselves confronted by the tall white scout. Stunned by the sudden appearance of the buckskin-clad white man, they were speechless at first. Jason spoke before they could recover from their surprise.

"I have come in peace. I have a message for your chief, Two Moon."

Still stunned, the hunters looked at each other with blank, confused faces. Then, as if hearing a signal, they looked frantically from side to side, expecting to discover soldiers. Three of them carried rifles slung on rawhide straps behind their backs and they reached for them.

Jason held his Winchester up and cocked it. "I come in peace," he repeated. "I have come to talk with Two Moon."

The formidable image that confronted them quickly persuaded the hunters, two of whom were little more than boys, that it might be best to hear what the white man had to say. Still there was a vein of defiance that prompted the necessity to voice their distrust. One, a short, solidly built man, obviously older than his companions, spoke for them.

"What are you doing here in our land, white man?" His tone was menacing like the hissing of a snake; the words sounded blunt and threatening in the Cheyenne tongue.

"As I told you, I have come to talk to Two Moon." Jason's face was passive, his eyes unblinking and fixed on the warriors.

"Where are the soldiers?" the warrior demanded. "You have come to attack us in our own land, kill our women and children!"

Jason remained stoic. "I told you I've come to talk with Two Moon. Now take me to him."

"Why should we? You are one man, alone. Why shouldn't we kill you, white man?" He looked from side to side at his companions. They all seemed to nod their heads in agreement.

Jason studied the warrior's face intently for a moment. "Because I come in peace, for one reason. Another reason is because I'd cut three of you down before you could get those rifles off your backs." He brought the barrel of his Winchester slowly around to bear on the warrior doing the talking.

There was a long moment of silence while the Cheyenne thought this over. Jason concluded that the man might be hot blooded but he evidently was not stupid because he accurately sized up the situation.

"I will take you to Two Moon because you have come in peace."

Jason fetched his horses and climbed in the saddle, his rifle cradled across his thighs. With the hunting party flanking him, he crossed the river and rode into the Cheyenne camp.

All activity in the busy village stopped when the small hunting party escorting the white scout splashed across the shallow ford. A group of women who had been scraping hides paused in their tasks to stare at the riders. Some of the men came out to watch, partly out of curiosity and partly to admire the two Appaloosas. As the party rode into the circle of tipis, the crowd of curious Cheyennes grew and closed in behind the riders as they made for the lodge of Two Moon. Jason rested his Winchester on his thigh, holding it straight up with a piece of white cloth tied to the barrel. He wanted to make sure the village knew he was coming in on his own under a white flag and not as a prisoner of the hunting party.

The hunters halted in front of a tipi in the center of the village. For a few moments they stood silent, all eyes on the white scout. Jason looked around him at the sea of faces looking up. In most faces he saw only wonder and curiosity, but in others there was open hostility. An angry word was spoken here and there among the crowd of onlookers and an undercurrent of angry mumbling began to build. Jason didn't like the look of it but he knew the best thing for him at that moment was to remain stoic and maintain a calm, fearless façade. Already a couple of young braves were examining his horses. He could well imagine the thoughts running through their heads. White didn't care much for the close inspection and kicked at one young warrior who passed a little too close to her hind legs. He leaped in time to avoid getting kicked, causing a ripple of laughter among the crowd.

One young brave pushed his way through the gathering until he was almost touching Jason's stirrup. He stared up at Jason in open defiance and undisguised hatred. When Jason glanced down at him, the warrior sneered. Jason would remember him well. He had the look of a young mountain lion and there was a distinctive scar that ran from his chin across his cheekbone. He looked as if he was about to pull Jason from his horse. Jason continued to stare impassively at the young brave but in his mind he was thinking, *If I get pulled off this horse, I'm going right down your throat.*

He was saved from having to take that action, however, for at that moment Two Moon emerged from the tipi. The mob of people quieted down at once as the chief stepped forward. He stood before Jason for a few moments before speaking. The hunter who led Jason into the camp spoke first.

"He says he has a message for Two Moon." He looked back at Jason for a moment then back to his chief. "He is either a very brave man or a very foolish one."

Two Moon nodded but still did not speak. He returned his gaze to Jason, who nodded to affirm what the hunter had said.

"I come in peace." Looking around him at the sea of hostile faces, Jason figured he'd better play all his cards. "I bring a message from my blood brother, Talking Owl." This caused a renewed murmur in the gathering. "He asked me to return a sacred bundle to the Cheyenne people."

"Where is Talking Owl?" These were the first words Two Moon spoke.

Jason looked around him at the people still closing in on him. "He is dead." There was a gasp from the

CHEYENNE JUSTICE

crowd and a woman's voice could be heard to moan. "I am sorry to have to bring the news of his death. I did the best I could for him, but he was too badly wounded to live. As I promised Talking Owl, I have brought the medicine arrows back to the people."

The crowd, especially the women, backed away a few steps at the mention of the sacred totem. Two Moon did not change expression but his eyes widened briefly before returning to their steady gaze. "You have the sacred arrows?"

Jason nodded. "In my pack."

Two Moon appreciated the fact that the white man had enough sense not to display the arrows before the crowd. His stoic expression relaxed and he invited the scout to dismount and talk with him. He had feared that Talking Owl was dead. Some others of that village had escaped and told of seeing the Keeper of the Arrows shot down by the soldiers as he tried to flee. He assumed that the white scout was part of the attack on the village, riding with the soldiers, and he was curious as to why he had brought the arrows back. Also, he would have to examine the arrows himself to determine if they were in fact the medicine arrows. The white man obviously knew the importance of the arrows but there may be some trick involved to gain the Cheyennes' confidence. Two Moon would have to see.

Jason stepped down and went to his pack. Exhibiting a great deal of care, he pulled the bundle from the pack, taking the precaution to wrap another skin around it to make sure none of the arrows could be seen. He could tell from the chief's expression that Two Moon was impressed. The chief turned and led him into his lodge. The scar-faced warrior reluctantly moved back to let Jason pass.

The air was still and warm inside the tipi. It would have been a great deal more comfortable to sit outside in the shade of the lodge, but Jason understood the need for privacy while the chief examined the arrows. Two Moon motioned for Jason to sit while he settled himself on a buffalo robe. He waited while a woman brought a pot of boiled meat and placed it before them and left the tipi. Two Moon motioned toward the pot and Jason took some of the shredded meat, even though he was not hungry. He chewed slowly while he watched the chief unwrap the bundle, looking carefully at each of the four arrows. It took but a moment for him to realize they were, indeed, the sacred arrows of his tribe. Satisfied that they were genuine, he was curious about the man who risked his life to deliver them.

"How are you called?"

"Jason Coles."

"Ah." There was a glint of recognition in his eyes. He had heard the name before. He carefully wrapped the arrows in the coyote-hide strip. "Why did you bring the arrows to me? Why didn't you keep them after you captured them?"

"I didn't capture them. Talking Owl gave them to me when he knew he could not return with them himself."

"You rode with the soldiers who attacked his village?"

Jason shook his head. "Nope," he said. Then, in Cheyenne, he replied, "No, I found him wounded on the Cheyenne River."

"Ah." Two Moon's face relaxed into a smile. "You did not shoot Talking Owl?"

"No. Talking Owl is my brother," Jason replied and held his wrist up to remind Two Moon.

Two Moon looked deep into the scout's eyes for what seemed like long minutes to Jason. "I see no deceit in your eyes, Jason Coles. What do you want in return for this honorable thing you have done for my people?"

Jason shrugged. "Nothing. I was just keeping a promise to Talking Owl."

"You want nothing?"

Jason shrugged again. "Maybe to get myself out of here with my hair still on my head."

Two Moon laughed. "I will gladly give you that."

Outside the lodge, the crowd of people still waited, quiet and patient, until the two men appeared. A small gathering of half a dozen or more stood off to one side, waiting to hear their chief's words. Conspicuous among these, the scar-faced warrior stood defiantly, his arms folded across his chest, his feet planted firmly.

Jason cast a wary eye in the direction of Scarface and his friends. He knew if trouble started it would come from that group of warriors. Then Two Moon turned to a young man in the gathering and motioned for him to come forward.

"This man is Red Hawk," Two Moon said. "He is Talking Owl's son."

Red Hawk came up to Jason and stood close to him, looking directly into Jason's eyes. Jason returned the steady gaze, unblinking. They faced each other for a long moment before the young man spoke. "I was told that my father was shot down when the soldiers attacked the village. Some of the people saw him go down."

"That's true," Jason replied. "He was shot but he wasn't dead. When I found him, he was trying to return the sacred arrows to his people but his wounds were too bad. I tried to do for him the best I could but his time was up. I promised him I would bury him and bring the arrows back for him."

Red Hawk considered what Jason had told him. Then he reached down and took Jason's hand and turned it over to examine the still-tender wound across his wrist. "My father traded blood with you?"

Jason nodded. Red Hawk turned to his chief, his eyes seeking Two Moon's guidance.

Two Moon smiled. "In my mind, this man speaks the truth. He has returned the arrows to us and asks nothing in return. He has taken a great risk in coming here but he did so because it was the right thing to do. He came as a friend."

Red Hawk seemed satisfied. He turned his gaze back to Jason then. "Then he is my friend. I say this before all gathered here." He clutched Jason's arm in friendship and said, "Thank you for your kindness to my father." Jason breathed a little easier.

Two Moon nodded his approval to the young man and then raised his voice for the people to hear his words. "This man comes as a friend to the Cheyenne. He has returned the medicine arrows to the people. I have looked into his heart and it is true. His name is Jason Coles and no harm must come to him. He came in peace. He will go in peace."

There was an instant howl of protest from the warriors standing with Scarface. Jason remained passive, showing no emotion but watching the obviously disappointed warriors closely. They had no doubt hoped Two Moon would take him prisoner for, in their minds, all white men were enemies.

Scarface could not contain his anger. He harbored an intense hatred for all whites, but when he heard the man was Jason Coles, that hatred was fanned to a white-hot fury. He had heard that name before. He pushed his way through the people, man and woman alike, standing in front of Two Moon. "This man you call friend, this Jason Coles, is the white dog who killed Stone Hand of Black Kettle's village. He is an enemy to the Cheyenne! I, Hungry Wolf, say he should be killed for his crimes against the Cheyenne people!"

Two Moon already knew the man who killed the legendary Cheyenne warrior was named Jason Coles

CHEYENNE JUSTICE

but he had also heard the white scout was held in high esteem by the Lakota and Osage for his honesty and courage. He looked at Hungry Wolf with the patience of a man who had many years of experience dealing with hotheaded young warriors. When he spoke, it was with the authority of chief of his people and his message was clear.

"This man is not to be harmed. He did not have to bring the sacred arrows back to us but he chose to do so. It would be wrong to do harm to a man who has done what he has done. He will go in peace."

Hungry Wolf was trembling with rage. He stood staring defiantly into his chief's face for a long moment before turning to Jason. "You are no friend of mine, white dog!" When Jason did not reply but stood firm, meeting the warrior's gaze, Hungry Wolf abruptly spun on his heel and stormed back to his group of angry companions. They followed him as he stalked out of the circle of lodges to fetch their ponies.

Jason thanked Two Moon and stepped up on Black. He picked up the lead line on White and the people of the village parted, making a clear way for him to ride out. He nudged Black and the Appaloosa started back toward the river in a slow walk. Jason looked neither left nor right as he passed out of the circle of lodges but, out of the corner of his eye, he kept a watch on the group of six warriors who had now reined their ponies up at the edge of the river. He had replaced his rifle in the saddle boot but he casually let his hand drop on the stock to make sure it was riding loose in case he needed it in a hurry.

He had just about reached the water's edge when a young warrior standing next to Hungry Wolf could stand it no longer. He suddenly kicked his pony hard and charged down at the white scout at full gallop. Jason prepared to defend himself. Since none of the others moved, he did not pull his rifle, figuring the young man just wanted to show how brave he was by riding right up to his enemy. Black's instincts told him to run when the Indian pony charged toward them but Jason held him back to a walk. It wouldn't do to run—that might cause the whole bunch to chase after him.

The warrior was within thirty yards of him now and he cut loose with a war whoop that pierced the still summer air. Jason turned to face him, striving to keep a casual expression on his face, expecting him to pull his pony up short and probably shout a few choice insults before galloping back to his friends. But the young man didn't stop. Instead, he rode right up beside Jason and tapped his leg with his coup stick. Jason reacted.

"Why you son of a bitch—counting coup on a peaceable man. I ain't gonna stand for that shit!" He grabbed the coup stick and yanked the surprised young man off his pony, leaving him flailing the air before landing with a thud in the dust. He then circled Black around the fallen brave and, with one swing, broke the coup stick across the young man's back. "I can't abide a show-off," he mumbled as he turned Black back toward the river, knowing he now had two bitter enemies in the Cheyenne camp.

After fording the river, he continued to hold the horses back to a walk as he guided them back up the coulee he had approached the village from. Once he had crossed the ridge beyond the river bluffs and was out of sight of the village, he picked up the pace to a fast walk. This was a comfortable pace for Black and one he could keep up all day while still covering a lot of ground. He struck out straight for the Powder. He figured he could reach it by dark, the days being a great deal longer this time of year.

As he rode, he thought over the events that had just taken place. It may have been a damn fool thing

CHEYENNE JUSTICE 37

to do, risking his neck to return a worthless bundle of arrows. But he didn't see how he could have done any differently. He had promised a dying man. And, though worthless to him, those arrows were sacred to Talking Owl and his people. He decided he wouldn't advertise what he had done when he got to Fort Lincoln—the army boys just didn't understand that sort of thing. They'd figure that, if losing the medicine arrows would have a demoralizing effect on the enemy, then you sure as hell wouldn't give 'em back. Jason realized that in spite of the fact that all whites were pretty much regarded as enemies to the Cheyennes, Two Moon didn't consider himself at war with the army at this time. Two Moon, like the Sioux chiefs, Sitting Bull and Crazy Horse, simply did not intend to go to the reservation as Red Cloud had done. Jason also knew that it was simply a matter of time before the Cheyenne chief would be at war. He would have no choice because the government was hell-bent on sending all free-roaming tribes to the reservation—or killing 'em in the process. It was a shame but that's the way it was.

As he had figured, he reached the banks of the Powder shortly after twilight, leaving him barely enough light to select a campsite in a clump of cottonwoods hard by the water's edge. He watered the horses and hobbled them where there was a little grass, then he built a small fire to boil some coffee and eat some of the antelope he had left. By the time full darkness set in, he was ready to turn in. As a precaution, he rolled up a blanket to look like a bed near the fire while he took another blanket and made his bed under a tree close to his horses.

The night passed without incident. The next morning, as the sun barely peeked through the trees, he poked up his fire enough to heat up some coffee to wash a few pieces of hardtack down his throat before saddling up. He was somewhat surprised that the night had passed peacefully. He was halfway expecting a visit from Hungry Wolf and his friends.

He started toward White with his saddle and she backed away, almost tripping herself on her hobbles. "Damned if you ain't the laziest horse, letting Black do all the work. I got a good mind to load that pack up with rocks." Not in the mood to argue with her this morning, he threw his saddle on Black again. With the saddle strapped on Black, White stood obediently while Jason put the light pack on her. After watering the horses, he climbed in the saddle and struck out for Fort Lincoln, a good week's ride to the east.

On the east side of the river, Black labored a bit when he climbed a rise in the bank. Suddenly the horse threw his head back violently and bucked. A split second later, Jason heard the shot. Several more shots rang out before he had time to react and he heard the distinct whine of a bullet as it passed in front of his face and the thud of two others against Black's side. As quickly as he could, he tried to pull Black's head around to guide him back down the riverbank but the horse was already mortally wounded and stumbled headfirst down the bank. Jason leaped from the saddle, pulling his Winchester out of the boot as he did.

"Son of a bitch!" He cursed himself for not having seen it coming. He scrambled to find cover behind the riverbank while trying to pinpoint the source of the rifle fire. A couple more shots sprayed sand a few feet over his head and he recognized the distinctive bark of a Henry rifle. They were at fairly close range and not very good shots, he thought, considering they had missed him and hit his horse three times. And he knew damn well they didn't want to kill the horses.

He looked back near the water's edge where Black lay on his side. "Son of a bitch," he muttered. "I'm sorry, boy." Glancing downstream, he saw that White had run about a hundred yards down the river and stopped. He crawled a few yards farther along the bank to a log that afforded a little more cover. Very cautiously, he eased his head around the log, trying to find where the attack was coming from. The move was immediately met with rifle fire that splintered the log, and he ducked back under cover. At least he knew where they were. There had only been time for a quick glance, but he had pinpointed the gully that concealed them.

As near as he could tell, there were no more than two rifles, but they had him pinned down where he couldn't get in a position to return their fire. And if he tried to retreat toward the river, he would have to cross about ten yards of open sand, and he would be too good a target for even poor shots. There wasn't much he could do except maybe wait all day for darkness, and Jason didn't care much for that plan.

After a moment's thought, he crawled back along the bank until he reached Black. The horse was lying still now and Jason could see there would be no necessity to end the animal's suffering. The sight of the dead Appaloosa sickened Jason—such a fine animal to be wasted in a lowdown dry gulching. "Damn, I'm sorry, boy," he whispered, "but I've got some plans for these boys yet." He reached into his saddlepack and retrieved the piece of white cloth he had tied on his rifle the day before. Retying it, he made his way back to the log. His movements must have stirred some of the long grass near the top of the bank because the log received another volley of rifle fire, sending splinters flying. There were also several dull thuds that Jason identified as arrows. They were probably the same six warriors he had seen with Hungry Wolf, and he was right about the rifles. Only two of the warriors had them.

Keeping low behind the log, Jason raised the barrel of his rifle and waved the white rag back and forth. The shooting stopped. He called out to his ambushers. "Don't shoot! I'm coming out, Don't shoot!"

There was a howl of triumph from the gully when they heard the white man surrender and the warriors rushed out to take their captive. Coles had been trapped on the riverbank, and Hungry Wolf knew the scout had no place to go. He was glad Jason did not make them waste any more ammunition. "Come out, then!" he called out. "We will not shoot."

"Glad to hear it," Jason mumbled as he stood up, his rifle leveled. The staccato hammering of the Winchester ripped the stillness of the river basin as Jason fired and cocked and fired again, so rapidly the startled Cheyennes had no time to react. In that instant of lightning-fast fury, he had no time to identify targets, simply pumping lead into bodies as they ran toward the cover of the gullies. He saw three bodies go down and a fourth caught a bullet in the shoulder as the bewildered warriors fled for safety. He climbed out of the gully and ran toward the bluffs in time to see the three survivors galloping away. They were soon out of range of his rifle, but Jason took one last shot at them anyway. He saw a puff of dust behind the last horse as his bullet fell short.

Satisfied he had seen the last of those three for a while, he returned to the gullies to check on the three bodies laying there. They were all dead. He turned each one over. The young hothead who had counted coup on him was one of the three but there was no Scarface. *Too bad*, he thought, *I sure as hell don't need an enemy like him.* Looking down at the bodies, he said, "I just said don't shoot . . . I didn't say *I* wasn't going to." He had no qualms about tricking them. He figured the no-good dry gulchers had it coming. Besides, they had killed as fine a piece of horseflesh as he had ever seen. They needed killing.

Catching White would be his next task. The Appaloosa was still standing where he had last seen her, seemingly unconcerned with the conflict that had just taken place, pulling up grass near the riverbank and occasionally looking toward Jason as if only mildly interested in his movements. Jason knew she was going to be difficult; she always had a mind of her own when it came to the amount of work she felt she was obligated to do. He started walking slowly toward her.

"Come on, girl," he called softly. He repeated it over and over, hoping to keep her from getting excited. She cocked her head and eyed him suspiciously, then turned and retreated a few yards further down the bank, where she again stopped and watched the man approaching. "Damn your ornery hide." He cooed the words softly in the same tone as before. "Come on, girl." He continued to walk toward her. She turned and slowly walked a few steps farther. He stopped. He could see he wasn't getting anywhere. Every time he advanced toward the horse, she retreated. He decided that if they kept that up, she'd eventually walk him all the way back to Fort Fetterman. He abruptly turned his back on her and slowly began to walk in the opposite direction. Glancing over his shoulder, he found that the horse was now following him. "Contrary bitch," he muttered and continued walking. She continued to follow. He couldn't help but smile. *I reckon she's like most women*, he thought. *She just don't like being bossed around*.

He continued walking until he was back at the carcass of his other horse, where he stopped and turned to face the mare. To his astonishment, White continued to approach and he stood there and watched openmouthed as she came right up to him and stood, obedient as you please. He held her halter and patted her on the neck, then scratched behind her ears. He was amazed at the horse's transformation. She might as well have said she had decided to accept him at this point. He wondered if it was because the competition with Black no longer existed. Was a horse smart enough to sense that? He didn't know, but she had sure as hell changed. He had never petted her much before, if ever. Maybe all she wanted was a little affection. Whatever the reason, man and horse agreed on a partnership on the banks of the Powder.

After pulling his saddle out from under Black with help from White, he threw it on the mare, along with the light pack she already carried. She made no objection, even standing quietly while he stepped up in the stirrup. With one long look back at Black, he shook his head sadly. It was a damn shame. Once again, he struck out toward the Little Missouri.

Chapter III

Andy Coulter looked up from the sock he was darning and squinted into the sun now settling down behind the roof of the bachelor officers' quarters. He was sitting on the small porch on the end of the quartermaster's shack, his back propped up against a post. A rider approaching from the west had caught his eye and he paused in his sewing to watch. Something about the way the man sat his horse looked familiar but he was still too far out to identify. Curious, he continued to stare. He knew he had seen the man somewhere so he put his sock aside and stood up on the porch to get a better look.

"Well, I'll be damned," he finally blurted when the rider approached the outer buildings of Fort Lincoln. "That can't be nobody but Jason Coles." He stepped down off the porch and started walking rapidly toward the headquarters building, where the rider seemed to be heading.

Jason pulled White up before the hitching post and remained seated in the saddle. He noticed the short barrel-chested man ambling toward him on legs bowed like someone had just pulled a horse out from under him. The man was obviously heading to intercept him, so he waited. When he was within about fifty yards, he recognized him. A faint smile creased Jason's face as he watched the old scout approach, but he said nothing.

"Jason Coles!" Andy called out. "What the hell are

you doin' out here? Are you lost?" The old scout's face was split with a wide grin.

"Hello, Andy. No, I ain't lost. I just thought I'd come out and see if you still had your hair." He dismounted and the two scouts shook hands and slapped each other on the back.

"Well, I reckon so," Andy laughed and pulled off his hat to expose his white, hairless skull. "Just as full and pretty as ever." They laughed at that and Andy said, "The last I heard of you, you was going to quit the army and raise horses in Colorado territory."

Jason smiled but his eyes took on a serious look. "That didn't work out. I reckon I wasn't meant to settle down in one place."

Andy waited expectantly but Jason failed to offer any details and Andy remembered that Jason seldom did when it came to his personal life. "Well, hell. Well, what the hell are you doin' here, anyway? You coming to work here?" Before Jason could answer, Andy continued. "Why don't you sign on with the Seventh? We could damn shore use a man who knows the Yellerstone country like you do."

Jason shrugged indifferently. "I got word that Colonel Holder wanted to see me about something. That's why I'm here."

"Holder? Hell, he's attached to the post adjutant. He ain't in the Seventh. He's riding a desk. Colonel Custer's our boss." Andy shook his head. "And he's a real pistol too, I can tell you. Custer's who you want to ride for, Jason."

"I scouted for Holder before—last time was out of Camp Supply in Oklahoma territory. He's a good man." Jason had heard of Custer on more than one occasion and, while he had never met the man personally, he didn't expect he'd care too much for scouting for the fiesty and flamboyant young colonel. There was that business with the Cheyennes on the

CHEYENNE JUSTICE

Washita, when he slaughtered most of a peaceful village and called it a great battle. Then, according to what Jason had heard, he rode off and abandoned a detachment of his own men when it looked like the Indians might be getting organized to counterattack. No, he thought, he'd just as soon not work for Custer. But Andy sure seemed to think the man was something special so he kept his opinion to himself. "I reckon I'd better see what Colonel Holder wants with me. I'm running a tad late. I got sidetracked on the way." He didn't feel it necessary to explain why.

After promising to meet Andy afterward at his room next to the quartermaster's shack, Jason went inside to find Colonel Holder. A young corporal directed him to a door near the end of the building and Jason knocked and waited.

"Come in."

He recognized the voice as Colonel Lucian Holder's. Jason opened the door.

"Coles!" The colonel got to his feet and extended his hand. "Come in, come in." He shook the scout's extended hand vigorously. "It's good to see you, Jason." Then his face took on a stern countenance and he frowned. "Where in hell have you been, man? I was beginning to think you were dead."

Jason explained simply by telling Holder that he had run into a bit of Indian trouble that took a little extra time to settle and that he had gotten there as soon as he could after everything was straightened out.

Jason looked around him at the tiny office—not very luxurious accommodations for a man who was supposed to be getting his star in a short time. Colonel Holder was quick to answer Jason's unspoken questions.

"This isn't much of an office, is it? They know I'm only here temporarily so they stuck me back here in this closet. I don't even have a clerk, for God's sake."

It was obvious the colonel's dignity had been thoroughly stomped on. "Where's Max Kennedy?" Jason asked. "I thought he came out here with you."

"The sergeant-major's been reassigned. I don't even have him anymore. I don't mind telling you, Coles, they've got me damn well impotent. It's that damn little poppinjay Custer. He knows I'm being called in to work for General Sheridan and he wants to make sure I don't know anything about the daily operations of the Seventh Cavalry." Holder glared at the tall scout for a few moments before his face relaxed. "That's why I sent for you, Jason. I've got an important mission to perform for General Sheridan and I need my own man, someone I can trust."

Jason raised one eyebrow slightly, the only hint that he was curious about the assignment. The gesture was not lost on Colonel Holder. He continued. "I don't mean to sound sinister or secretive. Let's just say I have my reasons for not making my plans public information. So I have to ask you to keep the real purpose of your mission between you and myself. The fewer people who know about it, the better."

"All right," Jason agreed.

"I know you and one of Custer's scouts, Andy Coulter, are friends. I don't want you to discuss it with him, either. I see no reason to let this get to be general knowledge."

Jason began to get impatient. "All right, I won't talk about it with Andy but, Colonel, what in hell do you want me to do?"

The colonel hesitated for a few seconds before leaning forward as if about to disclose a secret. "I want you to find a newspaper reporter in Indian territory."

"A newspaper reporter?" Jason could not disguise his astonishment.

Holder hurried to explain. "A reporter from the *Chicago Herald* has been making a big fuss about telling the Indian side of the conflict out here. Now she's hired a half-breed Sioux named Nathan White Horse to take her into the Big Horn country to try to talk to Sitting Bull."

"A reporter? Hell, Colonel, seems to me if a reporter ain't got any more sense than to— Wait a minute! Did you say 'she'?" Holder nodded. "She? A woman reporter? I didn't know there was such a thing."

"I'm afraid so, a Miss Abigail Langsforth. She's the publisher's daughter and a bit headstrong, so I'm told."

"Well, I reckon," Jason allowed, "and maybe a bit tetched in the head."

Holder leaned back in his chair once more. "You can see why General Sheridan is concerned. He's a personal friend of the publisher and the girl is like a niece to him. Of course she didn't tell her father what she planned until she wired him of her intentions when she got out here. Needless to say, no one here knew what she was going to do or we would have attempted to dissuade her. Now there's been no word of her, or the half-breed she hired, for over three weeks. Her father fears she's dead, murdered by hostiles or the half-breed. At any rate, he wants to know one way or the other."

Jason was astonished. "How long was she here at Lincoln?"

"Two weeks."

He thought about it for a few seconds more. "Why the secrecy? Have there been any patrols out looking for her?"

"No. General Sheridan directed me to keep this incident quiet for a couple of reasons. First, he thinks it best not to let word out that she's the publisher's daughter. It might give Sitting Bull a trump to play if he does have her captive. Secondly, we frankly don't have enough troops to mount a campaign to act as a rescue mission at this point."

Jason looked surprised. "How many troops do you need? I ain't ever seen so many wagons and horses in one place before." He had marveled at the apparent troop strength when he rode into Fort Lincoln. There were wagons lined up for a quarter of a mile. The place was crowded with cavalry and infantry. Looking out to the north, he had seen a large horse herd and two or three hundred head of cattle. "It sure looks like the Seventh is getting ready to mount a campaign."

There was a hint of a smirk on the colonel's face. "The Seventh is mounting a campaign, all right. Custer is leading an expedition into the Black Hills—an exploratory expedition he calls it."

"The Black Hills? Colonel, that's sacred country to the Sioux and the Cheyenne." He could scarcely believe the army would violate treaties with the Indians to stay out of the Black Hills. "Exploratory expedition? Exploring for what?"

The colonel's contempt for the flamboyant commander of the Seventh Calvary was evident when he answered. "I don't really know. Wildlife, rivers, possible locations for future forts—that's the word being circulated from Washington. It's my opinion that the main reason it was organized was to search for gold. Custer's taking a couple of mining experts with him. There have already been rumors of gold up in those hills."

Jason shook his head in sober thought. "Well, if there is, there's gonna be hell to pay. The army ain't got enough troops to keep folks out of there if the word gets out that there's gold in the Black Hills. And you know the Indians ain't gonna stand for it. That land's sacred to them. They believe that's where all the animals were born. They'll fight to keep that land."

"I know. You're absolutely right. But I'm afraid the politicians back East aren't really concerned with the rights of a bunch of savages. The country's suffering a recession now and a gold strike in the Black Hills would certainly help things."

Jason stroked his chin thoughtfully, the results of a gold strike in the Black Hills already painting a picture in his mind of the killing that had to follow. "I don't know anything about recessions or politics, but there's still gonna be hell to pay."

There was a moment of silence while both men thought about the consequences that might follow Custer's expedition. Then Colonel Holder continued. "Anyway, that's the reason we can't send a troop out to search for Miss Langsforth. Custer's all primed and ready to march off on another one of his glory-seeking campaigns with his reporters in tow." Holder, realizing he was letting his bile rise on a subject that was obviously repugnant to him, made a conscious effort to curb his comments. "Well, be that as it may. I'm not sure it would be a good idea to send anything less than a full regiment into the Big Horn country. Our scouts tell us that old Sitting Bull has amassed a sizable force of Sioux, Cheyenne, and Arapaho in that area. I'm afraid the hostiles have us outnumbered and, until we are able to reinforce our troop strength out here, we could possibly be embarrassed if we sent a regiment into the Big Horn country."

Holder paused for a moment, pressing his fingertips together like a steeple in front of his face. He watched Jason intently as the scout digested the information. "I've convinced Sheridan that one man who knew the territory and the Indians has a better chance of finding Miss Langsforth than a regiment of cavalry."

"I reckon you're probably right about that." He

thought about it for a few moments more. "Any idea where she headed when she left here?"

"None."

"Figured. Well, I need to rest my horse. She's been rode hard for the past few days. All right with you, I'll start day after tomorrow."

"Fine. I'll issue you a credit at the sutler's store and you can pick up whatever supplies you need." He stood up and extended his hand. "Jason, I know what I'm asking you to do is damn dangerous and I appreciate it. General Sheridan will be in your debt as well. He thinks a lot of that young lady."

Andy Coulter was waiting for him when he returned from his meeting with Colonel Holder. Andy had made himself at home in a small room that was once used to store rope and harness. His bedroll was spread against one wall and the rest of his gear was in a pile in the center of the tiny room. Jason's nose was assaulted by the strange combination of odors that permeated the room. After a few minutes, he adjusted to the strange bouquet but he didn't think he would care to tolerate it for longer than the one night he was going to be there. Andy didn't notice it. The mixture of hemp, leather, smoking tobacco, and sweat seemed to run to his taste.

"Well, pardner, what did the colonel want?" Andy was anxious to know what had been so important to send all the way to Fort Fetterman.

"Nothing much—wants me to take a message back to the Indian agency—nothing important."

"A message? He called you out here to take a message? What in thunder for? He could have sent somebody from here to take a message."

"Like I said," Jason offered, hoping Andy would let it drop, "I rode for the colonel before. I guess he just likes having people he knows to do his work."

"Sounds like he's a little bit daft to me. Listen,

CHEYENNE JUSTICE   51

why don't you go see Colonel Custer with me? He'd sign you on in a wink. Why, hell, we'd have a fine time. You and me and Squint Peterson. You know Squint, don't you?"

"I know of him," Jason allowed.

"He's scouting for Captain Benteen. They're out on a ten-day patrol right now. He's a helluva scout, damn near as good as I am. Why, Jason, you couldn't have got here at a better time. We're fixing to go out on a big expedition to the Black Hills. Colonel Custer is going to scout out that country to see what's down there. He's been gathering wagons and mules for weeks."

"I noticed. Ain't that gonna rile the Sioux a little? I thought that was sacred territory to them."

Andy smiled. "I s'pose it will, but hell, them hills is already full of miners. I hear they're striking color in every little trickle of water down there. You know, if that's true, they ain't nobody likely to keep folks out of them hills."

"I suppose you're right." He paused. "Although, last I heard, there was a treaty with the Sioux that guaranteed to keep folks out of that territory. Treaties don't amount to much, I reckon."

"Reckon not. So, whaddaya say? Want to go see Colonel Custer?"

Jason shook his head. "I guess not, Andy. Like I said, I've got a job to do for Colonel Holder. I guess I'll be riding out day after tomorrow." The prospect of taking part in a campaign of such proportions held no appeal for Jason. He had always preferred working alone when possible, and the Black Hills expedition sounded more like a circus to him.

Andy was clearly disappointed. "Damn. I'd tell Holder to find him a damn Injun to carry his message. . . . But that's me. I reckon you'll do what you want."

"I reckon."

* * *

He and Andy ate at the army's mess tent that night and again at breakfast the following morning. After that they parted. Andy had some business to take care of and Jason went to the sutler's to pick up the things he needed for his trip into hostile territory. Afterward, he checked White over thoroughly to make sure she showed no signs of fatigue. He checked her hooves carefully for any cracking or other damage, then made sure she was showing no swollen legs. He had to admire her condition. White was a stout horse and she had almost turned civil since becoming the only horse he rode. He almost hated picking another horse to carry his packs, but it was going to be a long trip and he couldn't load White down with the supplies he would need. He decided right away that he had better let her in on the decision making.

After handing his written authorization to the sergeant in charge of the horse herd, he went about the business of selecting his packhorse. In his opinion, there were not a lot to choose from, but he managed to find two horses he deemed suitable—one a shaggy-looking bay mare, the other a roan stallion. Both horses were broad chested and sturdy. With the sergeant's help, Jason cut the two out of the herd and tied them to a tree. Then he led White over, dismounted, and dropped her reins. She stood there for a few minutes, bobbing her head and grunting at the two horses, causing both mounts to stamp nervously. The decision didn't take long, for after another minute or two, she walked over and took a bite out of the stallion's hind leg, causing him to kick and jump sideways. She followed after and tried to take another nip. The stallion sidestepped around to the other side of the tree and White remained standing next to the mare. "Well, I reckon she's made her

CHEYENNE JUSTICE 53

choice," Jason said to the sergeant. "I'll take the mare."

When he had seen to his horses and his supplies, Jason rode over to the small area of tents where some of Custer's Sioux scouts were camped. All Colonel Holder had given him to go on was a name, Nathan White Horse, and he knew there was a better than even chance some of the Sioux scouts could tell him where the half-breed headed when he left Lincoln.

Several scouts were sitting in front of one of the tents when Jason rode into the camp. Conversation stopped as they paused to consider this tall white man stepping down from the saddle. One of the group, older than the others, stood up to meet Jason as he approached. Jason greeted him in the Lakota tongue and the man responded politely. His companions nodded their heads in greeting and waited to hear the purpose of the stranger's visit.

"I am called Jason Coles and I come to ask for your help."

The older Sioux nodded and replied, "I am called Black Elk. What is it you want?"

Jason sat down with the men and told them that he wanted to find Nathan White Horse and the white woman he had with him. The men were cooperative, but Jason sensed a general attitude of contempt for the half-breed son of an Oglala woman and an unknown soldier. Black Elk was the most vocal.

"The woman was crazy to go anywhere with Nathan White Horse. You will be lucky to find her alive." The others nodded in agreement.

"She paid him to take her to see Sitting Bull. Can you tell me where he is?"

Black Elk answered, "I can't say for sure. I have heard Sitting Bull's band has been camped on the Rosebud for the last two weeks. I don't know if he is still there."

"That's a lot of territory. Where on the Rosebud?"

"I don't know, but one of his favorite camps is a few miles above the place where the Elk River forks off from the Rosebud. Perhaps he is there."

Good a place as any to start looking, Jason thought when it became apparent he wasn't going to get much more out of the Lakota scout. "How can I know this Nathan White Horse? What does he look like?"

Black Elk shrugged. Evidently the half-breed had no distinguishing features that set him apart from other men. After a moment's thought, he said, "You will know him by his horse. He rides a paint with black feet."

Jason thanked the group and rode back to the headquarters building. After one more meeting with Colonel Holder, he took White and the packhorse out to graze with the army's horses. He would bed down there that night instead of returning to the post and Andy's stale little room. He wanted a clear head when he started the next day before sunup.

Chapter IV

At the bottom of a deep ravine, some distance southwest of Fort Lincoln, in the dark hills of Dakota Territory, two men guided their horses carefully along a rushing stream. A couple hundred yards away, in a stand of pines, a rough shack could be seen. The two riders stopped within hailing distance of the cabin. Looking from the cabin back to the creek, they could see two miners hard at work by a sluice box constructed in the stream.

"Hello thar!" One of the men called out and immediately the two miners scrambled out of the stream and grabbed rifles that had been propped close by. "Hello thar!" he repeated and the two riders waved their arms in the air. The greeting was met with a wary silence as the miners watched them from behind a huge boulder beside the stream. "We're friends . . . just passing through," he called out again.

"Well, come on in, friend. Just take it real slow so we can see your hands."

"No need to get all riled up," the rider who had called out said. "My name's Pike. We got a claim back up the creek a-ways. Just thought we'd get to know our neighbors." His companion rode silently behind him.

The miners remained behind cover until the two strangers had come within fifty yards or so. When it was clear that it was two white men and not Indians dressed in white men's clothes, the two miners stood up and lowered their rifles.

"No offense," Pike said. "Can't be too careful in these parts."

One of the miners answered. "Mister, that's the God's truth." He walked out to meet the visitors. "Seen any Injuns?"

"Nah. They ain't no Injuns nowhere around here. We'd'a seen 'em if they was." Still he did not dismount. Nodding toward his companion, he continued. "Me and my partner figured we got all the dust we need. We're heading out. How 'bout you fellers? You doing any good?"

The man's partner stepped out from behind the boulder then and hastened to answer. "Hell, you don't never git as much as you need. I reckon we'll have to look a little harder."

"I bet you got a little bit, though, didn't you?" When both men looked a little uncomfortable with the question, he immediately added. "No matter. That's none of my business."

A few steps more and the second miner was out in the open with his partner. He looked puzzled when the two riders slowly began backing their horses away, while still grinning broadly at him. When they finally became suspicious, it was too late. In the next instant, the narrow valley was filled with gunfire from the rocks behind them and the miners crumpled and fell, both facedown in the edge of the rocky stream.

Pike's horse reared slightly and he pulled back harshly on the reins to steady him. The miners were still alive while Pike and his partner turned their pockets inside out. "Where'd you hide the dust? Come on, it ain't no good to you now. Might as well save me the trouble of hunting it."

"You go to hell," the dying man managed to stammer with his last breath.

CHEYENNE JUSTICE 57

Pike picked up a large rock and bashed the helpless man's head in. "What about him, Selvey?"

He was answered by a scream as Selvey's skinning knife lifted the other man's scalp. "Nah, he didn't say nothing. We'll have to look for it."

A moment later they were joined by seven Sioux warriors, whooping excitedly around the bodies of the miners. Pike looked up at them, anger in his voice. "Next time you hold your horses till we get a little further away. You damn nigh hit us." He glanced at Selvey. "They ain't the best damn shots I ever seed, anyway." Turning back to the Sioux warrior, he said, "We've got to find the yellow dust. They got it hid around here someplace."

"Yellow dust is worthless. We will burn the shack and leave this place."

"No—hell, no," Pike retorted. "You can't burn the damn shack. We've got to hunt for that gold."

The warrior shrugged. "We go, then. You stay." After he and his friends had searched through the miners' belongings and taken what they wanted, they jumped on their ponies and left. Pike and Selvey remained to seek out the hiding places that they were certain they would discover.

"Damn fool Injuns want to burn everything." He grinned at Selvey. "Besides, this little rattrap might catch another little mouse. Huh, Selvey?" His partner answered with a foolish grin. "These two was easy. Them last two, up that narrow canyon, got too suspicious and took off. I thought we was gonna have to smoke 'em off of that there ledge behind the shack."

The morning he left Fort Lincoln it was cloudy and gray, and a light rain began to fall before the buildings of the fort were out of sight behind him. Jason didn't mind the rain. It had been awfully dry for a while and the rain felt cool and fresh on his face as he headed once more toward the west. He figured to take eight or ten days before striking the Rosebud south of its confluence with the Yellowstone. It was a long ride and, even then, he would just be at the place to start looking for this foolish woman. He figured the odds favored his mission as useless. Too much time for too many things to happen to the young lady, and most of them were bad.

He looked back at the bay mare following along obediently behind him. At least it appeared she had been trained to follow on a lead line and she didn't seem to mind her role as subordinate to White. The horse possessed one unique trait that was less than endearing. Jason didn't pay much attention to it the first day, figuring that her unsocialized behavior was due to the fact the army relied on grain to feed their horses. He had owned horses before that were unusually windy. His old friend Shorty Boyd used to say, "A fartin' horse is a working horse." After several days with no change in the mare's social graces, Jason resigned himself to the fact that he had picked a gasbag for a packhorse. Sometimes she would go half a mile, keeping time with the cadence, sounding like she was walking through a field full of frogs. He hadn't bothered to name her at that point, so it seemed only natural to call her "Thunder." White, for her part, seemed glad to leave the army's horse herd behind and head out on the open range again, and Thunder's expressive behind seemed not to bother her.

By the time he reached the Little Missouri, the rain had stopped and he rode on the next day under dry but cloudy skies. It was unusual weather for July and the gray overcast seemed to dull the outline of the horizon as he kept to a steady course to the west. At least the cloudy sky provided relief from the hot summer sun. He allowed White to set her own pace and he rode easy in the saddle as he crossed a rolling, endless sea of grass. He saw no other human

CHEYENNE JUSTICE 59

being—not even signs that there had ever been other human beings. The only other living creatures he saw were occasional herds of antelopes and black-tail deer. It was as if he were the only person left in the world, and Jason liked it that way. Sometimes he wished it were true and he realized that these were the times when he was most content.

The morning of the fourth day out of Fort Lincoln was sunny and clear and the prairie grass took on a brown sheen that had been missing for the past few days. When the wind swirled across the long grass it brought to mind the way a thick beaver pelt looks when you stroke it with your hand.

Two days more found Jason on the Yellowstone where the Tongue River forked off. He was at the base of the Big Horn Mountains and still he had seen no sign of hunting parties. He figured another two days riding should take him to the valley of the Rosebud, where Black Elk said he might find Sitting Bull's camp. When he made his camp that night, he was extra careful about his fire, building it in a gully so that it could not be seen. His natural instincts told him that he may not have seen any Indians but they were damn sure close around. He took even more precautions the following night after following the river all day. If Sitting Bull's camp was where Black Elk said it might be, he was close enough to stumble onto a hunting party from any direction.

If his memory served him, he could be no more than six or seven miles above the junction with the Elk River and he knew the village had to be close. He guided White into the bluffs that bordered the Rosebud and carefully made his way along the gullies until he came upon a narrow valley, covered with grass. It was easy to understand the origin of the name for the river, for the entire valley was sprinkled with wild rosebushes and they were all in full bloom. But he took no more than a few moments to appreciate the natural beauty of the valley—fragrant and lovely, it could be just as deadly as it was pretty if a Lakota scout spotted him.

He dismounted and scanned the banks of the river and the trees on each side. There were no tipis, no people. But they had been there; the signs were abundant. Jason rode on down the slope to the river.

It had been a sizable camp and Jason had no doubt that it was Sitting Bull's people. From the looks of it, they had not been gone more than two or three days and, from the way the grass was grazed down, he guessed they had remained there for several weeks before packing up and leaving the valley, heading southwest. He stood near the center of the worn patches in the grass left by the tipis, feeling the presence of the Lakotas as if they were still there. Their spirit was still strong there and Jason could sense it. With the toe of his boot, he stirred the ashes of an old campfire, uncovering some charred bones. Antelope, he thought, or deer . . . but not buffalo. The bones were too small for that. It occurred to him that he had not seen any sign of the large herds of buffalo since leaving Lincoln. Only a few years before, it would have been damn near impossible to travel that distance without at least seeing sign of the huge animals.

He looked around for only a few minutes more before stepping up in the saddle and starting out after the village. They weren't hard to follow. The trail left by the many ponies and travois was close to one hundred yards wide through the valley, up the tablelands, and into the bluffs. There it was transformed into a deep, but not so wide, ribbon as it approached the hills. Jason urged White to increase the pace to a fast walk as he left the valley and the wild roses behind him. More than likely Sitting Bull was heading to another of his favorite campsites and the trail seemed to point toward the Big Horn valley.

As he rode, he pondered his situation. He had no notion of a rescue plan even if he did find the girl. He figured he'd worry about that when he found the Sioux. The main thought in his mind at the moment was that he needed to find them and not vice versa. Unconsciously, he reached down to make sure his Winchester was riding easy in its sling.

Since he estimated the village had at least a two-day start on him, he assumed they had already reached their new camp. The trail followed what he remembered to be an often-used Indian route between the river basins and, if they stayed on it, their destination would more likely be a little further south on the Little Horn. It had been a little more than two years since he had been in this country but the land was still fresh in his memory. Nothing had changed that he could see, except there seemed to be a lot less buffalo.

He made good time that first day after leaving the Rosebud, and he figured that if he could do as well the next day he might catch up to the Lakotas by nightfall. As he anticipated, the village stuck to the common trail and headed for the Little Horn. He began to notice a reluctance in White to maintain the pace she had always been comfortable with before and he realized that he had been pushing her a little too much in an effort to catch up with Sitting Bull. She had had almost two weeks of solid, hard riding without more than a short rest each night. He looked back at his packhorse and her head was drooping a little and he felt a twinge of guilt for working his horses so hard.

"Well, girl, I reckon Miss Langsforth will have to wait another day," he said, and he reached down to pat White's neck. He didn't allow himself to speculate on whether or not that decision might mean prolonging the unfortunate young lady's hardship. In his honest opinion, that lady's fate had long ago been sealed. Either she was dead or a slave—one day wasn't going to make much difference. But one day's rest might mean the difference between life and death to his horses. If—and that was a big if—he was able to find the girl, he wanted his horses fresh and able to travel fast. When he reached the Lakotas' last campsite before striking the Little Big Horn, he stopped to rest his horses.

The campsite he selected was on a tiny stream, some two hundred yards down from the site where the village had camped. He found grass there and a few cottonwoods for concealment. He rested there all the next day. The following morning White was looking frisky again and didn't object when Jason threw the saddle on her. After a quick study of the terrain around him he took to the trail once more.

There they were. From where he knelt on the ridge, he couldn't see all of the lodges but he could tell that they extended for a long way around the bend in the river. There were more than two hundred lodges—of that he was certain. How many more he couldn't say. "Enough Injuns to go around," he muttered under his breath as he watched the busy village waking with the early-morning sun. It was time to make a decision.

Since first sighting the wispy columns of smoke on the horizon while still several miles from the river, he had pondered the question. Should he watch the camp on the chance he would spot Abigail Langsforth and wait for an opportunity to make a quick rescue, hoping to escape with the girl? Maybe. On the other hand, he considered riding straight into camp under a flag of peace. Sitting Bull was said to be a reasonable and intelligent man. Maybe he would hear Jason's request and permit him to take the girl peaceably. After all, Sitting Bull had sent word to the army that he was not at war with them. He just wanted them to leave him to hell alone. Jason would have to think through his options. He moved back down the ridge to the ravine where he had left the horses.

After thinking it over for a moment or two, he decided that boldly riding into Sitting Bull's camp might be a good way to get a behind full of lead. That decided, the next task was to find a good place to observe the camp in hopes of getting a glimpse of the girl. The next-best thing would be to catch sight of Nathan White Horse but he didn't expect that to happen. With a camp full of Indians, he couldn't see much chance of identifying one half-breed, especially from the top of a ridge a quarter of a mile away. But who knows? he thought. Maybe I'll get lucky.

It was going to be pretty risky trying to watch a Sioux village without having to manage two horses and Jason decided it would be too difficult to keep both horses hidden that close to the village. There was a lot of coming and going from the camp with hunting parties moving about. He would have to do his business on foot if he was to get close enough in the bluffs to see, even with the field glasses he had brought with him. So he retreated from the ridge and rode back into the hills until he found a deep ravine secluded enough to hide a horse. He left Thunder there and rode back toward the ridge. He selected a narrow gully that cut into the bluffs about a hundred yards from the spot he had picked to watch the camp. He dismounted and tied White's reins to a bramble bush, then made his way on foot to his lookout. He glanced back at his horse to make sure she was all right. *I reckon I can run a hundred yards quick enough if I have to,* he thought. *I'm damn sure I can if I've got a bunch of angry Sioux after my hide.*

He crawled into a shallow trench carved out of the bluffs between two rocks and checked the angle of the sun before taking out his field glasses. He didn't want the sun to cause a reflection off of the glass. Satisfied he could not be seen from the village below, he settled in to watch.

The hours passed as he watched the village. Twice he moved to new positions in hopes of seeing more of the camp. With the field glasses, he scanned the banks of the river from side to side. There was a great deal of activity—hunters going and coming, women working at preparing skins and drying meat. A group of women crossed over to his side of the river to pick some berries. Once two hunters rode into camp from the north and carried on an excited conversation with some of the other men of the camp. Jason guessed they were bringing news of a large herd of deer or antelope, for most of the men in camp quickly gathered their weapons and horses and rode out to the north. But there was no white woman in the camp that he could see. It was a waste of time, he decided. It was then that he saw something he had hoped not to see.

The day was spent. The sun started to sink behind the bluffs on the opposite side of the river. The hunting party that had left the camp in such a state of excitement earlier that afternoon had returned. Their hunt had been bountiful. He started to leave his position in a narrow gully when a bright garment caught his eye. A young Lakota woman emerged from one of the lodges and came to the river's edge to fill a water vessel. She wore a light dress, with a busy flowery pattern. She might have looked right at home on the streets of St. Louis had it not been for the beaded deerskin leggings she wore under the dress.

Jason trained the field glasses on the girl as she knelt by the water's edge. She was not a slight woman and the dress was still a loose fit. The previous owner of the garment must have been less than dainty indeed. Jason had not asked for a physical description of Abigail Langsforth but the dress looked like something he imagined she might wear. This was not a good sign. He continued to watch her as she turned to go back to her tipi. The dress was cinched tightly across the waist in back in order to make it fit.

"I was afraid of that," he murmured and rose to his feet, no longer concerned about being seen from the camp now that the shadows had deepened. It was the biggest probability from the start, he reminded himself. But his job was to try to find the young lady and, as yet, he had still not found her . . . or her body. That might be no longer possible. *Who knows what they might have done with her?* he thought. Still, he knew it was much more likely that she had been kept as a slave or that one of the men had taken her as a wife. "Damn," he mumbled. "Looks like I've got no choice but to ride into that camp and take my chances on coming out alive."

He went back to the ravine to retrieve his horse. White greeted him with a snort and whinnied softly as Jason led her down to the water to drink. Cookfires began to glow in the Sioux camp as the darkness slowly settled in on the valley, and he could hear the muddled noises of many different voices as they drifted to him across the shallow water. Sounds of a peaceful camp, he thought. In only seconds, it seemed, the darkness enveloped the valley as if someone had blown out a lantern. *I better go find my packhorse*, he thought.

He turned to leave but had not actually taken a step when he heard the sudden splashing of a horse fording the river from the far side. He froze. His hand on his rifle, he silently dropped to one knee and searched the darkness along the bank. There . . . out of the shadows . . . a horse and rider, making their way across—from the look of it, they were in a big hurry.

Jason looked about him to see if there were others who might be closing in on him from behind. There was no one and he realized that he was not under attack. The rider had not seen him . . . still did not see him. In fact, the rider appeared to be doing the best he could not to be seen himself. It was an Indian—that much Jason could tell. *Now, I wonder why he would want to cut out after dark*, Jason pondered. His curiosity up, he decided to find out. He jumped on White and started down the river on a line to intercept the rider where he would come out of the water.

White's natural competitive instinct made her want to catch the horse splashing across the river, and Jason had to hold her back so as not to get to the point of interception too soon. He could just make out the dark form whipping his pony for more speed and the pony was doing the best he could to gain the other side of the river. Jason timed it to parallel the other horse just as it reached the riverbank. About thirty yards from the horse and rider, Jason pulled one leg out of the stirrup and crouched low on the other stirrup so that, in the darkness, it appeared White was a riderless horse. Jason figured, whether the man was running or not, no Indian was going to pass up a horse that practically landed in his lap. He was right.

Startled at first, the rider jerked his pony sharply away from the charging horse that had so suddenly appeared out of the darkness. Then, seeing no rider, he kicked his pony hard and closed again with White. From almost under his horse's belly, Jason could hear the man's voice, trying to calm White. "Whoa, whoa." He managed to get his hand on White's bridle and gradually pulled both horses to a stop. Jason dropped silently to the ground and quickly moved around the horses. The Indian detected the movement behind him a split second before he found himself in midair, flailing helplessly.

He landed hard on his back, not quite sure in the darkness what manner of animal had attacked him. Panic-stricken, he tried to roll over and get to his feet, but Jason was on him like an angry panther, knocking him over again and pinning him to the ground, his knife pressed against his throat. The Indian lay still, resigned to his death. He was truly surprised when it did not come right away.

In the brief combat, Jason noticed that the man's horse was a paint, and he was looking for a paint. Black Elk had said that Nathan White Horse rode a paint. He spoke in the Lakota tongue. "If you lay still, I won't kill you." He pressed the knife harder against the man's throat.

"All right! All right!" the man answered in English. "I ain't moving."

Jason relaxed his hold a bit. "I'm betting your name's Nathan White Horse."

His prisoner, still frightened but relieved to find he was still breathing, replied nervously. "How'd you know that? Who the hell are you, anyway?" He now realized his attacker was a white man. "Listen, I could just sing out one time and you'd have about two hundred Lakota warriors on your ass."

"Well, friend, you'd better sing it loud the first time because the second sound is gonna come from the gap I'm gonna cut in your throat." He let Nathan feel the keen edge on his skinning knife as he drew a thin line of blood across his throat. Nathan stiffened but Jason held him. "Now, are we gonna have a peaceful little talk or am I gonna have to put a permanent smile across your gullet?"

"A little talk. That's all you want? A little talk? Then I go my way and you go yours?"

"Information. That's all I want."

"All right. Lemme up."

Jason covered him with his pistol while Nathan gathered himself together. He pulled the half-breed's rifle out of the sling and then motioned for him to mount up. With Nathan leading, they rode downstream for about a mile before Jason directed him to a stand of willows.

"Why did you bring me way down here if you just want to talk? Why didn't you just kill me back there when you jumped me?" Nathan showed more irritation than fear at this point.

"If I wanted to kill you, I would have done it back there." Jason replied in a matter-of-fact tone.

"Then why did you jump me?"

"I told you. I just want some information."

"Well, goddamn, you could of just asked, couldn't you? Where'd you learn a trick like that, anyway? Hiding behind your horse."

"From an Injun," Jason replied. Weary of the half-breed's incessant questioning, he ejected the cartridges from Nathan's rifle and threw it back to him. "Now suppose you let me ask the questions." He started to inquire about the girl but first asked, "Why were you sneaking out of that Lakota camp in the middle of the night? Are some of Sitting Bull's warriors after your hide?"

"Hell, no. They are my brothers. My mother was an Oglala."

Jason looked at his captive for a few moments, trying to figure him out. He seemed more white than Indian, at least in his language. It was strictly saloon style. "You were damn sure running from something."

Nathan seemed reluctant to explain but finally he admitted, "I was running from that damn woman." When it was obvious his answer puzzled Jason, he expounded. "Abby," he blurted. "That damn white woman."

Jason was kneeling on one knee in front of his

captive, his rifle resting in his arms. "Abby? You mean Abigail Langsforth?" Nathan nodded yes. "Pardner, maybe you'd best explain that."

Nathan White Horse was reluctant to talk about it but, at Jason's urging, he related his short history with the lady in question. "She came to me in town, outside the fort, and said she'd pay me to take her to see Sitting Bull. Well, I wasn't about to turn down fifty dollars."

"And everything else she had after you got out on the trail," Jason interrupted.

Nathan shrugged. "Well, the thought might have occurred to me. But I never intended to do the woman no harm. What kind of crazy woman would want to go out to Injun country anyway? I figured I might be able to sell her to some buck maybe. But there wasn't no use to kill her. She was a strong-looking woman, oughta be a good worker. Well, she showed up the morning we was supposed to leave, all dressed up like a man—buckskin pants, mule skinner's boots, and a wide-brim hat. And she was wearing a pistol on her hip. I shoulda knowed right then I'd cut a plug that was too tough to chew."

Jason settled back against a willow while Nathan went on. For his part, the half-breed appeared to forget that he was a captive; he just seemed glad to have the opportunity to vent his frustrations. Jason listened with amused fascination.

Nathan continued. "The first night out, I decided I might as well see what's what. So I waited till I figured she was asleep and then I snuck over to take a peek into that saddlebag she was using for a pillow. I hadn't even got one hand on it good when she whacked me upside the head with that damn Colt Peacemaker of hers. And I'm half Oglala. Hell, I didn't make a sound! Well, she set me straight as to how things were. She allowed as how she expected me to try to take advantage of a young girl like herself and she was prepared to defend her honor. She said she didn't never sleep, and I swear, I believe her. I never seen her with her eyes closed. I told her, hell, I didn't mean her no harm; I was just curious, that's all.

"Things kinda changed after that. After two or three days out, she started telling me about how she thought the Injuns was being treated poorly and she aimed to tell the world their side of things. Well, I told her I admired that. Before long, she was telling me how proud I oughta be fer being a Sioux. By the time we struck the Tongue, she was telling me what a fine-looking man I was and that she had took a shine to me. Well, that scared me plenty."

Jason couldn't help but laugh. "Well, that doesn't sound so bad to me."

"You ain't seen Abby."

"Is that why you were sneaking out of camp?"

"Damn right. That woman's crazy. By the time I found Sitting Bull's camp, she was talking about what a wonderful thing it would be if we got married and lived out here Injun-style. Hell, I'd as soon settle down with a wolverine."

Jason laughed again. This sure wasn't the picture he had framed in his mind of a frail little Eastern girl at the mercy of bloodthirsty savages. "Where is she now? Is she all right?"

"She's all right, I reckon. Right now she's staying in Two Humps's lodge while Sitting Bull decides what to do with her. Two Humps is Sitting Bull's cousin."

Jason pondered that a moment. "Is she tied up or being guarded?"

"Hell, no. They're hoping she'll escape. They'd love to be done with her." Nathan waved his arms wildly when he talked about her. "She keeps pestering 'em fer a council with Sitting Bull and he told her he don't council with women, 'specially white women."

"Damn," Jason exclaimed softly as he thought over the account he had just heard. Then to Nathan he said, "My job is to bring the young lady back to Fort Lincoln. I reckon that's what I'll try to do."

Nathan studied the dark figure before him in the shadows of the stunted willows. Confident now that he was in no danger from the man who had so effectively ambushed and disarmed him, he had some questions of his own. Foremost was just who this white man was who came alone this deep in territory controlled completely by the Sioux and Cheyenne free bands? Back at Fort Lincoln, he had heard Andy Coulter talk about a friend of his, a white scout who had hunted down that murdering Cheyenne renegade, Stone Hand, down in Oklahoma territory. He remembered the name—Andy mentioned it enough. "You're Jason Coles, ain't you?"

The question surprised Jason but he answered simply, "I am."

"Now what are you aiming to do with me? I answered your questions. Are you done with me?"

"That depends on what you've got on your mind," Jason answered.

Nathan understood the meaning of Jason's answer and he was quick to reassure. "I'm heading straight back to Lincoln. It ain't my business to tell anybody you're here. Like I said, I'm working for the army when I can. I ain't gonna mess around in your business."

Jason was satisfied that Nathan was straight with him and he probably had no intention of alerting the camp that an army scout was no more than a mile from them. The more he thought about it, however, the more he began to believe his only chance to fetch Abigail Langsforth was to walk right into Sitting Bull's camp and ask for her. And, if that was the case, it might be handy to have Nathan White Horse along.

Nathan wasn't too keen on the idea of going back to the village with Jason. In the first place, he didn't know if it was healthy for him to be in the company of the white scout. Sitting Bull might decide to shoot both of them. What he had told Jason earlier—about the warriors being his brothers—wasn't exactly accurate. When he was in their presence, he called them his brothers but they didn't look on him in the same light—in his presence or out of it. He didn't let on that he spent most of his time hanging around Fort Lincoln, hoping to be put on the army payroll. But he was afraid they suspected as much. In addition to these fears, he was not anxious to see Miss Abigail Langsforth again. However, when Jason mentioned that it might be worth another fifty dollars for him if he helped return the lady to safety he had a change of heart.

Jason wasn't sure how much of the half-breed's story he could believe, but if he was telling the truth regarding the lady's infatuation with him, she might be more willing to return to Lincoln with Nathan along. As far as the fifty dollars was concerned, if the colonel wouldn't authorize it, Miss Langsforth's daddy would probably agree to it to get his daughter back.

So the deal was made. They shook on it at Nathan's insistence and they made camp right there in the willows. Jason left Nathan to make a small fire for coffee while he rode back up in the bluffs to get his packhorse.

Chapter V

Sitting Bull set the bowl aside and wiped the grease from his fingers. "What is it that has made you so excited?"

The solemn old woman standing in the entrance of the tipi motioned toward the river. "Nathan White Horse is coming."

The old medicine man could not understand why she chose to interrupt his breakfast for this unimportant bit of news. "Why bother me with this?"

"There is someone with him. He looks like a white man."

This aroused his curiosity and he slowly got to his feet and went out into the early-morning sunlight. The two riders had already crossed the river and were making their way through the village toward his lodge. Sitting Bull strained to see the white scout sitting tall on the Appaloosa, the horse and rider towering over the lesser figure of Nathan White Horse. The stranger seemed oblivious to the murmuring throng of villagers that had closed in around him as he rode unhurriedly toward the old man standing in front of the tipi.

Jason pulled White up to a stop in front of the old man. Sitting Bull motioned the people back to give the scout room to dismount. His eyes quickly measured the man now standing before him. He was tall and lean, hardened by the prairie and mountains. That much was obvious—any man could see that.

But Sitting Bull looked deeper inside the man's eyes and determined an inner strength there that others might miss. "How are you called?"

"I am called Jason Coles. It is an honor for me to meet the great spiritual leader of the Lakotas."

Sitting Bull nodded and asked, "Why have you come here?" He glanced at his people gathered about, then over at Nathan White Horse for an instant before returning his gaze to fix on Jason. "You are a long way from home, Jason Coles. Are you bringing another message from the Great Father in Washington?"

Jason shook his head. "No. I have come to get the white woman who is visiting your village. She is far from home too, and I have come to take her back to her father."

"Ah, the crazy woman." Sitting Bull nodded his head slowly. "She is confused and needs to find her way."

Jason had to concentrate hard to keep from smiling. "This is true and the reason I have come for her—to take her back where she can find her way."

"It is good that you do this," he said to Jason, then turned to an older man standing near Jason's packhorse. "Two Humps, bring the crazy woman." Two Humps nodded and did as he was instructed.

In spite of everything Nathan White Horse had told him about Abby Langsforth, Jason was not prepared for the impact of his initial sight of the publisher's daughter. Nathan had said she was big but Jason assumed that meant she was a little above average size. Abby was big—almost as tall as Jason—with no evidence of fat on her. She was big boned and packed solid. In her buckskins and boots she could have easily passed for a man.

Jason tried not to show his surprise as she was led to Sitting Bull's lodge by Two Humps. As he expected, she was not a prisoner and, consequently, not bound in any way. The Sioux held a special fascination for people they felt were touched in the head. This, Jason suspected, was the sole reason the woman was tolerated—if, indeed, she behaved as Nathan had related.

Curious as to why she was being summoned by the great Lakota leader after her thwarted attempts to see him before, she strode confidently toward the gathering of people. She caught sight of the tall white scout right away and realized he was the center of attention. She glanced at Sitting Bull briefly, then her gaze locked on Jason.

"And just who might you be?" she demanded.

He knew he had flushed a little. He couldn't help it. He hoped she didn't notice. "My name's Jason Coles, miss. I've been sent to escort you back to Fort Lincoln."

"Ha! I suspected as much." She turned to fix Sitting Bull with an accusing glance. "He's been trying to get rid of me ever since I got here," she said, still glaring at the Lakota chief. Then, looking back at Jason, she informed him in terms unmistakable. "Well, damned if I'm going. I came here as a friend to help these poor Indians, to tell their story to the rest of the world, and I'll go when I damn well please."

After this brief introduction to the young lady, Jason was of a mind to tell her it suited him just fine. Stay with the Indians—it would damn sure be their ruination. He held his tongue, however, until he could calmly make one more try. "Miss Langsforth, you're wasting your efforts here. These people think you're touched in the head. They're not going to listen to you."

"Is that so? Well, even if they won't talk to me, I'm not going anywhere with you."

"Your daddy wanted me to come after you."

"I'm not going."

"He's going with me." He nodded toward Nathan White Horse.

She took a step sideways in order to see the man standing behind Jason's packhorse. Nathan had discreetly positioned himself between his horse and Thunder in hopes he would not be noticed. "Nathan!" Her eyes lit up at the sight of the half-breed. "I knew you wouldn't leave without me." Nathan's face drooped but he gamely flashed a weak smile in her direction. Abby's disposition brightened considerably now that her missing guide was back. She looked at Jason and announced. "Nathan and I will remain here with the Lakota people."

Jason said nothing for a few moments while he decided whether or not he should just say to hell with it and leave her to her own choosing. He glanced at Sitting Bull and found the chief as baffled as he was. Their glances met and the Lakota shrugged. Jason made up his mind. He looked back at Abby. "Nathan's going with me. If you stay here, they'll probably sell you for a slave to the Arapahos or the Cheyennes."

Abby jerked her head back indignantly. "They will not!" She looked at Nathan for confirmation.

"He's right, Abby, they might. I have to go back to Lincoln. I can't stay here." He knew he was not overly popular in the Lakota camp anyway because of his past dealings with the army. The more he thought about it, the more he began to think it was not such a bad idea to go back with Jason.

No one was happier than Sitting Bull when the lady finally agreed to return to Fort Lincoln with the white scout. It would be a great relief to be free of her, for he had truly been perplexed over what he should do with her. He was so pleased to be rid of her that he assured Jason that no one would raise a hand against him or interfere with the three of them. They were granted safe passage from his territory

CHEYENNE JUSTICE

and they left within the hour. Jason led out at a brisk pace, followed by his packhorse, then Abby on a red gelding, and Nathan bringing up the rear. Although his intent was to return to Fort Lincoln without wasting any time, had he known that word of his visit to Sitting Bull's village would be relayed to Two Moon's camp on the Tongue, he might have pushed his horses even harder.

Man Who Killed Two arrived in the Cheyenne camp early in the morning. He had ridden all night and his horse was exhausted when he approached Two Moon's camp on the riverbank. Without stopping to eat or drink, he went immediately in search of Hungry Wolf.

"Who is it?" Hungry Wolf asked, wondering what was so important that he should be awakened at that hour. His wife replied that it was Man Who Killed Two and that he appeared to have urgent news. Hungry Wolf got up from his bed and went outside where he greeted his visitor. "Man Who Killed Two, I thought you were away visiting your wife's relatives with the Lakotas. What brings you here so early?"

"I left Sitting Bull's camp yesterday and I came here as fast as I could. The white scout, Coles, was in the village when I left."

"Coles!" Hungry Wolf's eyes flashed with the hatred the mere mention of that name invoked. Unconsciously, his hand reached up and rubbed the wound still healing in his shoulder. "Coles is in Sitting Bull's camp? Are you sure?"

"I am sure. He came to take a crazy woman back to the white people. I came to tell you as quickly as I could. He is most likely on his way back to Fort Lincoln by now." Man Who Killed Two was not with Hungry Wolf when he ambushed Jason on the Powder, but his brother was one of the men killed in that ill-fated attack.

"Why didn't you kill him?"

"Sitting Bull gave him safe passage out of his territory. Since I was a visitor there, I could not go against his orders. But we can still catch him if we hurry."

Hungry Wolf spat on the ground. "Sitting Bull is getting as weak as Two Moon. Get the others. This dog must not be allowed to leave our territory alive." He turned on his heel and went back inside to prepare to ride.

He did not spare his pony as he led his small war party upriver. He would ride this one until it faltered, then he would change over to a fresh one and continue to push on. There was no talk among the war party of twelve warriors, all dedicated to the eradication of the white man from their lands. All, like Hungry Wolf, had family killed by the soldiers, though none matched Hungry Wolf in his hatred for the white man.

Hatred, like an all-consuming fire, burned constantly in Hungry Wolf's belly. And the focus of that fire had come to center on Jason Coles. It was Jason Coles who had slaughtered Stone Hand. It was Jason Coles who had slain Black Eagle. It sickened Hungry Wolf to hear others of his tribe defend Coles, saying that he had fought bravely and with honor on every occasion. Had he not acted with deceit when he tricked Hungry Wolf and his friends to expose themselves in the fight at the Powder, only weeks before . . . killing three of his companions and wounding Hungry Wolf himself? In Hungry Wolf's eyes, Jason Coles had become the symbol of everything he hated about the white man. He had come to believe that when he killed Jason Coles, it would take the heart out of the soldiers and they would wish to fight no more.

Hungry Wolf's passion for revenge had been born

before he had ever heard of the tall white scout. Like other young boys of his village, he had felt the resentment caused by the steady invasion of white people into his country. But his first exposure to the terror of a cavalry attack came on Sand Creek, where his father was cut down in the early-morning attack by the soldiers. They struck the peaceful village without warning. Hungry Wolf was only fifteen at that time and his father fell from a bullet in the back of his head as they ran for the cover of the riverbank.

He and his mother were among the survivors of that massacre and, with a few others, they made their way north to join their brothers, the Northern Cheyennes. A year later, as a boy of sixteen, he rode in the raids along the Bozeman Trail and in December of that year he was a member of the party that attacked Fort Phil Kearny.

Always one of the bravest and most daring, he was among the few who rode in close to the fort to lure the soldiers out to fight. It took several attempts and the killing of a sentry before the soldiers, led by the foolish Colonel Fetterman, gave chase and pursued the Indians into the ambush that rubbed them all out . . . every man.

It was an exhilarating time for Hungry Wolf. He, along with the other decoys, led the soldiers into the waiting Sioux, Cheyenne, and Arapaho warriors. In the short hours that followed, he fought with the ferocity of his namesake, using only a bow and his war axe. His only wound during the combat occurred when a soldier opened an ugly gash across his face with a whip. Hungry Wolf killed the soldier with his axe.

Now, as he pushed his companions hard to intercept the hated white scout, his mind was filled with thoughts of the many raids and battles over the years that had since passed. Without thinking, he reached up and felt the scar across his face and it somehow seemed to give him a sense of pleasure. He knew he would find this Jason Coles, and this time it would be different. He could not endure living with the humiliation he had suffered when forced to run for his life after the scout had wounded him in their first meeting. Coles must die!

Chapter VI

Jason knelt before the fire and poured himself a cup of coffee from the battered old pot resting in the embers. That pot had been through almost as many scrapes as Jason had, and it was burnished and black from the many hours spent seated in the ashes of countless fires. He glanced up at Abby sitting on the opposite side of the fire and motioned with the pot. She shook her head no. He settled back against a small tree trunk and sipped his coffee while he studied his two traveling companions.

Nathan White Horse lay on his side, his head propped up with his elbow, working on a piece of jerky. Jerky and coffee were all Jason offered on their first camp after leaving the Sioux village. If the girl could cook, she didn't offer to. There wasn't anything to cook anyway, save some salt pork. Seated comfortably, her legs crossed Indian fashion, she favored Nathan with frequent glances that he made a big show of ignoring. Jason couldn't help but be amused. She sure as hell wasn't subtle. To the contrary, she had obviously cut ole Nathan out of the herd and fully intended to put her brand on him. The thought of it brought a smile to Jason's face, while it seemed to terrify Nathan White Horse. Maybe it was because Abby was bigger than he was and Nathan felt smothered by the girl. Jason tried to imagine the reaction of Mr. Arlington Langsforth when his darling daughter brought Mr. Nathan White Horse home with her and declared him her fiancée. Why, he thought, he'd make a real dandy. Scrub him up a little, braid his greasy shoulder-length hair, and put him in a box-back suit. Maybe he could work for her daddy's newspaper. 'Course she'd have to teach him how to read and write first. He chuckled to himself. That girl has some strange tastes, he decided.

Abby Langsforth was a breed apart. Jason had never run into the likes of her before. She was as coarse as any man on the trail, cursing the red gelding every time he stumbled or stalled. But all during that first day's ride, she never once complained or lagged. The only difference between her and a man, that Jason could see, was an unusually small bladder capacity. Even with that inequity, she still did not delay their progress. Never announcing her need, she would abruptly break off the trail when a ridge or coulee was convenient, pop out of sight, do her business, and be back in line, sometimes before the two men realized she was missing. The first time it happened, they were passing between two low hills. Jason looked back to discover she was gone. Alarmed at first, he turned back and rode backtrail, looking for her. He rounded the turn in the ravine to discover the lady squatting beside the trail, her britches down around her boots.

"What the hell are you looking at?" she demanded, making no move to interrupt her business.

"Something I don't see very often," he replied and immediately did an about-face and rode back to take his place at the front. After that, whenever she disappeared, he gave her a couple of minutes before thinking about checking on her.

There had been no problem making the Rosebud on that first day. Jason planned to follow the river north for about forty miles and then swing over to the Tongue. Since it was obvious the girl was not going to hold them back, he figured to strike the

Tongue River in two more days. The sooner he got out of this part of the country the better. Even though Sitting Bull gave them safe passage, that didn't mean they were out of danger. Crazy Horse's band was camped somewhere in the Big Horn country, as well as some smaller bands of Cheyenne and Arapaho. If he was alone, it wouldn't bother him to remain in hostile territory indefinitely. But with Abby and the half-breed along, he felt like he was leading a parade.

"Well, I'm going to take a little look around before I turn in." He poured the dregs of his coffee on the ground and got up. "We'll get an early start in the morning."

Jason awoke the next morning to find Abby rolled up in her blanket and snuggled up close against Nathan. While they slept, he stirred up the fire and put some coffee on to boil. After he had taken a look around the camp, he returned to awaken his two companions. Abby opened her eyes when Jason's boot nudged her foot but she did not move right away. Nathan awoke reluctantly and rolled over to his side, whereupon he bumped into Abby. He almost bolted straight up on finding her sleeping next to him. He scrambled to his feet, looking as if he had found a skunk in his blankets. Abby winked at him and bade him a cheerful good morning, while Jason stifled a laugh.

They made good time that day and dusk found them almost thirty-five miles upriver. They would camp there that night and cross over to strike the Tongue before noon the next day. So far, there had been no sign of hostiles and Jason began to wonder if the trip back might prove to be without problems. He was gratified to find that after two days on the trail, Abby was still cheerful and holding her own—in fact, it was Nathan White Horse who seemed to complain the most. When they had made their camp by a small branch that cut off from the river, Nathan voiced one of his complaints.

He and Abby had changed positions in the line of travel due to the young lady's necessity to make numerous relief stops. Since Abby was now bringing up the rear, this placed Nathan directly behind Jason's packhorse. After a day behind Thunder, Nathan was ready to register his discontent.

"What the hell's wrong with that horse?" he wanted to know as he and Jason hobbled the horses.

"Why, what do you mean?" Jason asked, straight-faced, knowing full well what Nathan was referring to.

"Fartin'! That horse farts more than any damn animal I've ever seen. Ain't you noticed it?"

Jason didn't look up but finished hobbling White. "That's an army parade horse. She's trained to count cadence when she marches in parades. Sometimes she forgets she ain't in a parade." He got to his feet and looked at Nathan with no trace of expression on his face. "All army parade horses do that."

Nathan looked at Jason for a long moment before responding. "Well, I didn't know that." He walked away, scratching his head.

When Jason walked back to the fire, he found Abby and Nathan involved in a hushed argument over, it turned out, a rip in Nathan's pants. Abby insisted on sewing it up for him and Nathan was vehement in insisting it was not her place to "do" for him. Jason said nothing but he couldn't suppress a grin. Nathan huffed and grunted a couple of times and then removed himself to the opposite side of the campfire.

"Let me know when you get over your stubborn streak and I'll sew those britches up for you." Looking at Jason, she smiled sweetly as if he had walked in on her while she was disciplining a difficult child. She sat for a while, finishing her coffee, thinking about her two male companions. Jason, satisfied that the horses and their camp were secure, had already rolled up in a blanket and was well on his way to sleep. He was a curious sort, she thought, completely self-sufficient, needing no one. And, although softspoken and polite, she could see that he was as wild as any Indian she had met on her trip out west. He was as much a part of the land as the cottonwoods on the riverbank or the buffalo grass on the plains. She longed to be like that. For all her young life, she had been looking for her place in the world. Having never found it back East, she decided it must be in the prairies and mountains. Taking another sip of the bitter brew Jason called coffee, she thought back to her childhood. Glancing around at the sleeping scout and back to the sulking half-breed, she smiled to herself. What would Daddy think of his little girl if he could see me now?

Life wasn't always easy to figure out. Charlotte, her older sister by two years, was a dainty, almost fragile girl, with flaxen hair and the small delicate features that had the boys calling before she was sixteen. Why, then, did the second child from the same union of husband and wife turn out as gawky as the first one was graceful? It wasn't fair. Her parents knew she was going to be a maverick from the start—her mother had been eleven hours in labor before Abby made her entrance into the world. The big feet and hands of the toddler promised a not-so-dainty young lady in the future.

Her mother and sister continued to have hope for Abby in her early formative years, but those hopes were probably abandoned shortly after her fourteenth birthday. Abby remembered it well. It was the Spring Cotillion and would be her introduction to the social world of Chicago. Her mother and Charlotte had done the best they could for the gangly young lady. A lovely pink and white satin dress had been made especially for her first dance. She could never remember a time when she had felt dainty and feminine, but this was as close as she had ever been. After she was all dressed with the help of her mother, her sister, and her mother's maid, she was ready to go downstairs to gain her father's approval. She descended the stairs as gracefully as she could, trying hard to imitate the almost fluid movements of her older sister who repeatedly admonished her to glide her feet as if walking through a room filled with baby chicks—not stomp through the room as if the carpet was on fire and she was trying to put it out.

Arlington Langsforth had never been a subtle man. It required a blunt, ruthless businessman to forge his way into the ownership of a large Chicago newspaper. In typical fashion, he crushed the fragile dream of his younger daughter with one dry observation. Abby would hear those words of her father's in her mind's ear for years to come. Reading his newspaper when she attempted to glide into his study, he glanced up and studied his young daughter intently. She waited expectantly for what seemed a lengthy, heavy void. Finally he stated dryly, "About like hanging Christmas candles on a fence post."

Now, seated before a small campfire in the middle of hostile territory, she could smile about it for she had come to like herself as she was. She no longer envied her sister, married to a lawyer and the mother of three. She could ride and shoot a rifle as well as a lot of men and she was still just as much a woman—just a different kind of woman. That thought brought her mind back to Nathan White Horse. He was small and maybe a little shy of character, but she liked him and she figured he might be easily molded into a decent husband. On a practical note, her prospects of attracting a man like Jason Coles were not that sound, but she fancied herself to be a good catch for the likes of Nathan White Horse. She looked over at the half-breed, who had now turned his back to the fire. *You'll take some work, though,* she thought.

It was about six-thirty by the time Jason got everybody packed up and ready to ride. At this point on the river, he figured to be no more than ten or fifteen miles from the Tongue, so he led them out due east, into the sun. It promised to be a warm day, with no sign of a cloud in the morning sky, and Jason decided it best not to push too hard. The horses could use a good rest. Maybe, if things looked all right when they struck the Tongue and there wasn't a lot of sign, they could rest the horses there.

The sun was still high in the sky when they walked the horses into the shallow water of the Tongue to drink. Jason had ridden on ahead to scout out the riverbanks and he led them to a shady clump of willows where they could fix the noon meal. He brought out some salt pork from his packhorse and gave it to Abby to fry. He figured it might be time to give them something hot to eat to go along with the coffee and hardtack. He had seen a small herd of antelope on the far side of the river but he didn't deem it wise to risk a shot. Hardtack and salt pork would have to do.

"I'm sorry I don't have anything better to offer than army field rations," Jason said as he took some hardtack from a sack in his saddle pack. He walked back to the fire where Abby was frying the salt pork and knelt down to examine the hard crackers.

Abby, watched him intently for a few seconds then commented. "That stuff's got green mold all over it." She felt compelled to point that out because it appeared he was going to offer it to her.

"Yeah, I reckon. I'm afraid all I packed for victuals was from the army quartermaster's stores and this lot of hardtack was pretty old." He glanced up at her and smiled. "Little bit of mold won't hurt you, though. We'll just wipe it off. I'll show you how the soldiers fix hardtack up so you'll think you're dining on pastry back in Chicago." He laughed at the skepticism plainly conveyed in her gaze. When the salt pork was done and out of the pan, he put the hardtack in and fried it in the grease. When it was done on both sides, he produced a bottle of brown sugar from his pack and sprinkled it over the hardtack. The result was a fairly palatable offering that Abby found quite pleasing, considering their circumstances.

They rested there for the remainder of the day, giving the horses a chance to graze and water. The next morning they were rested and ready to ride again. Jason stepped up on White and waited a few minutes while Nathan and Abby climbed on their horses. Then he led them into the river and started across.

The first shot splashed in the water in front of him. It was a single rifle shot but, almost like a signal, it set off a barrage of rifle fire from the sandy mounds on the opposite shore and all hell broke loose, shattering the early still of the morning. White reared back in the shallow water and Jason almost came out of the saddle before he muscled her back and turned her around. "Get back!" he yelled. It was unnecessary because Nathan and Abby were already kicking their mounts frantically in an effort to escape the swarm of bullets that were buzzing and snapping across the narrow expanse of water.

"Make for the trees," he shouted. In the same instant, he saw Abby's horse tumble, throwing her over her mortally wounded horse's neck and into the knee-deep water. Nathan, a few yards ahead of her and flogging his horse mercilessly, never looked back as he drove for the cover of the trees. There was no time to return fire, even if he could have pinpointed their attackers. In a matter of seconds, Jason caught up to Abby and pulled her up behind him. He didn't wait for her to seat herself behind his saddle. He just yelled, "Hang on!" and grabbed her by the seat of her pants while she wrapped her arms around his waist and he galloped toward the willows where they had camped the night before. Abby, holding on for dear life, still found breath to curse their attackers.

They reached the safety of the trees not a moment too soon, for the air behind them was now split with Cheyenne war cries as Hungry Wolf and his warriors charged into the river after them.

Jason took but a moment to look the situation over. There were a dozen of them, painted for war. This was not a chance encounter. This Cheyenne band had come prepared to ambush them—and he didn't have to guess who led them. His rifle out now, he calmly picked off two of the foremost riders as they reached the middle of the river, slowing the others down for a moment or two. In those moments, he directed Nathan to a position on his right behind a log and put Abby behind them to hold the horses.

Now the Cheyennes rallied and ploughed on through the water, one of them pausing to snatch the rifle from the saddle sling on Abby's dead horse. As they gained the riverbank, Jason knocked another hostile from his pony, ejected the shell, and cut down the warrior who stopped to help his fallen companion. Hearing pistol shots behind him, he glanced back to see Abby holding the horses' reins in one hand and calmly firing her forty-five Colt Peacemaker with the other. Their combined firepower was enough to halt the Cheyennes' charge, causing the hostiles to disperse and seek cover. Jason had a few moments to evaluate their situation.

"Everybody all right?"

Nathan White Horse, still hugging the ground behind the log, nodded in reply. Abby, now on one knee reloading her pistol, replied. "Yeah, except the son of a bitches shot my horse and got my rifle."

Jason looked at her and then glanced at the half-breed behind the log. Of the two, he was glad he had her to back him. Looking back at her, he spoke. "You can drop one of them reins, I reckon."

She glanced behind her and noticed for the first time that Jason's packhorse was lying on the ground, blood oozing from her neck. "Damn, looks like we're down to two horses."

"Looks like," Jason replied. Glancing around him, he didn't like the position they were in. "We've got to find a better spot to hold them off. This one's wide open behind us. They work around us and it'll be Katy bar the door. We've got to move fast while they're making up their minds what to do." Hungry Wolf had lost four warriors when he tried to charge them. He would be thinking now about working around to surround them with the remaining eight men. "Grab that sack of cartridges and some of that hardtack off my packhorse and then lead Nathan's horse through the trees downstream. They ought to give us enough cover to slip out if we're quick enough."

Nathan scrambled back to his horse and he and Abby retrieved the supplies from the packhorse. Jason motioned for them to move out while he protected their withdrawal. There were no shots fired from the riverbank for a few minutes, but Jason fired a couple of rounds toward where he had last seen movement. These shots were just to notify their attackers that they were still there. When Nathan and Abby were safely down the bank and moving undetected downriver, he withdrew cautiously, watching the riverbank for any sign of movement.

Leading White, he stopped briefly beside the carcass of his packhorse to make sure Abby had taken his ammunition. *Poor ole Thunder*, he thought. *At least you went sudden-like. You were a pretty stout horse, even though you were noisy as hell.* That thought fostered another: *I wonder which end gasped the last breath.*

In a few minutes, he caught up with Abby and Nathan. With the trees as cover, they were able to climb on Nathan's horse, Nathan in the saddle and Abby behind. With Jason leading, they rode as quietly as they could manage until they emerged from the trees some seventy-five yards downstream. Then Jason kicked White for speed and she responded. He didn't have to tell Abby and Nathan to do the same.

They gained a sizable start before the yells of alarm behind them told them Hungry Wolf had discovered their flight. They rode as fast as they could manage through the cuts and gullies until they came to a deep coulee that led up to the bluffs. This was as good a place as any to take their stand, Jason decided. He guided White up into the coulee and dismounted. The ravine was about ten feet deep so his horse could be protected from hostile fire. He directed Nathan to take Abby to the head of the ravine, where they would have better protection and a better position to see anyone trying to come in behind them. He took up a position nearer the river, at the mouth of the ravine where he could get a clear field of fire. This would be the direction from which the attack would come. He watched for a few seconds while Abby and Nathan climbed up the ravine, and then he turned his attention back to his rifle and cartridges. He didn't have long to wait.

Jason counted on Hungry Wolf being so angry that he would charge blindly after them, thinking that they would continue to run. He read the Cheyenne correctly, for only moments had passed when the band of hostiles galloped blindly down the riverbank, screaming bloodthirsty war whoops. Jason shrugged his shoulders to loosen them up, then brought his Winchester up. "Time to go to work, son," he uttered softly.

Hungry Wolf, his blood running hot, was too intent on overtaking his prey to do any tracking. Consequently, he did not notice that his quarry had turned up into the deep ravine and he galloped on past. Jason, intent on reducing their numbers as much as possible, let the leaders go by, sighting down on the end of the line. He knocked the last two riders off. When the others heard the shots, they immediately jerked their ponies to a halt to see what had happened. This gave Jason stationary targets while they stared in disbelief at their fallen companions. He reduced their numbers by two more before they scrambled for cover. Four to three, he thought. The odds were to his liking now because he figured Abby to be as able as any man in their situation. He moved a few yards up the ravine in case they had spotted his position.

Now it was a waiting game while Hungry Wolf figured out what he was going to do. During the shooting, one of them must have seen his muzzle blast because, for the next few minutes, there was a series of shots from the hostiles. Jason could see bullets kicking up sand near the position he had just vacated. In a short time, they grew tired of wasting their ammunition and there was silence.

Beneath the riverbank, downstream from the ravine, Hungry Wolf and his remaining three companions were arguing. Yellow Hawk spoke. "This is not good. This man's medicine is very strong. He has killed eight of our brothers already."

"This is why we must kill him," Hungry Wolf argued. "We must avenge our fallen brothers."

"Yellow Hawk is right," Lame Otter said. "This man will kill the rest of us. He does not miss with that rifle. I say we should forget this foolishness and let him go in peace."

Hungry Wolf snapped back in anger. "I don't believe what my ears tell me! This is no spirit we are fighting. This is nothing but a white man. Are you afraid of one white man?"

"He has two others with him."

Hungry Wolf looked sharply at Yellow Hawk. "There are four of us." His angry glare came to rest on each one of them in turn. "The other two don't seem to have stomach for the fight. I tell you, we are fighting only one man." He paused, hoping to shame them. "You call yourselves Cheyenne warriors?"

Lame Otter gave in first. "I will stay, but we must be very careful." The other two agreed reluctantly.

"Good. He killed the others because we charged straight at him, giving him easy targets. This time we will make our way around, up through the bluffs behind him where we will have the high ground. Yellow Hawk, you stay here and keep him pinned down. Walks With Limp, Lame Otter, and I will get behind him. When you hear our rifles, you must be ready to shoot him if he runs out toward the river."

Nathan White Horse crawled up to the edge of the ravine and peered out at the tableland beyond. "We ought to get the hell out of here while we got a chance."

Abby looked up at him. "Hell, we can't go anywhere. They'd be on our tails again." She checked over her forty-five and made sure it was loaded and ready. "I can't hit a damn thing with this pistol. I emptied the cylinder back there and didn't hit one Indian."

Nathan continued to scan the bluffs around them nervously. "It's Coles they're after. They think he's big medicine. I bet they wouldn't pay us no mind if we cut out of here."

Abby looked up again, this time with a definite sign of annoyance in her eyes. "He is big medicine.

He's already cut their number down to four and with no help from us." She paused and fixed him with an accusing stare. "Come to think of it, I didn't notice how much shooting you were doing back there. I saw you hunkered down behind that log but I was too busy missing folks to see what you were doing."

Nathan, unmoved by her veiled accusations, crawled back to a deeper gully close to his horse. He checked the load in his rifle and then sat back against the side of the gully. "All's I'm saying is, we could get a good head start while he was holding them off. The important thing is to get you back safe." She didn't comment, but the look of skepticism in her eyes was obvious, even to Nathan. "If we stay here, we're gonna get ourselves killed," he added.

Disappointed but not surprised at his attitude, she crawled up toward the rim of the ravine for a better position to keep watch. *Some man I picked to mate with*, she thought. She looked back at the half-breed, securely tucked in a gully for protection. "Why don't you let me use that rifle? I can't hit anything with this pistol."

"Hell, no," was his curt reply, and he cradled his rifle closer to his chest.

"Little weasel," she mumbled as she returned her gaze to the bluffs. It had been quiet for maybe a quarter of an hour. She could not see Jason down below them because of a bend in the ravine, but she knew he was there. He had positioned himself between them and the Cheyenne warriors but he had cautioned her to be alert in case one of them tried to sneak around behind them. So she carefully watched the rough terrain above and to the sides of their ravine. She smiled to herself when she recalled that when Jason told them what to do, he talked to her rather than to Nathan.

She shifted her position and relaxed her hold on her forty-five, realizing that she had been unconsciously squeezing it so firmly that her hand was getting stiff. *I'm not afraid*, she told herself with some satisfaction, *I'm just tense*. She knew Jason Coles was not afraid and she felt a kinship with the tall white scout.

Her thoughts were interrupted by a flicker of movement off to her right. At first she wasn't sure her eyes weren't playing tricks on her and she stared hard at the scrubby bushes about fifty yards away. Her heart skipped an excited beat when, a few seconds later, she saw definite movement in the grass around the bushes and she knew that it was caused by more than one man. Although her heart was beating rapidly, she remained cool and cocked her pistol. Without looking behind her, she whispered back to Nathan, "Get ready, they're coming around behind us."

She was answered by a sudden thunder of hooves and she turned just in time to avoid getting trampled by Nathan's horse as he whipped the animal furiously, charging out of the ravine and out across the flat. Desperate and so intent on saving his own hide, he almost ran her over in his escape.

"Come back here, you little weasel!" she screamed after him, so angry she stood up, not thinking about her own safety. The events that took place in the next few minutes occurred so fast that she didn't know what happened until it was all over and she was trussed up like a hog for market. She didn't even hear Nathan's scream of horror barely seconds after he disappeared in the bluffs.

Hungry Wolf and Lame Otter had crawled to within fifty yards of the head of the ravine when they stopped to observe the ground before them. A slight movement of a man's head alerted them that Jason's companions were guarding his rear. Lame Otter considered the fifty yards of open ground between them and the ravine. "They are watching. If we charge them, we will be easy targets."

"I know, I know," Hungry Wolf replied impatiently. As deep as his lust for revenge was for the white scout, he could see the folly in charging across fifty yards of open ground. "We will wait for Walks With Limp to work around the far side. Maybe he will have a clear shot."

They did not have to wait long, for their plan of attack was laid out for them unexpectedly. When, suddenly, the man on the horse bolted up out of the ravine and fled and the other man stood up with his back to them, they acted instantly. The two warriors were on the remaining man in an instant. He turned and raised his pistol but it was too late. With one blow with his rifle butt, Hungry Wolf knocked him senseless.

While Hungry Wolf attacked the man with the pistol, Lame Otter raised his rifle and fired at the man on the horse. Nathan White Horse laid low on his horse's neck, his heart pounding wildly as he heard the angry snap of the bullets over his head. None found him and he drove at full speed down into the cover of a deep gully. Only then did he feel it safe to sit up in the saddle and then it was just in time to see the flash of the war axe a split second before it buried into his chest. As soon as he hit the ground, Walks With Limp was upon him to finish him off. There was still a flicker of life left in the half-breed when Walks With Limp took his scalp.

At about the same instant Nathan White Horse met his fate, Hungry Wolf stood over the prone body before him and prepared to deliver the killing stroke with his axe. He paused. The blow that had felled his enemy had knocked the broad-brimmed hat off his head. Hungry Wolf was stunned by the long, chestnut hair that fell about the face of his victim. Many white men grew their hair long but this looked like a woman's hair. His surprise saved Abby's life at that moment. She was big for a woman and he was fascinated by his discovery, but still he wasn't sure. He turned her over and looked carefully at her features. She was a woman but, to make sure, he reached down and crudely felt her crotch. He turned to Lame Otter, who was puzzled over Hungry Wolf's hesitation. "It is a woman. Maybe she is Coles's woman. She must have special value or Coles would not have tried to disguise her as a man."

Before Lame Otter could reply, rifle fire erupted down below them near the river and they knew that Yellow Hawk had engaged Coles. In the next instant, Walks With Limp appeared, leading Nathan's horse. "The other one is dead," he called out, holding up the bloody scalp. They waited until he had reached them. He looked at Abby lying on the ground before them and asked, "Is this one dead?"

"It's a woman," Hungry Wolf replied. "Give me that rope on the saddle and I'll tie her up. I'm going to take her back with me."

Walks With Limp was surprised. "Why?"

"This woman has some kind of special value. I intend to find out what it is. Then maybe I'll kill her." He worked quickly to bind her hands and feet. With Lame Otter's help, he lifted her up on Nathan's horse. "You had better go down the ravine and help Yellow Hawk. I'll be right behind you as soon as I take this horse and tie him with the others in the brush."

Lame Otter and Walks With Limp looked at each other. Lame Otter spoke. "I think it best to wait for you. It will be better if we all go together."

Down below them, Jason had heard the sudden eruption of rifle fire on the ridge above. Since he could not see Abby and Nathan, he could not know whether it was Nathan's rifle he had heard or one of the Cheyennes'. After three shots, it was quiet again and he decided to work his way back up the gully to a point where he could at least see Abby and Nathan. He had taken no more than two or three steps when Yellow Hawk opened up with his rifle, ploughing up dirt around the position Jason had left moments before. Crouching low behind the rim of the gully, Jason looked hard along the riverbank, searching for the source of the rifle fire. He hoped the gunfire he had heard earlier had in fact been that of Nathan White Horse. There had been no report from the Colt Peacemaker Abby carried, so he could only speculate on what had occurred above him. He had to count on the two of them—especially Abby— to cover his rear.

Once again he eased his body backward, almost to the depression where he had tied White, keeping a watchful eye on the riverbank. There! Between the trunks of two small willows, a rifle barrel slowly protruded. Jason raised his Winchester and sighted a few inches above the rifle barrel. He waited for the head to appear to aim the rifle. A moment later, Jason's rifle ball split Yellow Hawk's forehead. Now it's three to three, he thought, unaware of the developments that had taken place above him. The question to be answered now was how many were below him still and how many had worked around up on top? He was sure that only one rifle had fired on his position from the riverbank and he had heard but one rifle above. And he still did not know if the shots above were fired by Nathan or one of the Cheyennes. *I'd best move up to them*, he decided. The next moment was shattered by an explosion of gunfire that filled the narrow ravine with whistling death.

Lightning-like reflexes were the only thing that saved Jason's life. At almost the same instant, the scout and the three Cheyennes saw each other as the Indians crept around a bend in the ravine. Jason dived sideways, rolling to the bottom of the depression at the same time the three hostiles raised their rifles and fired as rapidly as they could pull the trigger and cock again. Jason's horse caught the full impact of the rifle fire and screamed wildly as she reeled and fell. Before she hit the ground, Jason rolled to a stop, brought his rifle up, and dropped Walks With Limp in his tracks. The dead warrior crumpled in the dust of the ravine. There was no time for a second shot before the other two dived behind the bend in the ravine.

Jason crawled up behind his fallen horse, using the dead animal for cover. He would lament the death of White later; now he was too busy saving his own neck. Behind their earthen rampart, Hungry Wolf and Lame Otter crouched low and considered the situation. From their position in the gully, they could see their dead companion's moccasined feet and leggings, his rifle laying a few feet from them.

Lame Otter was disenchanted with their mission. He had seen enough of the white scout's ability with his rifle. "This is madness," he whispered. "Now there are only two of us left. The white man's medicine is too strong. We should not have come after him. I am sorry now that I listened to you."

Hungry Wolf was almost blind with rage. He spat out his words of contempt for his companion. "Your cowardly talk sickens me! Go! Crawl back and hide in your wife's tipi. I will kill this white dog by myself." His eyes gleamed like dark coals, burning with the hatred he harbored. "Go," he mocked, "and when I return with the white man's scalp, I will dance and sing of your bravery."

Hungry Wolf's words of derision sparked a surge of anger in Lame Otter's breast but they did not cause him to lose his common sense. And his common sense told him that the two of them were no match for Jason Coles. "Go ahead, if you are so anxious to die. I think it is best to leave this man alone.

We have lost too many of our brothers already." He slowly began to withdraw.

Hungry Wolf's fury was almost more than he could control. In anger, he turned and raised his rifle as if to shoot Lame Otter. Lame Otter paused. Meeting Hungry Wolf's glare, he said softly, "You have lost all but two of us. Are you going to kill another by your own hand?"

"Auhh!" He growled in frustration. "Leave my sight!" He turned away from him. Lame Otter withdrew.

His anger and frustration had reached a boiling point deep down inside Hungry Wolf. His hatred for the white scout had been fueled by restitution he felt necessary for the execution of the Cheyenne warrior Stone Hand. Now it had been intensified by the defeat he had endured at the hands of the white man. He knew he would face humiliation if he now returned to his village without Jason Coles's scalp. His reputation as a war chief was damaged beyond repair, for warriors were not anxious to follow a chief who did not bring his followers safely back from battle. And he had lost ten of the eleven who had followed him. He could not leave this place with Jason Coles still alive. He would kill the hated scout and drag his corpse back to Two Moon's village behind his horse. Then he would kill the woman and feed her to the dogs.

"Coles!" He screamed out. "Coles! I have the woman. I will cut her heart out! First I will kill you!" Jason did not answer. He calmly checked the load in his weapons and waited. Hungry Wolf called out again. "I have the woman. She is alive for now but I will kill her. I will give you a chance to save her, Coles. Fight me! No guns. Fight me man to man with knives. What do you say, Coles? Are you a man or a cowardly coyote?" He waited a moment but there was still no answer. He reached over and pulled

Walks With Limp's rifle up to him. "Come out and fight, Coles. I'm throwing my gun away. A knife is all I need." He threw Walks With Limp's rifle out. It clattered against the wall of the narrow ravine. Then he drew his own rifle up, ready to shoot.

"All right," Jason replied, his voice calm, without passion. "I'll fight you." He threw his rifle out in the middle of the ravine. "I'm coming out."

As Jason stood up from behind the carcass, Hungry Wolf suddenly stepped out from the bend in the ravine, his rifle raised, an evil grin on his twisted features. The grin froze for a split second, then turned to shock when the shots from Jason's pistol ripped into his belly before he could pull the trigger on his rifle. Before the darkness claimed him, he managed to get off one shot but the barrel of his rifle was pointing straight up in the air when he fired.

From high up on the ridge, where he sat on his horse and watched, Lame Otter shook his head, dismayed. He had known what the outcome would be. Hungry Wolf was too hotheaded. Coles was big medicine. It could have ended no other way. He kicked his pony and started off along the ridge, leading the horses behind him, the woman tied securely across the saddle of one.

Jason could only watch the departing Cheyenne as he galloped out of sight. He was too far away for even a lucky shot, so Jason didn't bother. With his toe, he rolled Hungry Wolf's body over. The look of surprise was still frozen on the Cheyenne warrior's face. Jason reached down and pulled the rifle from his hands. It was a Winchester 74, a newer model than the one he carried. *And the soldiers are still carrying single-shot Springfields*, he thought. "Well, Hungry Wolf, I reckon we made a trade. A new Winchester for my Appaloosa. I'd a heap rather had my horse. I doubt if your rifle shoots any better than mine. And where you're going, it's too damn hot to suit White."

He climbed to the top of the ravine and stood gazing out across the rolling hills in the direction Lame Otter had gone. It was a big country to be on foot in. "Damn," he uttered when he thought about it. White was the last survivor of the fourteen Appaloosas he had gotten from the Nez Perces. And now he was on foot and the girl was a captive and he didn't know what had happened to Nathan White Horse. *I guess he ran off*, he thought. *Maybe he'll be back now that the shooting's over.* He didn't put much faith in that possibility, so he decided he'd better get started if he was going to trail the Cheyenne who rode off with Abby. The first thing he had to do was to get a horse and he had a pretty good idea where one might be.

The Indian who had shot at him from the riverbank must have tied his horse somewhere up the river, so he made his way back down the ravine to the water. There, between the willows on the riverbank, lay the body of the Cheyenne warrior, his rifle still aimed at the gully where Jason had been. Jason paused only a few seconds to gaze at the body, interested more in the man's tracks leading up to the willows. They told him that the Indian had walked along the water's edge. He followed the tracks back to a line of trees on a small bluff where he found sign that plainly showed where the horse had been tied. But the horse was gone. A broken willow branch told him that the pony, tied there, had broken loose, probably when the shooting started.

"Well, son, you're sure as hell on foot now." He wasted little time lamenting his misfortune. If he was going to track the Cheyenne, he was damn sure going to need a horse. And the only one he knew about had wandered off downriver, judging by the tracks that led down out of the bluffs. He was accustomed to unforeseen obstacles popping up in his line of employment so he spent not a second in despair. The horse had wandered; he would find him. It was just a matter of how long it would take and that depended on how scared the horse had been when he ran off.

The horse, a brown and white paint, had run for about a quarter of a mile before slowing to a walk. The tracks stayed near the river and Jason hoped they would continue along that path and not head out into the hills. The horse didn't make it easy on him. He wandered for several miles before stopping to graze in a grassy flat by a bend in the river, where Jason finally saw him. Man and beast caught sight of each other at the same moment. The horse watched Jason as the man walked slowly toward him then he took a few steps backward, still munching on the soft grass.

"Easy, boy . . . easy." Jason approached the Indian pony slowly and deliberately, but the paint eyed him suspiciously. It was plain to Jason that the horse was more than a little nervous about the stranger's advance. "Easy now. I know my smell ain't what you're used to, but if I can live with it, I reckon you can." The horse started to back around a tree, but the short reins caught on a low branch. Jason moved up to him and took hold of the bridle. The paint tried to jerk his head away but Jason held it firm. He stroked the horse's head and neck for a few minutes, letting the animal get used to his smell. Then he untangled the reins and started to climb on his back, but the pony sidestepped away from him. "I reckon I better climb on Indian style," he said and went around to the other side of the horse. Most Indians mounted from the right side. He jumped up on his back. The paint was skittish at first and bucked halfheartedly a couple of times, then settled down and accepted his burden.

Jason was not worried about losing the trail of the lone surviving Cheyenne—he would have very little trouble following a trail left by that many horses. He had lost most of the afternoon tracking the paint and hated to lose more time, but there were things he would need for an extended chase. He rode back to the site of the battle and collected the rifles and ammunition from the bodies near the ravine. He took the Winchester 74 that Hungry Wolf had carried and hid it with the others in a hastily devised cache at the head of a small gully. The Winchester got special attention. He wrapped it carefully in a piece of hide the Indian had used for a saddle blanket. That done, he stood up and took a careful look around him to burn the spot into his memory. He might one day pass this way again. Ordinarily, he would not have left the weapons, which included a serviceable Henry repeating rifle, but he was already far behind the Cheyenne and he didn't want to load the paint down any more than he had to.

He pulled his saddle from White's carcass and took the Indian saddle off the paint. The pony protested when Jason threw his saddle blanket on his back but Jason calmed the horse down and he stood still for the saddle. He took what ammunition and supplies he thought the horse could manage and started out after the Cheyenne. Walking the pony along the bluffs, he passed a deep gully that ran all the way down to the water. There he found Nathan White Horse's body. Jason gazed down at the man, insignificant in life, now even less significant in death. "Well, I reckon I'd a waited a long time for you to come back." He felt no responsibility for the dead half-breed and no inclination to bother to bury his body. "I reckon you ain't ever been of much use to anybody while you were alive. Maybe you can at least feed the buzzards now."

Lame Otter's trail led off to the north, up the river.

CHEYENNE JUSTICE

Jason had figured the Indian would be hightailing it back to Two Moon's camp with Abby and the horses, but the trail led in the opposite direction. He figured the Cheyenne intended to enter the river at some point and try to backtrack on him. He considered crossing the river and heading straight for Two Moon's camp in hopes of cutting the Indian off. But if he was wrong, he would lose even more time. Indians were not all that predictable, so he decided it best to stay on the trail.

Jason had walked into Two Moon's camp before, when he returned the medicine arrows, and had been allowed to walk out again. But that was before he had killed eleven of Two Moon's warriors. He didn't think it wise to try it again. He would trail Abby and, if she was in the village, he would just have to figure a way to get her out. He felt an urgency to rescue the young lady, but in the back of his mind he couldn't help but feel that Abby could take care of herself. In fact, she might be more than those unsuspecting Cheyennes could handle. He kicked the paint lightly and the horse responded immediately.

Chapter VII

At first afraid she was going to be bounced off the horse's back, she tried to hold on as best she could, squeezing her legs and arms against the animal's flanks. Her hands were tied together, as were her ankles, so it became more and more difficult to stay on the galloping horse. At last her captor decided he had put a safe distance between them and the white scout behind them and he slowed the horses to a fast walk. It was less difficult to hang on now but, since she had been thrown across the saddle on her belly, the ride was extremely uncomfortable. The horse had an aggravating gait that pounded on her bladder and she began to feel an urgent need for relief. With each bounce of the saddle, she got madder and madder. When she had first come to, after being whacked in the head with a rifle butt, her head had felt like it might be cracked. Now the urgency in her bladder made her forget the ache in her head. Finally, she could take it no more.

"Hey, you red son of a bitch! Let me off this damn horse!"

Startled, Lame Otter looked back at his captive but made no move to do as she had directed.

"Stop, dammit!" Abby bellowed at the top of her lungs.

Lame Otter was confused by the woman's tone. Not understanding a word of her ranting, or the blistering curses being hurled in his direction, he simply looked at her in astonishment. Surely, he thought, the woman must be crazy. He began to question the wisdom of capturing her. Maybe he should have left her with the white scout.

While Lame Otter was entertaining thoughts of abandoning his prisoner, Abby was becoming more and more desperate to relieve her bladder of its pressure. When the stoic Indian made no move to halt the horses in the face of her threats and curses, she decided she had to take the initiative. "You ignorant savage!" she screamed and threw her arms back while kicking the horse in the side with her knees, throwing herself backward. She landed hard on the seat of her pants and rolled several times, heels over head, before coming to rest in the knee-high grass.

Lame Otter pulled up hard on his horse's reins and wheeled around to stare open mouthed at the antics of this strange woman. While she staggered to her feet, he walked his pony back to stand before her, still staring, astonished.

Her face flushed with anger as she tried to make her need known to the Cheyenne. "Dammit, I've got to wet," she blurted. When he gave no indication of comprehending, she demanded, between clinched teeth, "Don't you understand a damn word of English?" Met with another puzzled look, she tried to make him understand with gestures.

This further confused Lame Otter. The woman was surely crazy, possessed by an evil spirit possibly. Maybe it would be best to shoot her before she broke free of her bonds and possibly turned into a crow or an eagle and flew away. Now she was making squatting gestures and making hissing noises with her mouth. He cocked his rifle. Then suddenly he understood. The woman had to relieve herself. He nodded solemnly to himself, relieved by his enlightenment.

Then he nodded to Abby to let her know that he understood.

She stood there and waited patiently for a few moments while Lame Otter smiled at her benevolently. When he made no move to dismount, she gestured toward her tied ankles. "Well?" she demanded.

Again the puzzled expression returned to his face but just for a moment. *Ah,* he thought, *she cannot release her water with her ankles tied together.* He dismounted at once and cut her ankles loose. She shoved her hands up in front of his face and demanded. "Cut!" He hesitated, reluctant to free the crazy woman's hands. "Cut!" she repeated. He cut. Then he backed away a few steps, his rifle ready.

"How the hell can I pee if I can't use my hands to get my pants down?" she growled as she hurriedly fumbled with her buttons. "Well, turn around!" When he did not understand, she made gestures until he did and dutifully turned his back on her. Mercifully, her tortured bladder emptied itself in the grass while her captor stood obediently with his back to her. *If I still had my pistol and I wasn't about to burst,* she thought, *I'd shoot your dumb ass.*

When she was finished, she hitched up her trousers and walked over to her horse. Lame Otter moved quickly to face her. Picking up the rope, he started to tie her hands again. "No!" she barked and pushed him away. Taking a step backward to maintain his balance, he raised the rifle and pointed it at her face. She stared him down with a look of defiance that all but unnerved him. "If I've got to go with you, you ignorant savage, I'll sit in the saddle." With that, she climbed on the horse and looked down at the confused Indian with a look of impatience.

Lame Otter did not move for a long moment as he studied the odd girl seated on the horse. This woman was the strangest white person he had ever come in contact with. Abby sat in the saddle, now looking

CHEYENNE JUSTICE

straight ahead, a no-nonsense expression fixed on her face. Having thought the matter over, he walked around behind her and, taking his rifle by the barrel, used it for a club to knock her off the horse. While she writhed in pain on the ground, he calmly tied her hands and feet again. When he was done, he hoisted her up over the saddle once more, mumbling, "Crazy woman . . . heavy."

Although Lame Otter permitted the horses to walk, he held them to a fast pace, one that would eat up some distance. He glanced over his shoulder often to search his backtrail. In his brief exposure to Jason Coles, he had come to respect the white scout's medicine. Added to that was a nervous discomfort at having the crazy woman behind him, even though she was securely bound. She kept up a steady stream of curses as she was bounced along. So absorbed was he in his backtrail that he failed to see the two men sitting on their horses in the shadows of a deep coulee, watching the approaching Indian.

He was abreast of the head of the coulee when his pony caught the scent of the two strange horses. The warning was too late and Lame Otter was forced to jerk back hard on the reins to avoid a collision with the other horses as they suddenly charged up from the shadows.

"Well, dang, lookee here. Where you goin', Lame Otter?"

Lame Otter, stunned by the sudden emergence of the two horsemen, thought first of flight but, in the next instant he recognized the two white men and his immediate fear was dissolved. However, since he knew the men for what they were, he was not ready to discard all caution. He nodded to them as they pulled up to flank him.

"Looks like you been doin some raidin'."

The man who spoke was Jack Pike, known to the

Cheyenne and Sioux as Black Hat. An army deserter, Pike moved among the free Indian bands, trading guns and whisky when he could get away with it. Lame Otter knew that Pike and his partner, a man called Selvey, were not to be trusted. Were it not for the fact that they were a seemingly unending source of rifles and ammunition, Two Moon would have had them killed long ago.

"I might be in the mood to do a little trading myself." Pike grinned, exposing a jagged row of teeth, stained brown from tobacco juice. He leered at the trussed-up woman draped across the saddle of one of the horses Lame Otter led. "What you got there? I thought, when I first seen you coming, you had a dead man, but that there's a woman, ain't it? A white woman at that."

Lame Otter tried to explain that he had a scout on his trail and he didn't have time to stop to parley, but Pike insisted that they had watched him coming for two or three miles and no one had showed up behind him yet.

"He will come," Lame Otter insisted.

"Who's tailin' you? Soldiers?"

"Jason Coles."

This caught Pike's attention. "Coles." he repeated. Pike had never encountered Jason Coles personally, but he had crossed his trail a few times and it almost always left dead people behind. But reputation or not, Jack Pike had never met a man he feared and he knew for damn sure there was never a meaner man born than Jack Pike. If he could talk, there was a dead lieutenant with a hole in the back of his head who could tell you how foolish it was to cross Jack Pike. Pike laughed every time he thought about it— the army thought the officer had caught a round from an Indian. "Coles, huh," he said again. "Well, ain't it lucky you run into your friends. Me and Selvey will take care of you. Won't we, Selvey?" The

CHEYENNE JUSTICE   111

man called Selvey responded with an animated nodding of his head and a foolish grin splitting his fat cheeks.

Lame Otter was not at ease with the situation he had ridden into. Pike and Selvey were not to be trusted. Still, they depended on trade with the Cheyenne people and they came to their villages as friends. Maybe it would be good to have their help against the white scout.

"Come on," Pike continued. "Let's sit down over here in the shade and talk for a while. Hell, if Coles is chasing you, he ain't nowhere in sight. You might of lost him."

Up to that point, Abby had held her tongue. When it was apparent that the two strangers were white men, although of questionable character, she finally yelled out. "Tell that damn Indian to cut me loose!"

This brought a startled laugh from Pike. "Ha! Listen to that, Selvey. What you got there, Lame Otter?" He got down off his horse. "I think ol' Lame Otter done trapped hisself a bitch coyote." He walked over to examine the Indian's captive. Grabbing a handful of Abby's hair, he jerked her head up so he could take a good look at her. "Ha!" he barked into her face and, dropping her head again, walked around to the other side of the horse. With no more emotion than if he was checking a horse's hoof, he laid a rough hand on her bottom, which was offered up to him in a vulnerable posture. Her reaction was swift but not quick enough to catch him as she tried to kick out at him. "Huh," he grunted, amused by her reaction. "Yessir, she's a woman all right, and a right sassy one, I'm thinkin'."

"You son of a bitch," Abby snarled. "You keep your damn dirty hands off of me!" She was sore, tired, and indignant, and she was determined not to show any sign of weakness no matter what. But she sensed an inherit evil in this man Pike. He was a far more serious concern than Lame Otter and one who would stand for no nonsense. She hoped the Indian would part company with these two with no delay.

"Let's have a look at you, honey." With that, Pike grabbed the back of Abby's shirt and pulled her off of the horse. Lame Otter started to move to protest but Selvey stayed him with a firm hand on his arm, smiling to assure him everything was all right. Abby landed on her feet but could not maintain her balance and went over on her backside.

"Damn you," she spat at him.

Pike laughed. "She's shore got spunk, ain't she?" He motioned Lame Otter over to him. "This here's your lucky day, Lame Otter. I could use a woman with that kind of grit and I've got something that'd be mighty handy for you." He turned to his sidekick. "Selvey, get that Sharps outta the pack and show it to our friend here." It only took Selvey a matter of minutes before he returned, handing the rifle to Pike. "This here is just what you need, a genuine breech-loading Sharps buffler rifle. I bet they ain't another one in your village. With this, you can knock a buffler down while them other bucks are still trying to git in range." He handed the rifle to Lame Otter. "This and fifty rounds of ammunition for the woman."

Lame Otter took the rifle, his eyes wide with astonishment. This was a good trade and one that took him by surprise. A Sharps buffalo gun and fifty bullets for one troublesome woman? He would be a fool to pass that up. He feared the woman anyway. It would be good to be rid of her and he would be spared the superstitious dread he would have felt if he decided to kill her. He gazed into the smiling face of Jack Pike, wondering why his offer was so generous. Not willing to give Pike time to reconsider, he quickly said, "We trade." Then, since the traders were obviously in such a benevolent frame of mind, he sought to take further advantage. "You trade for horses too?"

Pike's smile widened. "Yeah, I'll take the horses too. Selvey, show him what we got to trade."

Facing Pike, Lame Otter could not see the broad smile on Selvey's face as he stepped up close behind the Indian. All Abby heard was a short gasp as Selvey buried his long skinning knife under Lame Otter's rib cage. Her head started spinning and she had to look down at the ground to keep everything from going black before her eyes. Although she did not see Lame Otter's final moments, she could hear the Indian's gasps as Pike held him up while Selvey withdrew his knife and plunged it in his side again. She fought to keep from fainting as Pike, laughing as he worked his own knife, lifted the dying Indian's scalp.

Abby struggled to maintain control of her emotions. Going to pieces at this point would certainly not help her situation and might possibly make it worse. She was left to pull herself together for a few minutes while Pike and Selvey occupied themselves with an inventory of their ill-gotten gains. To make matters even more horrible, Lame Otter did not die well. His murderers did not even glance in his direction after they had relieved him of his weapons, leaving him to writhe in pain as his last breaths slowly subsided. She wondered that they did not at least put him out of his misery but she held her tongue, afraid to call their attention back to her.

When they had finished looking over their new horses and rummaging through Nathan White Horse's saddlebags, it was time to consider the woman. She steeled herself as they approached.

"Well, now, missy," Pike started, his evil face twisted with a crooked smile, "I reckon you'll be grateful for me rescuing you from that Injun." He reached down with his skinning knife and cut the rope binding her ankles. As he did so, he realized the blade was still bloody from Lame Otter's scalp and he paused to clean it on Abby's trouser leg. Then he stepped back to evaluate his prize. After a moment's pause, he said, "You ain't no raving beauty, are you?"

"You can go straight to hell."

Pike laughed. "In due time, I reckon. I ain't even shore why I wanted you, now that I got a good look atcha. I might have to git a mite more rutty yet."

Selvey drooled as he leered at the girl sitting on the ground at Pike's feet. Abby unconsciously pulled her legs back together. "I'm rutty 'nuff, Pike. I don't need to wait."

A quick flicker of anger flashed across Pike's face and he drew his hand back as if to backhand his partner. "You think I'll take your leavin's? You can go over there and court your hand."

"Ah, hell, Pike," Selvey pouted, but he went obediently back to the horses.

The smile returned to Pike's face and he looked back down at Abby. "Don't worry, sweetie, hit'll be me and you."

"Over my dead body," she replied.

"Well, I ain't never had it that way but it's all the same to me. I'll give 'er a try." He winked at her, still grinning. Then he abruptly turned to Selvey and started giving orders. "Let's git these horses on a lead line. We ain't got time to fart around here no longer. I don't wanna have that damn Coles taking potshots at us. Ol' Crooked Leg's Arapahos is camped somewhere on the Powder. We can trade these horses there."

Selvey did as he was told, still grumbling under his breath about the woman. He would grumble, but he had no misconceptions about his status in the partnership. Pike would just as soon kill him as look at him.

* * *

They left the Tongue and struck out to the northeast. Ahead of them, and to the west, storm clouds began to develop over the Big Horns. Abby, her hands and feet free of her bonds now, rode on Nathan White Horse's pony. While she appreciated the freedom she now enjoyed, she was not foolish enough to entertain any thoughts of escape. The minute she broke away, Jack Pike would send a bullet to catch her. If she had any doubts about it, they were dispelled within the first two hours of their journey.

Her bladder swollen to the point of pain, since it had been hours since she had been permitted to relieve herself, she determined to ease her discomfort at the next opportunity. It came when Pike led the small train through a ravine with clumps of thick brush growing on each side of the lower end. She pulled back on her reins, letting Selvey's horse go ahead of her. Selvey, half asleep in the saddle, paid no attention to her movements. There was no thought of escape. She planned to make one of her quick nature stops, just as she had done when traveling with Nathan and Jason. When abreast of the bushes, she turned aside and went behind them. She had barely disappeared behind the bushes and dismounted when the snap of a bullet was followed almost immediately by the report of Pike's pistol. Before she had time to unbuckle her belt, several shots followed, all close over the horse's back, where she would have been had she not dismounted. The horse reared and ran away and she could hear Pike's angry shouts and the sound of his horse's hoofbeats approaching. She was terrified. Knowing that her only chance of surviving his wrath was to get her pants down and squat, she hurriedly fumbled with her buttons and very nearly wet her trousers before she could assume the position.

His face black with rage, Pike wheeled his horse around the scrubby patch of brush to find the woman squatting, answering nature's call, an indignant expression on her face. It totally disarmed him and he pulled his horse up short and threw back his head and laughed.

"You damned near got yourself kilt that time, missy." The smile disappeared. "You pull another trick like that and I'll send Selvey with you when you got to piss." He sat on his horse and watched her till she finished. Selvey rode up beside him to see the show. Pike glanced at his partner for a few seconds, then he took his foot out of the stirrup and, with a stout kick, knocked Selvey out of the saddle. Selvey, confused, picked himself up from the dust and looked at Pike glaring down at him. Abby was reminded of a hound dog, unable to understand what he had done to warrant his punishment. "If you don't stay awake, I might have to shoot you," Pike warned. "Now get mounted and go fetch that horse."

After that, Abby asked permission to leave the trail whenever nature called. Every time she had to contend with the leering Selvey, skulking back, trying to get an eyeful. She complained to Pike about his degenerate partner's ogling but Pike didn't care enough to curtail it. Abby knew that Pike was going to make his move toward her when it pleased him to do so. She didn't know why he was content to wait, other than the fact he was intent on putting distance between them and Jason Coles, but she was thankful for his patience. When the time came, she prayed that she would be strong enough to fight him off. She had resolved in her mind that even though he might overpower her, he might succeed in satisfying his lust but he would damn sure not enjoy it. She also knew that the only thing protecting her from the degenerate Selvey was Pike's desire to be first. She didn't like to even think about that.

Pike studied the clouds that had been drifting over from the mountains for the past two hours. By now they had become increasingly darker and seemed to be building up all the way to the heavens. There had been no rain in these parts for weeks and many of the smaller streams were no more than dry beds. But sudden thunderstorms were common during the dry season and they were generally violent, sometimes lasting for days. Pike was thinking that this storm blowing up now might be just what he needed, so he turned his horse back toward the mountains and the black clouds.

Selvey, more alert now, was puzzled by his partner's change of direction. "Where the hell you goin', Pike? I thought we was gonna take these here horses to Crooked Leg's camp."

"We are, dammit. But first I'm gonna cover our trail. You just watch out for them horses and follow me."

Another hour brought them back to the river. By now, the wind was whipping the trees along the banks and the first random drops of rain had begun to fall, large drops that were almost a drink of water by themselves. Before long, the rain increased in intensity, falling almost sideways as the wind hurled the huge drops against the faces and arms of the three riders. Selvey called out to Pike to look for shelter but Pike continued on, leading them into the river and across. There was little shelter to be found—the trees were not substantial enough to offer much protection from the driving rain. All three were thoroughly soaked by the time they happened upon an overhanging rock ledge in the bluffs. It was barely large enough to cover three wet souls.

Pike pulled a slicker out of his pack to use for shelter and directed Abby up under the ledge with him. He sent Selvey to hobble the horses before he permitted the complaining little man to get in out of the rain. It was too wet to make a fire and there was no firewood handy anyway, so they sat where they were and waited out the rain. Pike offered to share his slicker with the woman but Abby declined, preferring to sit shivering against the side of the bluff. Looking from the leering Selvey to the snarling Pike, she could not imagine a time or place that could be more miserable than this. But she was not really frightened—keeping dry seemed to be the only thing on Pike's mind and she was grateful for that.

The shelter they had found was very small and it soon was filled with the stale, corral-like odor offered up by soggy flannel on unwashed bodies. Long-dormant scents of horses, sweat, skinned buffalo, and drinking binges seemed to have been called forth by the soaking rain like ghosts summoned to a seance. Abby stood it in silence for a long time but she finally had to voice her displeasure.

"Don't you two ever take a bath?" As soon as she blurted it out, she wished she hadn't said it. But Pike was not easily insulted.

"Hell, yeah," he roared with a grin. "I just took one."

"And that was one too many," Selvey added, pulling the wet flannel shirt away from his skin.

Abby moved closer to the edge of the overhanging rock—any farther and she would be out in the rain again. Pike reached out with one long arm and, grabbing a handful of her shirt, dragged her over closer to him. She recoiled as he stuck his face right next to hers. His breath was foul and heavy with the smell of rotten teeth and tobacco.

"You'll get used to my scent, darling," he said.

"Damned if I will!" She shot back defiantly and struggled to pull away from him.

He held her fast for a few moments, amused by

CHEYENNE JUSTICE

her futile efforts to free herself. "You better hope I fancy you, missy. 'Cause if I don't, why I'll just let ol' Selvey there have his fill of you and then I'll trade you to the Injuns." He yanked her face up close to his again and held her there for a few seconds. "You know, you ain't exactly the purtiest female I ever seen anyway. I might not get more than a stray dog fer you if I do trade you." Then he laughed and shoved her away.

She pressed up against the side of the ravine, taking several deep breaths in an effort to rid her nostrils of the stench of the man. He watched her for a moment, then turned his thoughts to other things.

"Hit looks like hit's lettin' up a little. Good thing too, 'cause hit'll be dark pretty soon and I want to make camp before dark."

Several hours behind them, Jason Coles came upon the body of Lame Otter. He knelt beside the body and looked at it closely. He had been scalped and it was a messy job at that. The wounds that killed him came from a knife in his back and in his side. Whoever killed him stripped him clean of weapons and ammunition. There were plenty of tracks and Jason studied the area carefully trying to piece the picture together. The Cheyenne had met someone—two men by the look of it—and they both rode shod horses. Traders, trappers, or possibly Indians on stolen army mounts—there was no way to tell but Jason's bet was on white men, judging by the boot prints and the tobacco stains on the bare patches of earth. And, from the pattern of footprints, it was apparent the Indian knew his murderers. "Some friends you got, you poor devil." Noticing something peculiar about one of the hoofprints, he knelt again to examine it more closely, tracing the outline of the print with his finger. Nicked, he thought. The corner of one of the horseshoes had a piece missing.

The Cheyenne's murder changed the game drastically. Jason had been confident that, even if he didn't catch up to the Indian before dark, he would almost certainly return to Two Moon's camp eventually, and Jason was prepared to go into Two Moon's camp to get Abby. Now he could only guess what the white men had in mind. One thing he knew for sure—he was now after a treacherous pair as evidenced by the way they had negotiated with the Indian. He had better watch his backtrail.

After searching the site of the meeting, he found where the tracks led out toward the northeast. He paused to study the sky before him. Don't like the look of that, he thought. Better get going. He stepped up in the saddle and urged the paint on in hopes of catching sight of Abby's captors before the rain hit.

Luck was not with him on this day. He had ridden no more than a few miles when the storm hit. He pushed on through a driving rain, following the trail left by the half-dozen horses until it disappeared in what had been a dry wash but was now a torrent of rushing water. He scouted the other side of the wash but the storm had erased all traces of the trail except for one lone hoofprint, pointed toward the river.

Jason stood in the pouring rain, looking around him in all directions. The hoofprint pointed toward the river but they could have gone in any direction. A cold trail was one thing—he could follow a cold trail—but no man could follow when there was no trail. There was nothing he could do but scout the riverbanks on both sides, hoping he might luck onto some sign. He had known horses that could follow a week-old trail left by the herd they had run with. It was worth a try, he decided, and there was little else left to try anyway. He climbed back on the paint and gave him a slight kick, letting him have his head, but the pony trotted a few yards and stopped to graze on a tuft of grass. "You ain't got no more notion than I have," Jason said and nudged the horse again. Might as well scout the banks, he decided.

After another hour, the rain stopped and he continued his search along the banks of the river until darkness made it impossible to continue. With no sign to be found he gave up for the night, hoping for better luck tomorrow. Reasonably certain he was the only human being within miles, he felt no need for caution, so he gathered up some dead limbs and made a fire to dry himself and his clothes. Wearing nothing but his boots, he unsaddled the paint and hobbled him close by his camp. Before returning to his fire, he stood there a few moments, evaluating his mount. The paint had proven to be a fairly stout horse, seemed to have a fair amount of stamina and had adjusted to the strange saddle on his back. He had kind of short legs but a broad chest that indicated a lot of heart. He also had dark brown markings around his eyes that made him look like he was wearing a mask. He would have been no match for White, but then few horses were in the same class with the Appaloosa. This one would do, he decided, and he returned to his fire to fix himself some supper.

The driest thing he had was his saddle blanket, so he spread that before the fire to protect his bare bottom from the wet grass. Not really hungry, he made some coffee and dined on a piece of jerky. While he sat before the fire, drinking his coffee, he speculated on possible places the two outlaws might be headed. He was pretty much certain the two white men were outlaws or deserters. For one thing, they obviously knew the Indian they had killed. Otherwise he would not have permitted them to get so close. Probably they were gunrunners, selling weapons to the hostile bands of Indians, which would explain why they felt free to travel alone in this territory. Aside from that, if they weren't outlaws, they would have brought

Abby back to find him. There was no telling what plans they had for the girl. Jason felt it at least a good sign that they had taken her with them. He could have found her body back there beside the Cheyenne's. He didn't spend any more thought on the possible fate of the lady—Jason usually made it a rule not to worry about things he was powerless to influence. He would do the best he could to find her and he would search until he did find her or find out what happened to her. That was the best he could do.

A little over fifteen miles upriver, Abby sat, cold and shivering, afraid to go to sleep even if she could, wondering if Jason Coles was still alive. At this moment, he seemed to be her only hope for survival. Her one encouraging thought was that, if he was still alive, Jason would come after her. She could not know that her one hope for rescue was no more than a half day's ride away, sitting naked on a horse blanket, nursing a cup of coffee.

Sunup the next morning found Jason in the saddle, scouting the riverbanks. From the sign he picked up before the rain washed everything away, he knew that the two men did not have any pack horses with them before meeting the Indian. Based on that, Jason figured they had probably just come from one of the several Indian camps in the Big Horn country. *Now what would they do?* he asked himself. They now were in possession of a woman captive and some horses. The obvious thing would be to go somewhere to trade the horses . . . and possibly the woman. He supposed they had enough sense not to take the horses back to a village where someone might recognize them, and they would probably want to get rid of them as soon as possible. Some of the Sioux scouts at Fort Lincoln had reported that several bands, Sioux as well as Cheyenne and Arapaho, were scattered between the Tongue and the Powder. Since he had to start somewhere, he decided he might as well search in that vicinity. His scouting along the Tongue had availed him nothing so he determined to waste no more time there. He turned the paint toward the east and headed toward the Pumpkin River.

Chapter VIII

Lieutenant Page Jeffers held up his hand to halt the column of cavalry following behind him. "Sergeant Ryman," he called out, and he waited while the sergeant pulled up beside him. "This is as good a place as any. We'll stop for the noon meal here and rest and water the horses."

"Yessir," Ryman replied, turning back to relay the lieutenant's orders to the scouting party of twenty troopers. After he had directed his men to a small assembly of cottonwoods near the edge of the river, he rode back to the lieutenant. "Can the men cook, sir?"

Jeffers nodded, then said, "Yes, we'll take an hour."

"Yessir. Want me to send somebody to call in the scouts?"

Jeffers shook his head. "No. They aren't that far afield. They should be able to see we aren't behind them and come back anyway."

"Yessir." Ryman wasn't surprised. The lieutenant didn't have a very high opinion of the two Crow scouts that had been assigned to the detail. He thought it was a waste of time to deploy the scouts when they seemed reluctant to operate out of sight of the column. Ryman understood the scouts' feelings. This country was crawling with Sioux and Cheyenne and Arapaho, and none of 'em was too fond of Crows. The lieutenant was right about one thing, though. Looking out toward the east, he could see one of the scouts. The Indian was standing still, looking back toward the troops. In a few minutes he and his partner would be back to the column. "Fannin, take the lieutenant's horse down to the river." He paused a moment to make sure the trooper responded quickly enough to his order before seeing to his own horse.

The column had been in the saddle since before sunup, some six hours before. Normally Lieutenant Jeffers marched only four or five hours before stopping for the noon meal but for once they had a warm trail and he had been pushing the detail hard in an effort to close on the hostiles. But in spite of the lieutenant's urging, there seemed to be no indication that they were closing the gap between them and the party of nine Indians. Finally Jeffers resigned himself to the obvious and realized the chase might take longer than he had hoped. He might as well save the horses.

The spot Jeffers picked to rest the men and horses had plenty of firewood and water so there were already several campfires crackling. They had only been out from Camp Carson for two days so the men were in pretty high spirits. Each man still had his supply of salt pork, hardtack, sugar, and coffee. They were all veterans of western campaigns so they would have resisted the urge to eat most of their rations on the first day out. Ryman had a feeling that this bunch was going to be hard to catch and that, before they were through, the detail might be eating one of the mules.

Fannin brought the lieutenant's horse back and tied the reins loosely over a willow switch. He settled himself beside the fire and got a slice of sowbelly from his mess kit. "How far you reckon the lieutenant's gonna chase after them Injuns, Sarge?"

"Till he says that's far enough, I reckon." His answer was curt but Ryman wasn't any more comfortable this deep in hostile territory than the rest of the men. The hostiles they were chasing had been sniping at the river steamers that brought supplies up the Yellowstone. That was not anything unusual, but this bunch—the Crow scouts said they were Arapahos—had killed two soldiers who had been sent ashore to cut wood for the steamer's boilers. The colonel was determined to punish the hostiles this time and he sent out three patrols. Lieutenant Jeffers was dead set on being the one to catch up with them and the scouts had picked up their trail easily enough. *Well*, Ryman thought, *he might just get us all dead if he keeps pushing farther and farther down this river.*

Of more serious concern to the colonel was the fact that the Indian snipers were armed with repeating rifles. Granted, they weren't very good marksmen but a steamboat is a pretty good size target. The boats were often transporting new troops on the river, and these recruits began to get the idea right away that the Indians were better armed than they were, which didn't help morale one bit. The army's standard issue for the infantry was the Springfield rifle. Even though it was a single-shot rifle, the Springfield was superior at long range in the hands of a man who knew how to use it. Still, that didn't help a raw recruit when an Indian warrior rode in close and banged away with a repeater.

Page Jeffers was a conscientious young officer. He had seen action in three engagements with the Sioux and he was confident that he could overcome a body of hostiles three or four times greater in number than his scouting patrol. Although in garrison at Camp Carson for only a few months more than a year, he had seen enough of the Indians' style of combat to know they were no match for seasoned cavalry in a pitched battle. In reality, their tactics were infuriating to the young officer—hit and run, raiding and hightailing it, never standing to fight.

"Coffee, sir?"

Jeffers glanced up at Ryman and smiled. "Thank you, Sergeant." He handed his metal cup to Ryman and watched as the sergeant filled it from a small kettle.

Ryman handed the cup back to the lieutenant and settled himself down against a tree trunk. He didn't say anything for a few minutes, seemingly occupied wholly with the sipping of his coffee. Jeffers had seen it before. His sergeant was about to either question his intentions or offer some unsolicited advice. Jeffers waited patiently. He respected the sergeant's ability to handle the men and he was not reluctant to give him credit for having more experience in the Indian wars than he had himself. Ryman had been assigned out here since the war back East had ended. Granted, he had seen more action against the hostiles but, in Page Jeffers's mind, that didn't necessarily make his judgement any more sound when it came to confronting the enemy.

"Well, sir," Ryman started, as if making idle conversation, "looks like we ain't making up much ground on that bunch."

Jeffers graced his sergeant with a condescending smile. "No, but we don't seem to be losing any ground either. And, if anything, the trail is getting easier to follow."

"Yessir. That's what's got me to thinking. It is getting easier to follow and I'm wondering why. It don't make no sense to me."

Jeffers stretched his legs out in front of him and shrugged his shoulders to work out some of the stiffness of the trail. "I don't think it's any great mystery. They don't expect anyone to follow them so they're careless about their trail."

"Well, maybe so." Ryman shook his head as if

thinking hard on what the lieutenant had just said. "It looks like they're too damn careless."

A wry smile creased Jeffers's face. "You don't think we should continue to pursue this band of renegades, do you?"

Ryman shrugged. "Well, sir. I wouldn't never try to tell the lieutenant what to do. I'm just saying that usually, when Injuns are this careless about their trails, they want you to find 'em, is all I'm saying."

"I understand your concern, Sergeant, but I feel sure this band is simply running away." Noting Ryman's doubtful expression, he continued. "Look, Ryman, these hostiles have been sneaking in to raid settlers and stage stations and shoot at the steamers for too long now. They raid and then run back into the hills where they think the army won't follow them. Well, this time they've got somebody on their tail who'll chase the bastards all the way to the Snake if necessary."

"Understand that, sir. All's I'm saying is they're acting mighty damn careless, like they was thinking about an ambush."

"Ambush?" Jeffers seemed surprised. "I hope they lead us straight to their village. We better not ride into a damn ambush. That's what those two Crow scouts are out there for." His face lightened a bit. "I think you've just been out here too long, Sergeant. You're starting to see Indians behind every tree."

"Maybe so, sir. I wouldn't disagree. I reckon I'm just kind of fond of what little bit of hair is left on this old head."

The noon rest over, the troop moved out again. The two Crow scouts rode out ahead once more to either side and about a quarter of a mile ahead. Since the trail was plain to see, it wasn't necessary for them to track. So they rode the flanks to keep an eye out for any other hostiles. Before riding out to their positions, however, they wanted to talk to Lieutenant Jeffers. It was their feeling that the column was probing too far into Sioux country and that it might be wise to turn back. Jeffers had little patience with them and advised them that he would decide when the column would about-face. Even though they did not protest, Ryman didn't like the way they looked at each other before silently mounting their ponies and riding out ahead.

Ryman looked back at the column of men plodding along behind him. Veteran campaigners, most of them, a typical troop of field soldiers. One might wonder, at first sight, if they were soldiers or simply an odd assortment of vigilantes. There were at least five different varieties of hats. Most of the men favored broad-brimmed campaign hats but few of them wore army issue. Consequently there were several different styles and colors. The usual uniform while in the field was the garrison casual dress blue shirt and light blue wool trousers. But at least a third of the detail wore buckskin pants instead.

That was one thing he liked about Lieutenant Jeffers. He didn't hold for much spit and polish, especially in the field. For an officer, he was well tolerated by the men. The only negative quality Ryman could find in the man was a sizable sense of arrogance when it came to fighting Indians. Jeffers thought he could take one regiment of cavalry and defeat the entire Sioux nation. The sergeant couldn't help but be reminded of another brash officer who had underestimated the fighting ability of the Plains Indian, and he was determined not to be a participant in another massacre like the one Captain Fetterman rode into back in '66. Ryman figured Jeffers would make a first rate officer, if he lived long enough. He just needed more time and experience out here. Three minor engagements with the hostiles—chasing three Lakotas who had killed a farmer's cow and two incidents while escorting a wagon train—that was the sum total of Jeffers's combat against the Lakota Sioux. It wasn't enough to establish a feeling of invincibility. *With a little luck,* he thought, *maybe we can keep him from taking us all to glory.* He turned his attention back to the front.

After two more hours and still no sight of the band of Arapahos, Private Fannin pulled up beside Ryman. "Sarge, reckon you ought to tell the lieutenant we're too damn deep in Injun territory?"

"Shut up, Fannin. Get back there where you belong and keep your eyes open." He hated to admit it but Fannin was right. Probably all the men were thinking similar thoughts but Fannin was the only one with gall enough to open his mouth. Further thoughts on the matter were interrupted when he saw the Crow scouts galloping back to meet the column.

Lieutenant Jeffers held up his hand and pulled up to await his scouts. He stood in the stirrups and scanned the country before them with his field glasses, searching for any cause for the Indians' rapid return. The rolling, treeless plains before them were devoid of any living creature. After a minute, he sat down again in the saddle and watched as the Crows pulled up before him.

"Soldiers, go back now. Too much danger ahead." This from the expressionless face of the Crow scout called Two Horses.

Jeffers seemed eager to question them. "What did you see? Have you spotted them?"

"No. Not see but good sense tell me go back." He groped for the words to explain his feelings of intuition in order to make the white soldier understand. "Don't have to see—Arapaho, Cheyenne, maybe. See here." He pointed to his heart. "Not here," pointing to his eye. Two Horses looked to his comrade for confirmation and the other Crow nodded his head vigorously.

CHEYENNE JUSTICE

Jeffers didn't say anything for a long moment. "Jeezus wept," he uttered then in disgust. He turned and scanned the horizon all around then returned his gaze to Two Horses. "I think you see here," he said, pointing to his backside. Two Horses shook his head, no. "My God, man. You can see for miles," Jeffers insisted. "There's no place to hide."

"Arapaho, maybe Cheyenne," Two Horses repeated stoically.

"Sergeant Ryman, what do you make of this?"

"Well, sir, these people have a way of feeling the presence of an enemy sometimes . . . and we are operating pretty deep in hostile territory."

The lieutenant looked at his sergeant as if the man had disappointed him. He looked back at the two Crow scouts for a moment before returning to Ryman. "Well, I'm not turning back just because two Crow scouts are feeling a streak down their backs, especially when I can clearly see the country I'm marching into. We'll go on. Send the scouts back out."

Ryman turned to instruct the scouts but, before he could speak, Two Horses shook his head. "No. Too many warriors. We go back now."

Jeffers's nostrils flared. "You're taking pay from the U.S. Army to find those Arapahos. Now, get your ass out there and find them!"

Two Horses was unmoved. "No, we go back. You want to find Arapaho? Keep going. You find 'em pretty soon now." Not waiting for the lieutenant's response, the two Crows kicked their ponies and galloped off.

Private Fannin, who had been listening to the exchange between his lieutenant and the scouts, called out. "Want me to shoot 'em, sir?" He raised his carbine to take aim.

Before Jeffers could answer, Ryman ordered, "No. Dammit, Fannin, put that rifle down."

"The sergeant's right, Private. No need to advertise our presence out here. Let them go. We don't need scouts anyway, as plain as this trail is. Sergeant, send two men out to ride point. I hope that damn savage is right about his feeling." He raised his arm again and signaled forward march and the column was in motion again.

Toward the middle of the afternoon, the trail cut back between two low ridges toward the river again. Jeffers halted the column and conferred with Ryman on the possibility of an ambush since the column would have to pass through the narrow ravine.

"Well, if they was of a mind to ambush us, this would be a dandy place to do it, sir, right where the men can see water just beyond." He looked around him at the ridges on both sides. "There sure don't seem to be much cover on them bare hills to hide anybody, though."

Jeffers studied the ridges for a few moments. "Well, no use taking any chances. Send a couple of men up ahead to scout out those ridges." In spite of his confidence that his men could handle a large force of undisciplined savages, he was beginning to have second thoughts about pushing on much further. He had fully expected to overtake the Arapahos before that morning, and already he was almost three days down the Tongue River. He thought about it for a few moments more and decided they had gone far enough. They had only drawn five days' rations and grain, so turning back after today would see them arrive at Camp Carson with empty bellies. "Sergeant, we'll go as far as the river, water the horses, and then return." To himself he thought, *Dammit, I hate going back empty-handed.*

Ryman was relieved. "Yessir," he snapped smartly and turned to the men behind him. "Fannin, you and McManus get up on those ridges and make sure we ain't riding into anything. And watch your behinds."

CHEYENNE JUSTICE

He waited a moment as Fannin and McManus pulled out of line and galloped out ahead. Then he went over beside Jeffers and watched with the lieutenant as the two troopers split up to climb the ridges on each side of the ravine. Jeffers followed the two with his field glasses as they slowed their mounts and worked their way along the tops of the ridges until they disappeared from sight. Every eye in the column was now straining to watch the ridges, the men quiet and listening. There was no sound except an occasional snort of a horse and a nervous stomping of a hoof. It seemed like a long time with no sight of the two troopers until one, then the other was seen loping back along the ridge tops.

"Clean as a hound's tooth," Fannin called out as he reined up before the lieutenant, McManus a few yards behind.

"Nothing?" Jeffers asked and, when Fannin shook his head, the lieutenant turned to McManus. "You see anything?"

"Nossir. There ain't really no gullies deep enough to hide no Injuns. I could see the trail down below. There ain't no Injuns in that pass. I reckon they just passed through on their way to water."

Satisfied, Jeffers gave the order to go forward and the column entered the ravine at a fast walk. Just to be safe, he cautioned the men to watch their flanks carefully to be on the lookout for anything suspicious. Fannin and McManus were right—there were no hostiles lying in ambush and the troop broke out of the ravine on the other side and descended a shallow coulee that led to the edge of the river.

Fannin, taking it on himself to assume the role of scout now that the Crows were gone, galloped ahead to the shallow water. He wheeled around and shouted, "Here's where they crossed!" Ryman rode up to join him. "They crossed right here, Sarge, and this trail ain't very old. Looks like the water ain't much deeper than shoulder high."

Ryman didn't say anything for a moment while he looked up and down the river and stared at the tracks plainly visible on the far side. *They sure as hell ain't concerned about their trail*, he thought. *I suppose they don't figure us to be crazy enough to follow them this far.* He turned back to get the lieutenant's orders.

"Looks like they're hightailing it back home as fast as they can ride, Lieutenant. I reckon we can water the horses and head back to the post."

Jeffers was studying the bluffs on the far side of the river. Three days in the saddle and he hadn't even gotten a glimpse of the hostiles. He was weighing the choices before him. He had said he would go to the river and no further, but the desire to see his enemy was strong and he was tempted to follow them across the river in hopes they would make camp soon. It was getting late in the afternoon and the thought that they might be just ahead was enough to entice him to see for himself.

"Sergeant, we'll ford the river and follow that trail up to the top of those bluffs. Let's get moving, it's getting late."

Ryman jerked his head around to look at the lieutenant. He didn't say anything for a few moments. "You gonna keep after 'em?"

Jeffers was impatient with the question. "That's what I said, Sergeant." Then he softened his tone a bit. "Just to the top of the bluffs to have a look at the country beyond."

"Yessir," Ryman answered. He turned to face the troopers, most of whom were dismounted, holding their reins while the horses drank. "Mount up. We're going across. Fannin, you look like you want to play scout. Go on out at point—and don't lead us into no holes. I don't feel like taking a bath right now."

They entered the water single file and started

across, Fannin leading. The footing was firm and the water came up no further than just above their stirrups in the deepest part. Fannin reached the other side and turned to watch the rest of the column, some twenty yards behind. Ryman glanced up at him just at the moment the arrow struck Fannin's chest. Ryman could hear the thump of the arrowhead when it shattered Fannin's breastbone, even above the rippling of the water around him. For a moment he was too stunned to react. One moment Fannin was sitting on his horse, grinning and waving to his comrades to come on. The next moment the arrow shaft seemed to materialize from nowhere—it almost appeared that the arrow had come from inside Fannin and had suddenly protruded outward.

Ryman's paralysis lasted for only a second before the reality of the moment took hold of him and he sprang into action. Behind him, he heard one of the men cry out as another arrow found its mark. Then he was aware of a swarm of arrows piercing the water around the troopers. Another cry rang out from a wounded man, and a horse screamed and foundered, thrashing about in the middle of the river. Then the river bottom exploded with rifle fire and he was suddenly in the midst of a hailstorm of flying lead.

Ryman pulled his carbine off his shoulder, almost losing it in the river. Looking frantically around him, he tried to locate the source of the hostile fire. Behind him was chaos as the stunned troopers tried to escape the deadly fire, not knowing which way to run. Directly in front of him, Lieutenant Jeffers was blindly firing his pistol at the riverbank. In another moment, Ryman sized up the situation. The ambush was set up behind them and on both sides of the column so that they were caught in the middle of the current and could run neither upstream or downstream.

Barking out orders at the top of his voice, he yelled to his men to follow him, but he was too late to stop some of the men who had tried to escape to either side, only to ride right into a killing swarm of lead. There was only one route of escape and that was to plow on across the river and try to gain the cover of the bluffs. "Across!" he yelled while trying to control his horse with one hand, with the other firing wasted shots from his carbine. "Make for the other side! Follow me!" Lieutenant Jeffers quickly joined in and urged his men to make for the far bank. They kicked and pleaded with their horses, begging for speed, and the frightened animals struggled in the belly-deep water, straining for the other side.

Upon reaching the comparative safety of the bluffs, Jeffers and Ryman remained exposed to the blistering attack from across the river while they directed the rest of the troop into defensive positions among the cuts and gullies that ran down from the bluffs. When the last man staggered into safety, leading his horse, the lieutenant and his sergeant took cover and the troop began to return fire.

"How many lost?" Jeffers gasped.

Ryman wasn't sure. In the chaos of the crossing he had seen one body floating downstream and another knocked from his horse, but he had been too busy to see everything. "I don't know for sure. Two I saw—three counting Fannin. We'll just have to count heads."

When the head count was completed, there were five troopers missing. "Damn!" Jeffers exclaimed softly when he heard. Five men dead and he was now backed up in the bluffs. He had been suckered by a undisciplined band of savages and his men were pinned down by the rifle fire from directly across the river. While the soldiers were clamoring for cover among the gullies, their attackers had moved from their hiding places and advanced to new positions

CHEYENNE JUSTICE 137

along the riverbank. From the long line of rifle fire pouring in upon them, keeping them low behind what cover they could find, Jeffers could now see that he faced a force of considerably more than the nine Arapahos he had been chasing.

There was no time for self-blame as the lieutenant did his best to direct his men to return fire, admonishing them to conserve their ammunition. At the start of the patrol, each man had drawn one hundred rounds of carbine ammunition and twenty-five rounds of forty-five pistol shells. So the ammunition was not low by any means but he didn't like the position they were forced to defend and he was afraid the siege could last a long time.

"How many do you make it out to be?" Jeffers asked Ryman when the sergeant crawled up beside him after making a check on the condition of his troops.

"Hard to say, but from the way they're spread out along that bank, I'd say at least forty or fifty." He hunkered lower to the ground when a bullet kicked up sand just above his head. "We're in a mess, all right."

"How are the men?"

"Hell, they're doing as best they can, I reckon. They're all veterans. They've been shot at before. Evers and Schumacher are wounded but they're all right." He ducked his head again as another bullet kicked up dirt between them. "God damn that son of a bitch!" He crawled up to the brim of the gully and fired several shots at the spot he thought the shots had come from. Knowing that he was wasting ammunition when he couldn't see his target, he fired anyway to release some of the frustration he felt.

After the first forty-five minutes or so, the firing from the Arapahos tapered off to occasional bursts of rifle shots whenever a trooper carelessly exposed part of his body. Now two hours had passed and the sun began to descend below the bluffs, throwing the gullies into shadow. It would not be long before the river bottom would be immersed in total darkness. Ryman wasn't looking forward to that. It would be a long night and every man would have to stay alert. There was always the chance that the hostiles would tire of the siege and ride away during the night, but Ryman didn't give that thought much of a chance. Why should they? Hell, they held all the cards. They knew as well as he did that there wouldn't be any rescue column coming to reinforce the besieged troopers—they were three days' ride from the fort. Ryman also knew, from personal experience, that the tales that Indians didn't fight at night were simply myths. So the troopers' only chance for survival was to hold the Indians off till they got bored with the battle. They were not likely to charge—that wasn't usually their style, since they didn't like to suffer the heavy casualties that military face-offs usually brought. So the soldiers would have to sit tight and pray the hostiles got tired of waiting them out. Ryman promised himself one small liberty in the event they had to hold here until their ammunition ran out and the hostiles overran them. When it came down to the end, he was going to make sure he told Lieutenant Page Jeffers what an arrogant ass he was for leading a twenty-man patrol this deep into hostile territory.

Evening began to settle in, still with sporadic gunfire between the battle lines. One of the men, Private Greenwell, called to Sergeant Ryman that he thought he had seen Fannin move. The trooper had laid where he had fallen on the riverbank, the arrow imbedded in his chest, for over three hours. Ryman ducked low and, in a crouch, made his way over to the end of the gully to get a look for himself.

After staring, unblinking, at the fallen trooper for several minutes, he was about to conclude that

Greenwell had simply seen a dead man's contraction. Then he saw Fannin's hand slowly reach up and touch the arrow shaft as if to pull it out. He was too weak, however, and the effort to raise his hand seemed to exhaust him. The hand dropped back to his side.

"He ain't dead," Greenwell said. "I'll make a run for him."

Ryman stopped him with a hand on his arm. "No. I ain't gonna lose another man right now. He's laying out in the open. They'd cut you down before you got halfway there. It'll be dark in another thirty minutes. We'll get him then. Another half hour won't make much difference." So they waited.

Lieutenant Jeffers made the rounds to each man's position as the light faded away in the valley and only long streaks of orange and dark blue remained above the ridges. He cautioned each man to keep a sharp eye to guard against a surprise attack and to make sure he knew the exact position of the men on either side of him. "I don't want us to start shooting each other during the night, so if you're going to change your position make sure you tell the man next to you."

As soon as it was dark enough that the outline of the river became lost in the softness of the night, Greenwell and McManus crawled over the rim of the gully and made their way to the wounded man. Fannin cried out in pain when his two comrades picked him up and the sound brought an immediate response from the hostiles. Within seconds the air was filled with gunshots as several troopers targeted muzzle flashes from the opposite bank of the river.

Fannin was almost out of his head with pain. There was no medical orderly with the column and the one man who had had some training in the care and bandaging of wounds was the body that Ryman had seen floating downstream during the ill-fated crossing. At times Fannin seemed lucid and then he would seem to be hallucinating and ranting about a dark angel who would smite the savages with his scythe. They figured he wouldn't last till morning, especially if he was seeing dark angels around him. The arrow was buried deep in his chest and, after a futile attempt to dislodge it, during which Fannin collapsed into unconsciousness from the pain, they concluded the arrowhead had bent around the bone and had best be left to the surgeon—if Fannin was still alive when they returned to Camp Carson. There was nothing they could do for him except try to make him as comfortable as possible. For the rest of the night, he drifted in and out of consciousness. During one of his lucid moments, he thanked the sergeant for not leaving him out in the open to die.

Not long after total darkness set in, they were aware of movement in front of their position and every man tensed to repel what might turn out to be a frontal attack. Every eye strained to see in a night so deep that a man could stand ten yards away and be totally invisible. Occasional muffled sounds reached the men dug in under the bluffs. Fingers rested nervously on triggers, knowing the savages would be using knives and bows, not wanting to reveal their advances with muzzle blasts. Suddenly a scream rang out on the far end of the line of troopers, followed by the blast of an army carbine. One Arapaho was dead, a bullet through his gut. But the price had been one trooper, his throat opened up by the daring hostile's knife.

Knowing the Indians would probably make a try for the horses, Sergeant Ryman posted two men to guard them. The horses were crowded together in the back of the gully and Ryman didn't want to take a chance on the possibility that some of the hostiles might be able to descend the steep wall of the bluff behind them.

CHEYENNE JUSTICE

Another half hour passed and there was another attempt by an Indian to slip in and kill a trooper on the opposite flank from the one just killed. This time the trooper targeted was alert and quick enough to dispatch this warrior with his Colt forty-five. The hours creeped slowly by, occasionally punctuated by a sudden flight of arrows that rained down around the weary soldiers. But there were no more sneak attempts. Ryman figured they had decided to wait for daylight. Everything was quiet then; the only sound reaching the besieged cavalry were the insect noises along the river and an occasional night bird's call.

A muffled cry was heard from the opposite side of the river, then nothing again. Minutes passed. Then, downstream, a grunt reached them and Ryman and the lieutenant speculated on what the sounds meant. In a few more minutes a sharp cry of some kind rang out briefly before going silent again. It sounded somewhat like an abbreviated war cry.

"What the hell are they doing?" Jeffers mumbled.

Ryman answered. "Damned if I know. Maybe they're getting theirselves worked up to attack us." As if underscoring his remark, they heard a low grunt in the darkness before them.

"I think they're trying to work on our nerves," Jeffers concluded.

"You might be right." Then he added, "They're doing a right smart job on mine."

Whatever the reason for the sounds, there were no more that night beyond the general noise of movement across from them, which indicated to the lieutenant that they were getting into position to attack at first light.

The first faint rays of sunlight that probed the heavy darkness of the river bottom found a sleepless cavalry patrol nervously waiting for the dawn and the fury it promised to bring. Every man strained at his post, trying to penetrate the gloom that was rapidly fading away. It seemed that, hours before, when the darkness was a cloak for the sinister movements of the savage Indians, it was a foreboding and threatening thing. Now, as that darkness lifted, there was almost a reluctance to let it go. There was a feeling of nakedness, knowing that the sun's rays would expose the meager defense of the patrol. They knew they were outnumbered three or four to one. Their only avenue to the water was across an open riverbank and most of the canteens were emptied during the long, sleepless night. The horses were already restless at being so close to water and not being allowed to drink. There had been no cookfires during the night for obvious reasons, and there was no wood available to them to build fires even if it had been allowed. So, tired and hungry and nervous, they waited and watched.

Even as the sky lightened and the ridges beyond the river became visible, there remained an eerie quiet over the river bottom. A heavy mist rose from the water causing the opposite side of the river to remain obscure. Sergeant Ryman crawled over beside Lieutenant Jeffers and checked the load in his carbine for at least the tenth time since the darkness started to lift.

"It shouldn't be long now," Jeffers said. "I haven't heard a sound for hours."

"It's too damn quiet to suit me," Ryman agreed. "I don't know what they're up to but they're being mighty quiet about it."

Up and down the line, he could hear the muffled sounds of his men shifting around in their dug-in positions, situating their rifles in scooped-out firing trenches, eyes riveted on the wall of mist hovering over the river. "Keep a sharp eye," he cautioned. "Some of them devils will be sneaking in under the cover of that mist."

CHEYENNE JUSTICE

Still there was no sound and no sign of movement. They waited. Now the first rays of the sun extended down to touch the river bottom and the mist began to slowly dissipate. "Hold your fire till you can see a clear target," Jeffers ordered. "We can't afford to waste ammunition."

The silence was almost unbearable. At Ryman's elbow, Greenwell complained. "Why don't they come on?"

Ryman didn't answer. His eyes strained to see through the rapidly evaporating mist, and as he stared, his eyes burning from lack of sleep, he thought he saw a form materializing on the far side. At first he thought his eyes were playing tricks on him, but the form began to take on shape and he realized it was a man. He raised his carbine and took aim. It was a long shot so he hesitated to pull the trigger. *Come a little bit closer*, he said to himself. In seconds, the fog faded to reveal a tall man dressed in buckskins. Ryman lowered his rifle. He thought once again that he was seeing things, that his mind was playing tricks on him. But in a few more moments, the mist swirling around the appellation's feet and legs melted away and he realized that it was no mirage he was looking at. The man didn't look like an Arapaho. Seconds later he realized it was a white man. A few more seconds passed and the ghostly form spoke.

"Hold your fire," the stranger called out. "I'm coming across." There was a few moments' pause. "Can you hear me? I'm coming across."

The significance of the man's ghostlike appearance hit him with thunderous impact—the hostiles had gone! Ryman stood up and ordered, "Hold your fire! Hold your fire!"

"What the hell . . . ?" Jeffers started but didn't finish, for by that time Ryman had walked out in front of the gully.

"They've gone," Ryman told him. Turning back to the river, he called out, "Come on across!"

Daylight was rapidly filling the river bottom now as the lone figure on the far bank led a brown and white paint to the water's edge before stepping up in the saddle and starting across. The beleaguered men crawled out of their rifle pits and, one by one, walked out on the hard-packed sand, scarcely believing their deliverance from what had promised to be a massacre. With bleary eyes they watched the progress of the mysterious rider as he unhurriedly forded the shoulder-deep water. They looked around them in confused amazement as the sunlight revealed still more. Not ten yards from the spot where Fannin had lain wounded for hours was the body of an Arapaho warrior. Directly in front of their position, at the water's edge, another body lay, his legs in the water from his knees down. Ryman looked in wonder at the bodies and then back to the tall stranger now climbing up the shallow bank.

"You boys got any coffee?"

Lieutenant Jeffers was almost in shock. "The hostiles . . ." was all he could get out at first, still unable to understand what had happened.

"They left a couple of hours before daylight," was the simple explanation.

Ryman stepped forward, offering his hand. "Mister, you're welcome to all the coffee you can drink. Roy Ryman's the name."

"Jason Coles." He took the extended hand.

An almost festive atmosphere settled over the small command as the threat of imminent death was lifted. After assurance from Jason that the Arapahos had indeed left the area, Jeffers gave the men permission to gather firewood and have a hot breakfast. While the bacon and hardtack was being prepared, Jason gave the lieutenant and Ryman an explanation for the sudden change of heart by the Arapahos. Jason Coles's accounting, as usual, was simple and abbreviated on the first run-through, but with Sergeant Ryman's probing and questioning, a fuller version was extracted from the soft-spoken scout.

Jason explained that he was trailing two white renegades who had kidnapped a woman, and he had heard rifle fire late last evening. He broke off to investigate and was surprised to find the cavalry patrol so deep in hostile territory with no more than the few men he could make out from his position up on the ridge. He could see the Arapahos below him in the bluffs and it was apparent to him that the soldiers were in a box they couldn't get out of.

Jeffers interrupted. "But there must have been fifty or sixty hostiles."

"There wasn't but forty that I could see," Jason countered, and then he continued. After sizing up the situation, he concluded that he would be of little help if he tried to ride through to the soldiers. He could be far more effective by himself after dark. He figured that, if he could take out a few of their warriors without them knowing what hit them, he might be able to spook them into thinking some mysterious force was telling them that maybe it was bad medicine they were making and they'd best fight another day.

As soon as it was dark enough, he scouted around until he found their horses beyond the second ridge. There were only two warriors left to guard the horses and, in the darkness, it wasn't too difficult to get the jump on them, using his knife to kill them both. He took their scalps, figuring to further confuse the Arapahos, making them wonder if one of their natural enemies, like the Crows or Pawnees, was at their backs.

"One of the horse guards had a bow and that made my work a little easier. I ain't what you might call a crack shot with a bow but I'm a fair shot and I can hit something if I get close enough."

He cut the hobbles on about half the horse herd and chased them off. Then he went about stalking the rest of the warriors. He worked his way in behind them on the bluff, slipping up to within his bow range. He killed one who had left the others to relieve himself. Then he worked his way around to the downstream side of the war party and waited until he got a shot at another one. "It was pretty close in there after that so I went downstream a ways and came across to this side. I figured to wait till they found their friends dead and their horses gone."

"You were on this side of the river?" Jeffers asked. "Why didn't you come on in, then?"

"Well, to tell you the truth, Lieutenant, I didn't fancy getting myself shot by one of your boys."

Ryman interrupted. "That was four killed. What about those two?" He pointed to the two bodies on this side of the river.

"Like I said, I was laying low. I saw that one buck come across the river—it was so damn dark he damn near stepped on me when he sneaked by. He was fixin' to take that boy's scalp with the arrow in him—I thought the boy was dead—but I couldn't see any sense in sitting there letting him take his scalp."

"Angel of darkness." McManus spoke up. He had been standing at Ryman's elbow, taking in the conversation. "There's Fannin's dark angel he was ranting about. I reckon he wasn't just talking out of his head after all."

Jason was puzzled by the remark but went on. "The other buck came across looking for the first one, I reckon."

"So you were on this side of the river all night?"

"Well, no. I was over here until I heard them find the bodies of the ones I killed. When I heard them pulling out, I crossed back over and followed them to make sure they were going to stay gone. I reckon that's the whole story."

Lieutenant Jeffers was astonished. The man had singlehandedly routed a band of forty Arapaho warriors and without doubt had saved many of the lives of his troop—maybe all of their lives. As Coles had so succinctly pointed out, the Indians had them in a box, and fighting their way out would have been costly. Though Jeffers had heard stories of Bridger and Carson and a few others who had established reputations as frontier scouts, he was not familiar with the name of Jason Coles. But one thing for certain—he would never forget it.

"Well, Mr. Coles, my men and I certainly owe you our thanks."

"Why, not at all, Lieutenant, I'm sure you'da done the same for me."

After the men had eaten breakfast, some of them were detailed to cut poles for travois to carry the wounded back to the post, while others were charged with the chore of burying the dead. Once the bodies were in the ground, the troopers rode their horses back and forth over the graves to keep the hostiles from finding them. It was past seven o'clock when the detail was ordered to mount and prepare to move out.

Jeffers tried to persuade Jason to accompany the column back to Camp Carson—having seen the man in action, he was anxious to enlist him as a scout. But Jason explained that he was already engaged in a mission for Colonel Holder at Fort Lincoln that had turned into an urgent rescue attempt, because he was already a day behind Abby Langsforth's abductors. He respectfully declined Jeffers's offer of employment but asked a favor of the lieutenant.

"When you get back to the fort, will you send a message to Colonel Holder for me? Tell him the

Langsforth girl was snatched by two renegades and that I'll do my best to find her."

Jeffers assured Jason that he would be happy to comply. The scout sat on his paint for a few moments while he watched the column of tired but alive troopers file out of the river bottom and ascend the bluffs, retracing their march of the previous day. When the last soldier disappeared beyond the ridge, he turned the paint back across the river to pick up the trail of the Arapaho war party. Right now, he thought, I need a little luck. The storm had washed out all sign on the two renegades' trail, so he had to rely on hunches—and he had a hunch the war party had come from a village somewhere close. He had taken note of the fact that many of the war party were well armed with repeating rifles, and that meant somebody was actively supplying them. That somebody could be the two who rode off with Abby. At least that gave him someplace to start looking. He urged the paint with his heels, starting off at a fast walk after the Arapahos.

Chapter IX

"You try that again, you dirty little bastard, and you'll get worse than that." Abby glared at Selvey, who was now bent over, clutching his private parts and grimacing with pain. He had just experienced the girl's swift and not too subtle retaliation for his attempt to fondle her breast. Before, he had restricted his actions to undisguised leering whenever Pike wasn't around, but this time, with Pike down by the stream, Selvey's lust for a woman emboldened him to make physical advances. He paid a dear price for his brief contact. For two days, Abby had managed to discourage Pike's desire with her bluster and defiance, but she wasn't sure how much longer she would be able to keep him at bay. She sensed that Pike's delay was in no small part related to his fear of inadequacy—she did not doubt for a minute that it was primarily due to the strong front she presented. It was her feeling that he was afraid he would embarrass himself if he was not successful in assaulting her. If he failed, he would be mortified and would probably be forced to kill her and Selvey too. And he was reluctant to put himself in a position where he had no white woman to trade.

Selvey didn't worry her—she was confident she could defend herself against his fumbling attempts. But Pike would be different. She was certain the man was not only evil and without moral fiber, but also possibly insane. If he did decide he was ready to make a move toward her, she feared there was really nothing she could do to stop him. She only vowed to herself that she would make it as costly as she possibly could.

In a few minutes, Selvey's pain subsided enough to permit him to stand up straight again. He stared at Abby through eyes squinting in anger. "I got a good mind to carve you up," he threatened, drawing a skinning knife from his belt.

"You little turd. I just might tell Pike you tried to rape me. Then we'll see who gets carved up."

He sneered at her and made a couple of feints in her direction with his knife, but she stared him down. "Huh," he snorted. "I wouldn't want none of you anyway, you homely bitch." He put the knife away and moved away to sit by the fire. He knew full well that Pike would kill him if he dared to violate the woman before Pike was through with her.

Pike returned to the camp and stood for a moment, silently staring at the girl. Then he turned his glance to Selvey, who was sitting slightly hunched over by the fire, still feeling the remnants of the agonizing pain administered by Abby's well-placed kick. "What's the matter with you?" Pike demanded.

"Nuthin'," Selvey replied, glancing at Abby out of the corner of his eye. "I just got me a bellyache. I don't feel so good."

Pike continued to stare at his partner, the contempt in his eyes undisguised. "Well, you're gonna have a butt ache if you don't get them horses took care of."

Selvey grumbled softly to himself, but he got to his feet and shuffled off to saddle the horses. Pike pulled a piece of bacon from the frying pan and blew on it to cool it before stuffing the entire piece into his mouth. While he chewed, bothered not at all by the rivulets of grease that flowed from the sides of his mouth and down his chin, he stared coldly at Abby. She did not blink or drop her head, but returned his glare defiantly, even though she feared inside that this might be the moment he was making up his mind to have his way with her. After a long moment, he apparently made a decision and abruptly got to his feet and kicked dirt on the fire.

"Git your ass up. I want to make Crooked Leg's camp before noon."

They rode in silence for most of the morning with Pike leading Abby, riding Nathan White Horse's pony, behind him. Selvey, leading the extra horses, brought up the rear. Pike permitted the girl to ride with her hands and feet unbound. He had even grown tolerant of her frequent stops to relieve her bladder. If she even entertained thoughts of escape, she soon abandoned them. Pike knew there was no place for her to go. The country was open for miles around them so there wasn't sufficient cover to hide in. Besides, if she decided to suddenly bolt for freedom, he would most likely simply shoot her, or the horse, depending on his mood at that moment. So she rode, docile and unprotesting as thoughts of Jason Coles occupied her mind. Where was he? Was he tracking them at this moment? Or had he given up after the storm washed out their trail? She knew he was her only hope as she considered the bleak future that awaited her.

Along about midday, Abby spotted a ribbon of trees in the distance that traced the path of the Powder River. They rode on until reaching the banks of the river and then turned north to follow it. Pike knew approximately where Crooked Leg had camped so he continued up the river until he came to a low line of bluffs where the river bent around a high sand spit, thick with small willows and brush.

"I reckon this here's close enough." He guided them in among the trees and dismounted. "Crooked Leg's camp ain't but about a mile further up." He motioned for Selvey to get off his horse. "I'm gonna ride in with them horses first and talk to old Crooked Leg. You stay here with our guest. I'm gonna trade the horses first before I tell him about the white woman." He glanced at Abby and grinned. "I reckon I might make a better trade if he don't get a look at you first."

Selvey laughed. "Reckon you're right about that, Pike."

Pike's grin disappeared. "I'm aiming to sell 'er untampered with so I'm telling you to keep your hands off of 'er."

"Ah, Pike. If you ain't gonna tap 'er, why can't I just git a little? Them damn Injuns won't know whether she's been bred or not till we're long gone."

"Damn you, Selvey, they'll know. You keep your hands off 'er. I find out different, I'll cut your gizzard out."

"All right, all right. Whatever you say."

"I won't be gone long," he warned. Satisfied that his spineless companion understood, Pike turned his attention to Abby. Without asking her to dismount, he reached up and jerked her off her horse. Taken by surprise, she had no time to resist and consequently landed rather roughly on the ground. Selvey snickered. Pike grabbed her by the back of her shirt and dragged her over against a tree. "Fetch me that rope," he instructed Selvey. When it was handed to him, he tied her hands and feet together.

Still smarting from her rough dismount, Abby tried to resist but Pike was too strong. "What are you tying me up for? You're leaving him to watch me anyway. What if I have to pee before you get back?" There was no anxiety in her tone, merely irritation.

"Pee in your damn pants," Pike shot back. "Watch her, Selvey." Pike didn't explain that he tied her up because he was afraid she was more than a match for Selvey. When he was satisfied that she was bound securely, he stood up and stared down at her for a few moments. "I might trade you fer a pretty little Arapaho girl."

He continued to stand over her, staring. Abby began to feel uncomfortable with his intense gaze. She could almost see his mind working, wondering if he should have taken her after all. The longer he stood there, the more worried she got. She was thinking that she would rather take her chances in the Indian camp than have this foul-smelling renegade touch her.

"What the hell's keeping you?" She made an effort to break his thoughts with her usual bluster.

His hard face slowly broke into an evil grin. "Damn, you are a mouthy bitch. Maybe I'll just give you a proper good-bye." He knelt down beside her and, pulling her neck toward him, suddenly clamped his mouth over hers.

She tried to pull away but he held her firmly by the back of her neck while he smothered her with his rancid kiss. She could not breathe for fear of inhaling his foul stench. He tried to insert his tongue between her tightly pressed lips but she fought to keep her mouth closed. Suddenly she relaxed her lips and he eagerly thrust his tongue in her mouth. She clamped down as hard as she could with her teeth.

"Waugh!" he roared and tried to jerk away. It only increased his pain for she held on with the tenacity of a snapping turtle. Then she released him and he staggered backward, his injured tongue throbbing with each beat of his pulse. "Goddam you!" he screeched, spitting blood at her. She glared at him defiantly and spit several times to rid her mouth of his vile taste. He slapped her hard across the face then slapped her again. She took the blows silently, refusing to grant him even so much as a whimper. Humiliated, he turned on his heel and stalked to his horse. "Watch her, Selvey!" He jerked his horse's head around and rode off in the direction of Crooked Leg's camp.

In the first few minutes after Pike had ridden off, Selvey busied himself building a fire. After it was burning to his satisfaction, he decided to entertain himself by taunting Abby. "You ought not to of bit ol' Pike like that. I reckon now he'll probably trade you off to some redskin—maybe some buck wants a slave for his squaw. If you'da played your cards right, Pike mighta kept you with us."

Abby said nothing for a while as she studied the simpleminded little man. She made a decision. "Selvey, I favor you more than that crazy Pike."

"What?" he blurted, not sure he had understood her.

"Hell, yes," she said. "Pike's too rough to suit me."

He looked at her, disbelieving. "Shit. I ain't as dumb as I look. You don't favor neither one of us."

She shook her head. "That's not exactly true. I could give myself to you but for one thing."

"What's that?" he asked eagerly, his interest immediately rising.

"This morning when you tried to touch me, the only reason I kicked you was because you ain't had a bath in months."

"A bath? What's that got to do with it?"

"Well, a girl likes to make love to a clean man. Didn't you know that?"

"Hell, no." Selvey's blood was definitely beginning to warm. "The only puddin' I ever got was dirtier than I was." He stared at her, scarcely able to believe her smiling countenance. He glanced over his shoulder as if making sure Pike wasn't behind him. "You ain't sayin' you'da let me this morning?"

"I'm saying I'd let you right now before Pike drags me off to that Indian camp."

CHEYENNE JUSTICE

Selvey's brain was threatening to explode. "I don't know. Pike would kill me."

"Pike won't know."

"Damn!" His common sense was rapidly draining toward his belt buckle. Selvey could never remember a woman wanting to make love to him. Even those he had paid were still reluctant. He moved over closer to her. Being careful to stay out of range of her feet, even though they were tied together, he reached out and very slowly laid his grimy hand to rest on her bosom. She did not flinch but smiled warmly up at him. He remained in that posture for a long time, his face a perfect portrait of simple and pure stupidity.

After a few moments, she spoke to break him from his apparent trance. "We could have ourselves a little party before Pike gets back." His eyes widened with the thought. "But I want to enjoy it too, so you need to wash up first."

For an instant his blissful facade faded. "A bath?" His expression was the same as if she had specified that it had to be taken in fire.

"You don't have to take a whole bath. Just go down to the river and wash your face and hands." She flashed a wide smile. "I'll tell you what. Untie me and I'll cook us up some salt pork and fry that hardtack in the grease. We'll have us something to eat and then we can work it off. We'll have us a real party."

Selvey, his hand still planted on her left breast, was starting to squirm like a puppy, no longer able to contain himself. "All right," he blurted. "Just my hands and face, right?" She nodded yes. He immediately went to work on the knots and, within a few seconds, she was free. While she stretched her arms, he started toward the river. "Put some of that brown sugar on the hardtack. I like that."

"I will," she said and went to his saddlepack

where he kept the supplies. He had a brief second thought and paused halfway down the bank, his hand on his pistol as he looked back at her. She pulled a heavy iron skillet out of the pack and knelt before the fire. Relieved, he turned and fairly ran down to the water's edge where he hurriedly began splashing water over his face and arms.

Selvey was beside himself with anticipation of what was to come. The woman was not by any stretch of imagination pretty, but then he didn't really care. He had never had any woman who was pretty. When you had a craving for bacon, you didn't give a damn if the hog was pretty or not. A sobering thought invaded his joyful anticipation. Pike would kill him if he found out. "To hell with Pike," he muttered, looking again at Abby kneeling by the fire, tending to their dinner.

"Well, I reckon I'm as clean as I ever get," he announced as he walked back up to the fire.

She smiled up at him and said, "Have some bacon." She stood up and swung the heavy iron skillet as hard as she could. It landed squarely against the side of his head. Selvey went down in a heap. He laid there, struggling to gather his wits, his ear and the side of his face seared by the hot frying pan. Abby didn't give him time to come to his senses. Wielding the skillet like a hammer, she came down hard on the stunned man's head, driving him into the dirt. The hollow sound of the iron skillet on Selvey's skull almost sickened her but she held on to it with both hands. He struggled helplessly, trying to get up on his hands and knees while she forced herself to come down with the skillet once more. He went face down in the dirt again and lay still. She stood over his prone body for a few moments, praying that he did not move again. When he did not, she flung the skillet away from her and wiped her hands vigorously on her trousers.

CHEYENNE JUSTICE 157

Constantly glancing at the stricken man to make sure he didn't move, she moved quickly, gathering what things she could in her frantic haste to escape. As fast as she could, she saddled her horse and when she was ready to ride she returned to stand over Selvey again, looking hard at the unconscious man, wondering if he was dead. With great caution, she reached down and took his rifle and pistol, jumping back as soon as she had them in her hand, afraid he might suddenly grab her. He didn't move. She started to mount her horse when she thought, *I need some food*. Not wanting to spend another minute in that place, she ran to the saddlepack Pike had loaded on one of the horses and, without taking time to be selective, took it and threw it behind her saddle.

Snatching up Selvey's canteen, she jumped on her horse and kicked him hard. Her first impulse was to ride as far and as fast as she could so she did not let up on the horse for a half mile or more. She didn't know if she had killed Selvey or not but she intended to be long gone when Pike returned. With no notion where she was or where Fort Lincoln might be, she decided she would just ride east. It had to be somewhere in that direction.

Jason poked the ashes of the dead campfire with the toe of his boot. Judging by the coals still smoldering underneath the ashes, he knew he had closed the distance between him and the Arapaho war party. They had cooked their breakfast here that morning, no more than a couple of hours earlier. He had ridden the paint hard since before sunup, and he was finally close. He would have to be more careful from this point on and keep a sharp eye for any Arapaho scouts who may have lagged behind to make sure they weren't being followed.

The trail had left the Tongue the day before and cut a path to the east. Jason figured they must be heading to a village somewhere on the Powder. He stepped up on the paint and gave him a nudge. The horse responded immediately. By his reckoning, the Powder could be no more than a half day's ride from the campsite he had just left. He let the paint settle into a gait that suited him, keeping to the low side of the rolling hills whenever possible, always watching the horizon ahead. It wouldn't do for one of the Indians he followed to spot him and realize he was alone. Since they probably weren't in good humor after being spooked out of their ambush of Lieutenant Jeffers's patrol, they might not be any too hospitable.

The sun was still not directly overhead when he sighted the river ahead and, for the first time since trailing them, caught sight of the hostiles. Keeping a safe distance behind, he trailed the band for another hour until they reached a sharp bend in the river and he got a glimpse of the village. It was a sizable camp of Arapahos, fifty or sixty lodges spread out along the west side of the river. On the other side, Jason could see a horse herd of several hundred ponies.

There was a great deal of excitement in the Indian camp when the war party rode in. Jason took advantage of the distraction to scout out a closer place to watch the village. It was not easy to get close because the campsite had been well chosen to prevent surprise attacks from an enemy. There were some trees along the banks of the river where the tipis were located, but the hills and bluffs before that were open with no cover but tall grass. If he was even going to get close enough to use his field glasses, he was going to have to do some crawling. So he tied the paint in a thicket of bullberry bushes on the side of a ravine a good half mile from the river and then made his way back up the ridge on foot. Crawling to a position where he could sweep the main part of the village with his glasses, he lay in the grass and watched the people of the camp welcome the returning warriors.

From the looks of the camp, they had been there for some time. The grass across the river was grazed down and the ponies looked fat and rested. There were a good many skins staked out to dry and the women were busy scraping them. It was a busy camp. But there was no white woman, at least not that he could see, and the two white men he searched for were not there either. Another cold trail, he thought, and he cursed the storm for obliterating the tracks of Abby's abductors.

As he lay there, trying to decide what to do now that this trail had led to nowhere, a movement under the cottonwoods along the river caught his attention. He turned to see a rider making his way along the riverbank, approaching the Arapaho village from the south. It was a white man. Jason raised his head and scanned the banks behind the man. He was alone. The trail Jason had followed before the storm was from two shod horses, plus the extra Indian ponies, one of which carried Abby. This man was alone. Jason didn't think it was very likely that this could be a different man—it had to be him. He was leading the extra horses, no doubt to trade with the Arapahos. But where was Abby? And where was the other white man?

He had to consider the possibility that Abby had already been sold to the Arapahos and she might be inside one of the lodges—maybe guarded by the missing white man. Or, more likely, this one had her hidden somewhere, not wanting the hostiles to know about her. If that were the case, then his partner was probably guarding her. He reasoned that he would know soon enough when the man rode into the village so he lay there and watched.

When the rider emerged from the trees and approached the southernmost lodges of the village, a woman looked up from her work on a buffalo hide. Jason could tell that she was alarmed, for she ran to alert her people that a white man was coming. Almost immediately, several of the warriors whom Jason had trailed to the camp jumped on their ponies and raced to intercept the stranger. Even from that distance, Jason could see that the stranger was frantically making the peace sign. It was obvious that he had not been in the Arapaho camp recently. Apparently they recognized the man for they surrounded him and escorted him to a tipi in the center of the village.

This told Jason what he wanted to know. This was one of the men he searched for and Abby, if she was still alive, was being held somewhere downriver by his partner. This had to be the case. Otherwise, the Arapahos would not have been so surprised when the white man showed up. *No need to lay around here any longer*, he thought. He would circle around to the south and cut the white man's trail and that should lead him straight to Abby. Luck was with him.

Slowly, keeping low to the ground, he backed down the other side of the rise he had hidden behind, being careful not to disturb the tall grass on the crest. Once he was far enough down so that he could stand up without showing a profile, he made his way quickly back the way he had come. Moving carefully, he crossed over the ridge and descended the side of the ravine to the thicket where the paint stood, quietly pulling at the grass around the bushes.

He untied the pony and started to mount when he was stopped in his tracks by the sudden flight of a covey of birds on the other side of the ravine. He stood still and listened. Something had flushed them. What? A fox, maybe . . . or maybe not. All at once a familiar feeling took hold of him and he sensed that he was in danger. Then he heard the low call of a lark on the opposite side of the ravine. He was being hunted!

Wasting no more time, he quietly climbed up in the saddle and started the paint along the bottom of the ravine at a slow walk, listening and watching the high ground on each side of him. He had only two choices—to go back down the ravine the way he had come or to ride north, away from the river. The choice took no deliberation since he felt reasonably sure they were on both sides of him—they had tracked him into the mouth of the ravine behind him and had split up to trap him in the ravine. Maybe luck was not with him after all. All he could figure was that some hunters must have stumbled across his trail into the hills. It had to be sheer accident on their part because his tracks, before finding this ravine, had been intermingled with those of the war party he had followed to the camp. His only chance was to make it out the north end of the ravine before they could get there to cut him off. The only good thing about the situation he found himself in was the fact that they were too far away from the camp to summon other hostiles to participate in the chase.

From his many years of living with the danger that rode with a frontier scout, he could see the chase developing in his mind's eye. Everything was still quiet but they were pacing him, much as a fox patiently paces a prairie hen until she bolts. *Well*, he decided, *I reckon it's time for this hen to bolt.* With that thought, he suddenly kicked the paint into full flight and the horse didn't disappoint him. On the ridges above him he heard an almost immediate response as war whoops rang out on both sides.

The little paint worked hard and steady, sensing he was in a race as he flew over the small gullies and cuts with never a misstep. From the whoops of the warriors above him, he determined that it was not a large party chasing him—there was no way to tell for sure, but he guessed there were no more than half a dozen. Even though the paint had the heart for it, Jason could see that the hostiles, riding on the level tops of the ridge, would intercept him at the end of the ravine. As he galloped toward the narrow opening at the top of the ravine, he could see that he would come out barely a few steps ahead of them.

Now he caught glimpses of his pursuers as their ponies jumped and weaved in their headlong dash to cut him off. He flinched as an arrow flashed in front of his face and he was aware of others passing harmlessly behind him. The race was too fast and too roughshod to permit accurate shooting. Jason knew that if an arrow found him, it would be pure luck. He didn't have time to speculate on the reason they were using bows instead of rifles. Maybe they didn't have rifles, or maybe they had used up their ammunition while hunting—he didn't care why. At the moment, his concern was to reach the end of the ravine.

Fifty yards more. He could see that it was going to be a dead heat. He couldn't outdistance them. He pulled his rifle from the saddle boot and kept kicking his heels into the paint's sides. There was a sharp turn where the head of the ravine broke out on the ridge above. As he approached it, he pulled back on the paint, slowing the horse a little. When the pony hit the turn, Jason threw himself off and hit the dirt rolling over and over. Startled, the horse continued to charge up out of the ravine. Jason scrambled to his feet and ran after the horse, reaching the end of the ravine at almost the same moment the hostiles galloped by, chasing the paint.

There were four of them and, when Jason brought his rifle to bear, there were two less. Realizing too late that they were chasing a riderless horse, the two remaining hostiles turned back to discover their companions lying dead, their ponies galloping off into the hills. Confused at first, then angry, they charged back toward the white man standing calmly awaiting them. Unhurriedly, he shot one and then the other.

This was no time to be on foot so close to a hostile village of Arapahos, so Jason started out after his horse at a trot. The paint had continued on for almost a mile before coming to a stop, where he casually began to graze. Jason could see the paint ripping at the grass, then looking up at the man trotting toward him, seemingly unconcerned. Jason glanced to the west. All four of the Indians' ponies had scattered toward the hills. As he jogged along, he found himself hoping the paint didn't develop an urge to join his brothers. Evidently the pony had decided to adopt Jason because he stood there, patiently waiting until Jason caught up to him.

"Good boy," Jason cooed, stroking the paint's neck. He slid the rifle back in the boot and stepped up in the saddle. "I don't know how much time we've got before somebody rides out to find out what all that shooting was about, but I reckon it would be best to keep going for a ways before doubling back. I don't want that whole damn village following me." He galloped off toward the hills after the Indian ponies to make sure they didn't turn around and head back to the village. He knew he was losing time but he thought it necessary to chase the horses then try to cover his trail before turning back to the river and Abby.

Jack Pike was angry. Crooked Leg, that old son of a bitch, wanted rifles and bullets. He didn't want to trade anything for the horses Pike brought in. He said he had plenty of horses. Pike tried to tell him that he didn't have rifles this time, he had three horses. That's what he needed to trade, dammit! Then he told the chief that he had a white woman captive and he might be willing to trade her.

Crooked Leg said, "Why would I want a white woman?" The old son of a bitch! He took the horses anyway. *When I get back,* he told himself, *I'm gonna have me some of that homely bitch, then I'm gonna carve her up good before I let Selvey have her.*

He paid little attention to the shots heard beyond the bluffs. There were hunting parties going and coming all day. There had been four shots. Probably one damn Injun shooting at a rabbit, he thought. No wonder they were short of ammunition. He had to promise old Crooked Leg that he'd come back with more rifles and bullets or the old cutthroat might not have let him leave. "Damn!" he swore when he thought about it. They had been lucky that last time, he and Selvey, when they bushwhacked that freight wagon loaded with ordnance. He let Selvey scalp the driver and the guard—Selvey liked scalping people. It would be right handy to run up on another wagon like that. He and Selvey needed some more merchandise to trade with.

Something didn't look right as he approached his camp. Then it struck him that one of the horses was missing. "What the hell . . ." he muttered, and drew his pistol from his belt. Looking cautiously from right to left, he rode up to the edge of the camp and stopped. "Selvey!" he called out. He heard a low groan and followed the sound with his eyes. There, under a tree, Selvey lay, looking half dead. The girl was nowhere to be seen. He rode on in and dismounted, his pistol still ready.

When he had satisfied himself that the girl was not hiding and waiting to ambush him, he went back to the stricken man lying against the tree trunk. "Selvey, what the hell happened?"

Selvey's eyes fluttered for a few seconds. When he tried to speak at first, nothing came out but a wheezing sound. After a moment, he seemed to come to his senses. His voice weak and strained, he spoke. "Pike, I think she cracked my head."

Pike, looking around at the skillet laying in the sand and a half-cooked piece of salt pork a few yards from it, responded impatiently. "Yeah, I can see that. She oughta cracked your head. You untied her, didn't you?"

"She was gonna give me some, Pike, I swear. I don't know why she up and hit me."

Pike just looked down at his partner for a long moment, the anger and disgust building up to a peak. "You dumb shit. Why would any woman want to give you any? Open your mouth," he ordered. Dutifully, Selvey opened his mouth as wide as he could manage. Pike casually stuck the barrel of the forty-five in Selvey's mouth and pulled the trigger. "I've had enough of your whimpering," he said.

Pike didn't waste any more time there. He picked up the half-cooked piece of pork, wiped the sand off, and ate it while he packed up Selvey's horse with what supplies were left. It was not until then that he realized the saddlepack left by the fire was Selvey's. She had taken his! The bitch had taken his! It was not the little bit of pork and hardtack that concerned him. There was a pouch of at least four ounces of gold dust in that pack. He had killed a man and his partner for that dust. It was his property, and that ugly bitch had stolen it. Selvey didn't even know about that pouch of gold—when they had drygulched the two miners, he told Selvey there wasn't any gold.

His business was finished with Crooked Leg, he knew that. The old bastard was getting too hard to deal with. Well, that was all right with Pike. Crooked Leg didn't have anything he wanted to trade for anyway. He might go back to his business with the Sioux, although he didn't like the way he was being treated by the Sioux lately. Maybe it would be better to trade with Two Moon's Cheyennes. They still appreciated his help in ridding the Black Hills of the white miners, and they paid in gold dust. But one thing he promised himself was to track down that homely bitch who made a fool of him and Selvey. He vowed to make himself a tobacco pouch out of one of her breasts.

Chapter X

Abby hopped down from the saddle and stretched her back and legs while her horse drank from the shallow river. She looked back the way she had come, half expecting to see Pike galloping after her. Ahead, the country looked the same as that she had just traveled through, never changing. She had been careful to keep the position of the sun over her left shoulder. Otherwise, it would be pretty easy to end up riding in a circle.

She knelt down at the water's edge and splashed some water on her hands and face. Then she unbuttoned her shirt and splashed some of the cool water on her chest and neck. It reminded her of Selvey and she wondered if the little rat was dead or alive when she had fled. The thought caused her to stand up and look long and hard at her backtrail. She rested her hand on the rifle butt protruding from the saddle boot. "I hope to hell they do come after me. I'll settle their hash for 'em." Her bluster had become a habit over the last few weeks. This time it was for the purpose of shoring up her spirits. If she had permitted her innermost thoughts to surface, she would have had to admit to the dread she harbored that the two bloodthirsty renegades might appear at any time.

Up in the saddle again, she paused to look upstream and then downstream, and then at the rolling prairie facing her. "Abby, girl, you ain't got the slightest idea where the hell you are . . . or where you're going, for that matter." The quiet was almost overpowering. Were it not for the soft gurgle of the water, there would have been no sound at all, and suddenly the vastness of the land seemed to close in on her and she felt her throat choking off her windpipe. "Stop it!" she scolded. There was no time to become frightened and she patted the butt of her rifle again for reassurance.

There was no choice for her but to keep riding, even though she had the feeling that she might blunder into a band of hostiles on the far side of every hill. She knew well enough what was behind her so she urged the horse into the water and walked him downstream. Since she had no idea where she was going, one direction was as good as the other. Her intention was to ride down the middle of the river for a mile or two in hopes of throwing Pike off her trail.

She had ridden not quite a mile when she came to a place she deemed suitable for leaving the river. A grassy knoll extended out almost to the water before giving way to a sandy bank about three yards wide. She guided her horse up the bank and onto the grass, where she dismounted and cut herself a switch from a young willow. Using the willow switch as a broom, she went back and carefully swept the hoofmarks from the sandy bank. Feeling smug about her ingenuity, she mounted again and resumed her trek to the east and, she hoped, civilization.

"Well, Mister, it sure looks like your friend has dissolved the partnership." Jason stood over the corpse lying at the base of a cottonwood tree. The man's brains were splattered all over the tree trunk behind him. It wasn't the work of Indians, that was plain to see, so it had to be the man's partner.

Jason had circled back below the Arapaho village and picked up the white man's trail down the river.

It was easy to follow. But the piece of business he had with the four Arapaho hunters had caused him to lose more time than he had planned. He didn't see that he had had any choice in the matter. He did what he had to do at the time. Though unavoidable, it caused him to find the renegade's camp several hours after the man had already returned from the Indian camp. Abby was not there, but maybe that meant she was at least still alive. The puzzle facing Jason now was to try to paint a picture of what had happened here.

He studied the tracks carefully and determined that his man had ridden out to the east. There were three horses but two of them carried riders, so evidently Abby was still a hostage. The third horse carried a light load, probably a packhorse that belonged to the fellow under the tree. The tracks could not tell him if all three horses rode out together but he assumed that they had. Satisfied that he had gleaned all the information he could at the campsite, he climbed aboard the paint and started out after the two riders. As he rode by the already stiffening body under the tree, he offered one final comment. "Looks like your friend didn't think enough of you to put you in the ground. And I sure as hell don't. Besides, buzzards gotta eat too."

The trail was easy to follow. There had been no attempt to disguise it—evidently there had been no consideration toward the notion that someone might be tailing them. As he kept his eye on the trail before him and his senses keen for any danger from an unexpected quarter, he pushed the paint forward at a ground-eating pace. He had a fleeting thought about Abby's welfare, wondering how she might be holding up. He discarded the thought immediately, knowing that it never helped to worry over things that he could not control.

Jason rode on for a couple of hours when he approached the northern end of a low butte that stretched for about a half mile to the south. He pulled the paint up and studied the tracks for a few moments. One of the riders had veered off and headed around the end of the butte. The other rider and the packhorse went straight up and over the butte. Jason looked at the country ahead and considered the general direction the trail had taken for the last hour. Why did they split up, he wondered, and why did one of them go the long way around? It didn't take but a moment to sink in. He realized that the two of them were not riding together. The man leading the pack horse was trailing her.

Abby had escaped—that was the only thing it could be. When she approached the butte, she rode around the end of it. The man chasing her took a short cut, trying to gain ground on her. This put a little more urgency in the chase and he hurried the paint up the slope of the butte. The pony took to the incline with the surefootedness of a mountain goat.

On the other side of the butte, the trails joined again and continued on in generally an eastern direction, although Abby showed a tendency to lean toward the south a little. It was late in the afternoon when he came to the river. Here's where she decided to cover her trail, he thought, because, when he crossed, there were only two sets of tracks that came out on the other side. To further complete the picture for him, tracks ran upstream and down. Jason decided the man he tracked had ridden upstream first and then, when he didn't find where Abby had come out of the water, he turned around and searched downstream. Jason scouted the tracks upstream first, just as the man had done.

He hadn't gone two hundred yards before he reached the point where the man had turned around. Impatient cuss, he thought. Jason did not see any sign that the man had missed and, while he normally

CHEYENNE JUSTICE

would have scouted the riverbank for a while longer, he decided he would stay with the tracks and he turned back too. He walked the paint slowly downstream, his eyes searching the open riverbank for the one little piece of evidence that would tell him what he wanted to know. He looked at the riverbank as Abby might, trying to guess where she might consider it safe to leave the water. He continued searching along the river's edge, just as the man leading the packhorse had done several hours before. There was also the possibility that Abby had left the water on the same side she had entered, but he doubted it. Abby was running—trying to get back to Fort Lincoln was his guess. But if she continued in the same direction she had been riding, she was more likely to end up in the Black Hills.

Up to now, there had been no likely spot to disguise her exit from the river, for the banks were bare and wide and her tracks would have been evident even to the rankest greenhorn. But then the river took a little turn around some overhanging trees and a little grassy knoll almost reached the edge of the water. The bare sand was only a few yards wide here before the grass began. This would have been the first likely spot, he figured, and by this point she would probably have been impatient to get out of the river and resume her flight. The problem was, there were no tracks across the short stretch of sand and he had yet to see the horse that could leap from that riverbed, over the sandy bank, and land in the grass.

The man he followed had not even stopped to consider it, for the tracks never wavered but continued on down the river. Still Jason had an instinct for such things, so he dismounted to look the spot over more carefully. Something about the sand looked too smooth to be natural. When he took a closer look, he knew right away his instincts had been right on target. She had come out here and had swept the tracks clean. He looked around until he found the broken willow branch and the discarded switch where she had thrown it.

"Good girl," he muttered, smiling as he looked up to follow the tracks of the two horses disappearing down the riverbank. The next few minutes were spent on his hands and knees until he found a print in the soft grass. He traced the impression of it with his finger, then looked in the direction it pointed. Southeast, he thought. Little by little, she had constantly changed her course more to the south. He was sure she had Fort Lincoln in mind, but unless she changed her direction pretty soon she was going to miss it by a helluva lot.

Being a stranger to the country, Abby had no concept of the distance to be covered. She remembered how long it took her and Nathan White Horse to reach Sitting Bull's camp, but part of that time was spent in finding it. For that reason, she kept hoping that beyond every ridge, on the far side of every line of rolling hills, behind every low butte, she might strike the Missouri. She knew she would recognize the Missouri when she reached it. Big and wide, it would be easily discernable from the smaller, shallow rivers she had come to so far.

Now her hopes were becoming strained, for she saw mountains stretching across the horizon before her and she began to doubt her sense of direction. She had not remembered those mountains when she and Nathan were going in the opposite direction. She knew she should be south of the trail they had ridden then, but she didn't think she was that far south. What mountains were they? The Big Horns? Maybe she had gotten turned around and started out in the wrong direction that morning. She had been near exhaustion when she finally stopped and slept last night. No, she told herself firmly. The Big Horns were far behind her. Lost or not, the sun still rose in the east and she was riding toward the sun. She pushed on toward the mountains.

After two days riding and no sign of anyone following her, she began to feel less threatened and gradually her nerves settled down. "I believe I lost the son of a bitch," she announced to her horse. Her concern shifted from her immediate safety to the challenge of finding her way back to Lincoln. And she was confident now in her ability to do that. She was certain to reach the Missouri eventually and then it would be simply a matter of following it north. "If the damn thing hasn't dried up," she stated.

Of immediate importance now was the matter of food, for the supplies she had taken from Pike's packhorse were now running out. There was no coffee left and the salt pork had been finished at supper the night before. She hefted the little pouch she had found in the bottom of Pike's haversack. "I'd trade you right now for a sack of potatoes."

Well, I can hunt, she told herself. She fancied herself an adequate shot with a rifle and she figured that if a man could hunt to survive, then she damn sure could. Having seen no sign of Pike behind her for the last two days, she felt it would be safe to risk a shot. It seemed to her that she was the only living person on the face of the earth. Who would hear it if she fired her rifle?

As she approached the higher hills, she saw more and more signs of the presence of game and even some glimpses of antelope herds in the distance. But she was never close enough to take a shot. By the late afternoon, she was beginning to feel the gnawing in her stomach that told her she was going to have to find something to eat before very much longer. It would be getting dark in a couple of hours, so when she came to a stream that cut through a narrow pass she decided to make camp there for the night where she would have water and some grass for the horse.

She entered the stream and turned her horse to walk slowly up the center, looking for a suitable place to spend the night. She had not gone fifty yards when she pulled back on the reins and held her horse still. There, not a hundred yards away, two black-tailed deer, a buck and a doe, stood drinking at the stream's edge. Moving very slowly so as not to spook them, she drew her rifle from the boot and carefully took aim at the deer closest to her. "Easy, boy," she whispered as her horse shifted from one foot to the other. When he was still again, she pulled the trigger. The bark of the rifle startled her and her horse jerked back briefly before settling down again. Her shot hit the buck, wounding him in the back leg. The impact spun him around and he fell. She urged her horse forward but the deer struggled to his feet and tried to hobble off after the doe, now disappearing through the brush beside the stream.

"Damn," she uttered and pulled back on the reins again to take another shot before he reached the cover of the shrubs. Her second shot missed entirely but she quickly cocked the rifle and her third shot caught the deer behind the shoulder. Still the deer made it to the bushes and out of sight. She galloped after it.

The dying buck had made it to the cover of the brush by the stream and no farther. When Abby galloped up through the bushes and discovered her trophy, her first sensation was a flush of triumph. She had made meat, her first kill. There was a feeling of self-confidence along with the pride of knowing she could survive in this wild country as well as anyone. Her elation was tempered only a little with the sober thought that, now that she had killed it, what was she going to do with it? She had never skinned anything before. There were scant occasions for skinning wild game back at her father's newspaper in Chicago. Her growing hunger told her that she would figure it out.

The first thing she must do was to get her kill out of the bushes where she had room to butcher it. This proved to be a bit more difficult than she imagined. The buck didn't appear to be that big—the antlers counted only four points. But when she attempted to pick him up, she found she could not lift the animal. She dropped his legs and went around to his head and, taking a firm grasp on the antlers, tried to drag the deer free of the brush. At first that didn't work either but finally it occurred to her to use the horse's strength to drag the deer out.

By now the light was fading as the shadows covered the narrow pass, so she decided to camp right where she was. She soon had a fire going and her horse hobbled where it could chew on the bark of the bushes by the stream. Nathan White Horse had showed her how to start a fire with his flint and steel and, while she had spent a good part of the night trying to make enough sparks the first time, she had since improved her technique.

Having no idea where to start her butchering, she studied the carcass before her. Finally she decided she would cut the skin around the neck to separate it from the body. Then she would start on the deer's belly, split it down the middle, and try to peel it off like she was taking off a coat. That seemed a sensible approach to her, so she set into her work with a hungry vengeance.

It wasn't as easy as she had hoped and she worked away at the stubborn hide, straining and cursing. Not bothering to disembowel the animal, she cut and pulled at the hide until she had managed to expose a considerable area of flesh. She was too hungry to continue her struggle to completely skin the animal, so she left it half peeled and cut some strips of flesh to roast on a stick over the fire. While her supper was cooking, she went back to work on the hacked-up carcass, cutting strips of flesh from the shoulder and haunch. She wanted to make a supply of meat to carry with her but she had no way to preserve it. She knew that the Indians dried meat in order to keep it but she wasn't sure how they actually did it. Anyway, she didn't have time to stay in one place long enough to dry meat. So she would cook enough for now and then think about finding more food later.

The first strip of roasted venison she ate was only half cooked because of her impatience. But she decided it was the best meat she had ever tasted—a royal feast, in fact, enhanced by the fact that she had killed it, skinned it, and cooked it. She ate her fill of the sizzling hot meal, continuing to eat long after her hunger was satisfied. When she was content, she went down to the stream and washed her hands and face. Unconcerned about Pike or any other mortal, she rolled up in her blanket by the fire and was soon asleep.

Morning found Abby rested and ready to be on her way. Another night safely passed, with no threat on her life, gave her reason to believe she had indeed escaped Pike's vengence. He may not have even thought it worth the bother to come after her in the first place. Of course Selvey had incentive to want to find her and gain his revenge for the frying pan she laid him out with. But she squandered no more thoughts on the matter. It was a beautiful morning and her spirits were up as she saddled her horse and prepared to ride.

She had considered eating more of the deer meat but the carcass had already begun to bloat and she had no appetite for it. So she breakfasted on a couple of hardtack crackers and guided the horse toward the north end of the pass. The Missouri might be on the other side of these mountains, she told herself, by now not really believing it.

Although her situation was grave, she found herself admiring the country she was traveling through. The rolling treeless hills of the past few days had given way to higher hills and ridges covered with green trees. The stream she followed sparkled with the early rays of sunshine that lit the treetops on the slopes beside her. The peace of the narrow valley seemed immune from any form of violence, a haven from the world of savage Indians and the likes of Selvey and Pike. She felt in the best spirits she had been in for many days.

The narrow pass proved to be longer than she expected, for she rode for two hours, following the winding course of the stream. But still there was no end to it. Fearing that it was causing her to lose her eastern progress, she looked for some way out of the pass without climbing up the steep sides. Finally she came to a cut where a branch of the stream forked off eastward again and she decided to follow it in hopes it would lead her to the other side of the high ridges above her.

The branch narrowed to no more than three or four feet wide in some places where the rushing water cut through massive rock formations. Abby's horse could barely find adequate footing in many spots, causing Abby to consider going back to the main stream. But having gone this far, she decided to continue until the horse could not get through. Reaching a point where she had to dismount and lead the horse, she was ready to turn back when she sighted a clearing about two hundred yards ahead. A few yards farther through the narrow opening in the rocks, she could see a wide valley beyond. Her spirits lifted once more, she hurried the horse along toward the clearing.

She was almost out of the narrow pass when she

first spied the cabin. It was actually little more than a shack, but the sight of it caused her heart to leap into her throat. She almost cried out and had to caution herself to be careful. *Maybe Indians built cabins too*, she told herself, even though it just didn't look like anything an Indian would build. She continued slowly down into the clearing and stopped to look the situation over carefully before proceeding any further. Her rifle out, she scanned the little clearing from left to right. There seemed to be no one around and there were no animals, no horses. Maybe the place was abandoned. Then her eyes settled on a wood trough in the water and she realized that it was a sluice. This was a miner's shack. Her heart pounded again, for this meant that it was no Indian cabin.

"Hello," she called out. "Hello the cabin."

There was no answer save the echo of her voice coming back to her from the rock walls of the pass. Then the heavy silence returned to the clearing. It was abandoned, she decided, and led her horse on down to the cabin, where she tied him to the end of a log protruding from the wall of the rough shack. "Hello," she called again and slowly pushed the door open with the barrel of her rifle. Peering into the dark interior, she took but a moment to realize it had been empty for a while.

She shoved the door open wide. Her heart sank a bit with the disappointment of finding no one there, but at least it was a sign of civilization. *The gold must have played out*, she thought. Maybe there was a mining settlement close by. She stood in the center of the crude shack and looked around her. There was a table made from split logs and two chairs, one of which was lying on its back on the dirt floor as if someone had gotten up quickly and knocked it over, never bothering to right it again. A bucket sat in the

CHEYENNE JUSTICE 179

corner with water in it. At the back of the cabin was a fireplace with a short chimney, made of stones from the stream. The mud had crumbled around a few of them and they had been pulled out of the fireplace. In a corner by the fireplace Abby found a couple of packs, similar to the army haversacks that soldiers carried, but they were empty. "No woman," she muttered. It was obvious there had been no female's touch about the crude abode.

There was nothing for her there, no reason to waste any more time. But she had an urge to pause there for a while, maybe a day or two to rest and find food before continuing her journey. Maybe it was just because it was a structure, a building erected by white men, some semblance of civilization. *I'll stay here for a while*, she determined. *The prior owners abandoned it, so now it's mine to use as long as I want.* The decision made, she went outside to unsaddle her horse.

Outside the cabin, she looked around the clearing to determine the best place to hobble her horse. The site picked for the cabin was no more than a pocket in the side of the high ridge behind it. Standing in front of the shack, she could see a narrow trail that led up the slope, evidently to a narrow ledge about sixty or seventy feet above the stream. Curious, she decided to follow the path to see where it led.

Breathing hard, for the path was steep, she made her way up to the ledge. Whatever the purpose of the path, it had evidently not been used very much, for it was grown over in places by low brush. She stepped over the smaller branches and pushed her way through the larger ones. At the top of the path she stopped to look around. Seeing nothing at first, she started to turn around and return to the cabin. Then she saw it.

A gasp stuck in her throat and she almost dropped

the rifle she had clutched so tightly as she climbed up the path. The body had been there for some time. As she stood there, helpless to move for a few moments, she glanced beyond the putrid body and saw a second body. She had found the owners of the cabin. Her first impulse was to leave there at once but she forced herself to move closer to examine the lifeless forms lying against the rock wall of the ledge.

They had been white men. Now they were mutilated carcasses. Both men had been scalped, their bodies stripped almost entirely of clothes so that their bloated bodies resembled some macabre form of giant insect. One of them had had his skull smashed to pulp, the apparent instrument a large stone by his body, stained brown with his blood. Suddenly Abby felt dizzy and her stomach began to heave violently. She staggered a few steps away and dropped to her knees, unable to stop her stomach from emptying its contents.

She wasn't sure how long she remained there on her knees. It seemed a long time before she felt her legs would support her again. Slowly, she got to her feet and, without looking at the dead men again, turned and retraced her steps back down to the shack. All the way down the path, she told herself she did not want to stay in this place another hour. She would saddle her horse and find another place to make her camp.

By the time she reached the bottom and the peaceful serenity of the stream again, she had begun to rationalize her situation more calmly. She could think more clearly away from the grotesque scene on the ledge. The two miners had evidently run up the path, trying to escape the Indians. She remembered talk among the soldiers at Fort Lincoln about the miners pouring into the Black Hills looking for gold. Maybe she was in the Black Hills, which meant she was quite a distance south of Fort Lincoln. They had said

CHEYENNE JUSTICE 181

there would be hell to pay because the Indians held that land as sacred land. The two previous owners of this cabin had paid that terrible price for whatever gold they may have found. But now her practical mind took over her thoughts. Wouldn't this cabin be the safest place she could be right now? The Indians had already been here and killed the miners. There was no reason for them to come back here. It made sense to her. She decided to stay for a few days. She would be fine here . . . as long as she did not climb the path to the ledge again.

With new resolve, she set about making herself comfortable in her temporary home. Confident in her ability to provide food for herself since her success with the deer the day before, she decided to go hunting in the morning. This time she might try drying the meat for the continuation of her journey back to Fort Lincoln. She felt self-sufficient again. "It'll take more than a couple of old dead miners to scare me," she announced with her old self-confidence.

The two Lakota warriors sat on their ponies, high up on the ridge, and contemplated the activity at the cabin in the small clearing below them at the foot of the mountain. Small Bear, the elder of the two, spoke.

"You were right. I was not sure this one was a woman. She looked like a man with long hair."

On the afternoon of the day before, the two warriors had heard three rifle shots and rode to investigate. They discovered the trail of one horse leading into a mountain pass and followed it along a stream that flowed along the floor of the pass. There was still light enough to see when they came upon the camp of the lone rider. It proved to be a white man, or so they thought at the time. Small Bear wanted to ride down and kill the intruder immediately, but his companion, White Bull, was not so anxious. There was something curious about the white man and he persuaded his friend to wait so they could watch for a while. Small Bear reluctantly agreed and they moved to a point above the white man's camp where they could determine the man's intentions in their country.

It was plain to the two Lakotas that the shots they had heard earlier were fired at this campsite, for there was a hacked-up carcass of a deer lying near the stream. It seemed a strange and inefficient way to skin a deer and they decided the person they were watching had never skinned one before. They wondered what the man's business was here in the sacred hills. He did not kill the animal for its hide, and the head was not taken for a trophy. It was obvious the deer had been killed for food and yet most of the animal was left to rot. Looking over the man's camp, they saw no packhorse carrying mining tools. They concluded the man must be lost.

The longer they watched the man, the more curious he seemed until White Bull began to think he was not a man at all.

"A woman?" Small Bear had exclaimed. "What would a white woman be doing in this country alone? If it's a woman, she doesn't wear women's clothes. I say it's a man, and a very foolish man at that." Although unconvinced, he agreed to spare the intruder's life momentarily so they could watch him for a while.

The next morning they followed Abby up the stream after stopping to look over her campsite. Everything they saw told them that the person they followed did not belong in the mountains. Continuing upstream, they lost her trail in the rocky pass and after a while decided to double back to see if they had missed some sign. Small Bear finally discovered a print in the sandy bottom of a small branch that forked off toward the miners' shack.

It had become an intriguing game with the two warriors as they tracked Abby through the narrow cut and watched her reactions when she stumbled onto the cabin. Of special interest was her reaction to the bodies of the miners they had killed several days before. Watching this, White Bull was more convinced they were observing a woman. Small Bear was still unconvinced and could see no reason to delay the execution. "If it is a white woman," he had said, "she will run away from there as fast as she can." But the woman stayed and White Bull persuaded his friend to watch her for one more night.

Now, as the two warriors sat on their ponies observing the strange antics of the white woman below them, there was complete agreement that it was, indeed, a woman they had followed for two days. Abby, stripped down to her bare skin, was happily splashing around in the cold mountain stream. The chill of the water caused her to almost lose her breath and she danced and hopped, flailing her arms wildly, in an effort to keep her blood circulating. She continued her wild gyrations until she was satisfied that she had had a thorough bath. Then she stepped out of the water, shivering, and dried herself, using her shirt as a towel.

"Grant's balls," she exclaimed, repeating a muleskinner's oath she had overheard while passing the stables at Fort Lincoln. "I don't know if I could stand another bath in that water." She laughed at herself, still shivering in her nakedness. Slipping her feet into her boots, she went over to the wooden sluice and used it for a clothesline to let her shirt dry. While she waited for the sun to finish drying her skin before putting her underclothes back on, she picked up her trousers and held them up to inspect them. Since they were the only pair of pants she had, she was reluctant to wash them. "I might need 'em in a hurry," she stated. It struck her funny, looking at the worn pair of men's trousers and, on a girlish impulse, she laughed and began to dance around, holding the pants as if they were her dancing partner.

Small Bear and White Bull watched in fascinated silence for a long time, glancing at each other occasionally to exchange puzzled expressions. Finally Small Bear spoke.

"I think her mind has gone."

"Maybe so. Maybe the spirits play with her mind. I heard there was a crazy white woman in Sitting Bull's camp many nights ago. He asked his people to let her go unharmed. Maybe this is the same crazy woman. Maybe she has big medicine and that is the reason Sitting Bull permitted her to go in peace."

Small Bear was not so certain. "It is just a woman, an ugly woman at that. Let's put an arrow through her chest and see if she has special medicine."

White Bull was not comfortable with that solution. "It is not a good idea to kill one who is touched by the spirits. I say leave her alone and maybe she will go away."

When the two Lakota warriors returned to their camp, they sought out their chief, Lodge Smoke, and told him of the crazy woman at the miners' shack. Lodge Smoke, a wise and patient man, listened with interest as White Bull and Small Bear told of the woman's antics by the stream.

"Was the crazy woman looking for the yellow dirt that the white man craves?"

"No," White Bull replied. "And she seemed to kill only that which she could eat. Although," he added, "she was very wasteful with it."

Lodge Smoke nodded thoughtfully as he considered what his two warriors had said. "I think you have done a wise thing, leaving the woman alone. I think it is the same crazy woman who was in Sitting Bull's camp and he said that she should not be harmed." He paused as if thinking about what he had just said. "Still, I think it would be best to watch this crazy woman for a while. If she does no harm, it is best to do no harm to a person the spirits have touched with their hands—even a white person."

And so it was that Abby decided to stay in her newfound cabin for a few days longer when she found that game was within her easy access, often coming within a few yards of the cabin to drink from the stream. Unseen and, consequently, unknown to her were the Lakota warriors who passed by on the ridges above her cabin almost daily, pausing to watch the crazy woman for a while before moving on. Those who happened by in the morning were fascinated by the strange ritual she performed in the stream. Abby, weary of the dirt and grime of long days before when there was no opportunity to bathe, now delighted in the clear mountain stream that flowed almost at her door. Before, when riding with Nathan and later with Jason—and certainly while she was a captive with Pike and Selvey—there were many streams and rivers, but there was no privacy to allow her to bathe. So she took advantage of the opportunity and bathed in the cold stream every morning. It became a game with her to keep from freezing while she waited for her skin to dry so she danced and cavorted around the rocks until she was dry enough to get back into her clothes. It served to exhilarate her and, unknown to her, fascinate the unseen somber figures watching from the mountainside.

To the Lakota scouts, her ritual obviously surpassed simple bathing, for she did it every single day. There was little doubt that the woman was touched by a spirit and White Bull was convinced it was the spirit of the water who possessed her. It was obvious, he concluded, that she purified her body each day in the chilly waters and then performed her religious dance to appeal to the spirit of the water.

Chapter XI

Jack Pike sat hunched over against a huge pine tree, his rain slicker pulled over his head, watching the steady pattern of raindrops on the surface of the river. "Damn you!" he spat, cursing the very heavens above him for the second sudden storm during the night. He had been careless in making his camp and consequently he had paid for it with wet blankets and clothes. Pike didn't care for even the thought of getting wet, especially bathing. He was convinced regular bathing weakened the skin. As opposed to bathing as he was, however, that was not the reason for his surly mood this morning. The rain had made it impossible to find any trail the woman might have left and his impatience to overtake her was eating through his craw like acid.

He had continued down the river for more than two miles, looking in vain for the point where Abby might have left it. At first discounting the possibility that the woman might be smart enough to cover her trail when she came out of the river, he finally conceded that this was in fact what had happened. So he had crossed the river and made a careful search of the opposite side, still finding nothing. The closer it came to sundown, the madder and more frustrated he became. When darkness finally forced him to end his search for the day, he reluctantly pitched a hasty camp and turned in to wait for daylight again, only to be awakened by a thorough dousing in the middle of the night. The second storm hit at daylight and it didn't appear it would let up anytime soon.

Now, as he sat cursing the rain and the woman he had been unable to overtake, he was forced to admit to himself that he was beaten on this day. There was no trail to follow. It only strengthened his resolve to find Abby if it took him the rest of his life to do it. The woman was alone somewhere within this vast country and she would have to show up sooner or later. And when she did, he would be there to take his revenge.

For now, he could think of nothing better to do than find Lodge Smoke's village. There were only a few Sioux bands that still tolerated him and Lodge Smoke's band had been the most profitable for his business. This thought caused him to curse those Indians who had warned him that he was not welcome in their camps. *The bastards,* he thought. They should appreciate his help in dealing with one of their biggest problems. The Indians were mad as hell at the miners pouring into the Black Hills and he had tried to convince the Sioux and some of the Cheyennes that he was only interested in helping them get rid of the whites.

In spite of his current frustration, he was forced to smile when he thought about his arrangement with Lodge Smoke and Crooked Leg. He helped them find the scattered mining camps and often went in first as a decoy to lure the white men out in the open. He insisted to the Indians that he was only interested in helping them keep their sacred hunting grounds—all he wanted in return was all the worthless yellow dust they found at the camps. When he was in the Arapaho camp two days before, Crooked Leg told him that their hated enemy, Colonel Custer, was even now leading a large column of soldiers into the Black Hills. Crooked Leg had angrily complained that the soldiers had no right in the sacred land.

CHEYENNE JUSTICE

There were sure to be more white men following. Pike had pretended to share the chief's anger while thinking to himself, *The more the merrier*. There would be more gold dust for the taking.

Those thoughts helped to improve his mood somewhat and he saddled his horse and prepared to head out toward the mountains to find Lodge Smoke's camp. He considered himself a miner. "I just got a different way of mining," he said aloud, a grin now creasing his face. "And now I don't have to give Selvey a share."

When last he had been in Lodge Smoke's village, the Sioux chief had been camped above the fork of the Powder and the Little Powder. So Pike set out, following the river, continuing on in the direction he had traveled before when looking for Abby. The chief had moved his camp further north, so Pike found it less than a half a day's ride from where he started out that morning.

Lodge Smoke's people were accustomed to Pike's occasional visits so there was no alarm when he was spotted approaching the village. For those who had seen him before, Pike was easily recognized from a distance. He was a tall, lean man who wore buckskins, long since turned almost black from smoke and grease, and a black hat with a wide brim. The Sioux called him Black Hat because the brim flopped low in the front and back, its wideness exaggerated by the thinness of Pike's face. His eyes were set deep behind a nose that seemed as sharp as an axe.

White Bull, standing beside his chief, watched their visitor approach. "Black Hat," he stated with no emotion beyond a touch of contempt. Lodge Smoke only grunted in reply. White Bull was never happy to see the white hairface. He did not trust him. "I am sorry to see that man in our camp again."

Lodge Smoke said nothing for a moment. He realized that many of his people shared White Bull's distaste for the white man who claimed to be a friend of the Lakotas. He made an effort to defend Pike but it was without conviction. "Maybe his heart is true. He has helped to draw out some of the miners."

"He only wants the yellow dust. He cares nothing for our people. I say let him keep no more of the yellow dust and then see how much he wants to help our people."

Seeing the chief and White Bull standing in front of Lodge Smoke's tipi, Pike rode straight into the camp and pulled up before them. Using sign language and his rudimentary knowledge of the tongue, he told Lodge Smoke that he had come to visit his friends, the Lakotas. If the reception was cool, Pike took no notice of it. He was more interested in whether there had been any recent war parties into the hills and if the warriors had gotten the yellow dust for him.

Disliking the man intensely, White Bull could not resist the urge to taunt him. "Yes, there is a crazy woman living in an old shack who gave me a sack filled with the dust." He held his arms up, indicating the size of the sack. "It was too heavy for my horse so I emptied it in the stream. Then the sack was much easier to carry." The pain reflected in Pike's face brought a smile of satisfaction to White Bull.

Pike fairly whined when he protested. "Chief, I thought we agreed to give me the yellow dust."

Lodge Smoke shrugged. He failed to see why the white man placed such value on the heavy dirt. "There is plenty of dirt everywhere. Why carry it around in a sack?"

"But, dammit, this here's special dirt," Pike protested. "I can get you rifles with that dust . . . new rifles . . . repeaters."

"Why would any man trade a good rifle for a sack of dirt?"

Pike shook his head, bewildered in the face of such

CHEYENNE JUSTICE 191

obvious innocence. "Just don't throw any more of it away." Still fuming over White Bull's story and not certain if it was true, he asked, "When will you be sending out another war party?"

"We hunt now. Soon the summer will be over and we must have enough meat for the winter." It was apparent that Lodge Smoke was not interested in scouting for miners at the moment.

Pike was adamant. "Hunt? Hell, there's plenty of time to hunt. You've got to find them miners and kill 'em. They're gonna take your sacred hunting grounds away from you. You've got to kill 'em all."

"And give you all the yellow dust," White Bull said sarcastically. "These miners are your people, white man."

"They ain't my people. I ain't got no people." Aware that both men were staring at him, he quickly added, "I'm a friend to the Lakota."

His disgust for the dingy white man was too overpowering for White Bull to tolerate any longer. He turned abruptly and walked away. Pike watched him for a moment, then turned his attention back to Lodge Smoke.

"He was just japing me about that crazy woman with the big sack of gold, warn't he? That was all a big story to get my goat, warn't it?"

Lodge Smoke shrugged, showing his disinterest. "No, no yellow dirt. The crazy woman had no yellow dirt."

The significance of the chief's casual answer suddenly hit Pike right between the eye. His eyelids narrowed and his nostrils flared. "Crazy woman? There really is a crazy woman?"

Lodge Smoke was mildly surprised that this piqued such an intense interest in the white man. He nodded yes.

"You wouldn't be talking about a crazy white

woman? This here crazy woman you're talking about, she's an Injun, is she?"

"Crazy woman is white. White Bull and Small Bear says she looks like a man."

"Damn," Pike murmured to himself. A smile slowly began to develop across his homely features as he realized his good fortune. It might be too good to be true. He had to make sure. "This here crazy woman—she's a right handsome little gal, is she?"

"No. This woman big."

Pike was fit to bust. Lodge Smoke thought for a moment the sour-faced white man was going to laugh, something the Lakota had never seen him do. In an instant, Pike's smile faded and the pinched, sinister facade returned to his features. "That ain't no crazy woman. That woman belongs to me. She's run off and I've been trying to find her. Where is she?"

"I think it is best to leave this woman alone. The spirits talk to her. White Bull says she does no harm."

Pike flared up. "Leave her alone, hell! I told you, that woman belongs to me and I damn shore intend to git her back." His eyes were now no more than slits, recessed in the dark face that cast a menacing glare on the Sioux chief.

Lodge Smoke was not intimidated. "I think you forget where you are." He calmly glanced to each side at the busy village surrounding the white man. Like White Bull and most of the other men in his village, Lodge Smoke decided he had had his fill of this evil-smelling white man. "You are still alive only because I let you live. Now I think it is time for you to leave my village. You may go in peace this time, but if you come again, my warriors will kill you."

Pike recoiled in shock. He had never expected to be cast out by the Sioux chief. "You need me, dammit. Where are you gonna get rifles and bullets?"

CHEYENNE JUSTICE   193

He began to stammer, his threatening expression of moments earlier now one of disbelief. "You got no call to turn on me. I'm a friend."

"You bring more promises than rifles. The Lakotas need no white man. Go and never return to our country." He turned his back and went into his lodge.

Pike was left stunned by the sudden cancellation of his welcome. Then, becoming angry at the treatment just suffered, he started to reach for the pistol in his belt. He immediately thought better of the notion when he glanced around him at a growing number of warriors who had heard the last loud fragments of the conversation. The warriors, White Bull foremost among them, began to gather around him and he realized that he had best hold his temper and ride out while he still could. In spite of himself, he couldn't help but spit out one last feeble display of defiance.

"I'm going, but that damn crazy woman is my property and I aim to take her with me." He climbed up on his horse and jerked the animal's head around. "I'll find her. I know where to look."

Pike wasted no time in clearing the Indian camp. He did know where to look for the woman. He had gotten enough information from White Bull and Lodge Smoke's conversation to know that Abby had moved into one of the miners' shacks in the mountains. There weren't but one or two shacks that were not burned by the Indians. She had to be in one of them.

Jason stood before the scorched pile of timbers that had once been a miner's cabin. In his estimation, it had been some time since the burning of the shack. Already, weeds were beginning to pop up between the charred logs. It was his guess that the lone skeleton he found closer to the creek had been taken by surprise while the man was panning. There was a large crack in the back of the skull that just about matched the sharp edge of a war axe. He had been a small man, one who had lived a hard life, judging by the crooked bones of the left arm, evidence of a long-ago fracture that didn't set properly, and the curved backbone, bent after long years of toil. *Must have been an old man*, Jason thought. He looked around him at the makeshift corral where a half-smashed wooden cage caught his eye. "A chicken coop," he murmured under his breath. He brought a chicken coop with him, all the way from St. Louis, or Ohio, or wherever he came from. The picture seemed clear in Jason's mind—one old man, alone in these silent hills, with his mule and his chickens, looking for the strike that would send him back east to die in comfort. Instead, he met his end at the hands of the Sioux . . . or maybe the Cheyenne or Arapaho. The sign was too old to tell which. "You didn't have any business out here anyway," he said, looking down at the bleached skeleton. "Not much point in burying what's left of your bones. I reckon the closest a man gets to Heaven out here depends on how high the buzzard flies that eats his carcass."

He led his horse to the edge of the stream and paused there while the paint drank. He was about to step up in the stirrup when his eye caught sight of another hoofprint—this one no more than a day old. Still holding the reins, he knelt down to examine it. It was fresh, all right, and it was from a shod horse. Someone else had ridden by the burnt-out cabin just before him. Curious, he searched the bank of the stream until he found more prints. Following them along the rocky bank until they led across an open stretch of sand, he suddenly stopped short. There, in the smooth sand, was a familiar print. The left front shoe had a nick in it. The last time he had seen that print was on the Powder River, and it was heading downstream searching for Abby. He had stumbled upon the white man's trail once again.

Jason stood up and looked over the scene again. The man had not caught her yet. His tracks told a simple story. He rode alone, leading one horse. There were no fresh tracks around the remains of the cabin. He had ridden by and stopped briefly to take a look, then continued on downstream. Jason himself spent only a few minutes more before stepping up on the paint and riding off, following the stream.

No more than six miles, as the crow flies, from the burnt-out miner's shack, Abby Langsforth sat before the doorway of her adopted cabin and cut up strips of meat to hang on the branches of a wild cherry tree to dry. It was time to get under way again, so she had decided to try her hand at drying meat to take with her.

She felt safe here in this pleasant little valley but she was not naive enough to believe she could survive a winter in these mountains. She felt girlish and lithe here in her private little world. Here she was no longer the homely sister. She was the prettiest girl here. She was graceful and alluring. She wished Jason could see her as she saw herself in this special place. Why had she thought of Jason Coles? she asked herself. What did Jason care about her one way or the other? For that matter, what did she care what Jason Coles thought? And yet there was a part of her that hoped she was more to him than a job he was hired to do. He was not like any other man she had ever met. Strong and silent, he was also sensitive. He might be able to see into her heart and see her as she saw herself in this little valley. Then she conjured a picture in her mind of Jason relentlessly searching for her. He would find her and she preferred to think he came for her because he cared for her and not because it was his job. "It's my valley and I can think what I damn well please," she concluded and put thoughts of the tall scout out of her mind for the moment.

How long had she been away from civilization anyway? She could only guess because she had lost track of the days. So much had happened. It had been around the middle of June when she left Fort Lincoln in Nathan White Horse's company. It must have been in July when Jason came to find her. Could it still be July? The nights were already chilly and the mornings brisk. It was time to go. Still, she felt quite safe here. She was convinced that the Indians had never returned after they murdered the original owners of the cabin. Why should they? However, it was time to find her way home. She knew she had to, although part of her wished she didn't have to leave.

She glanced down at her hands and realized she had been holding the same piece of raw meat for some time. She shook her head as if to wake herself from her daydreaming. Suddenly everything seemed to be too quiet, as if all living things had paused, and immediately her instincts told her something was wrong. Alarmed, though not understanding why, she turned to reach for her rifle, which was propped against the side of the cabin.

A cry caught in her throat and she felt as if her lungs were squeezed empty of breath. He stood between her and her rifle, his hand resting on the barrel of the weapon, his own rifle in his other hand. He was not tall but he seemed to tower over her as she sat in the doorway. Sitting cross-legged, her lap full of raw meat, she knew she was helpless. He could kill her before she got to her feet. Deserted by her usual bluster, she was terrified as she felt her gaze locked by the piercing dark eyes set in the bronze of his face. His black hair was worn in two braids and adorned with a solitary eagle feather.

The dark eyes that had held her gaze softened and,

CHEYENNE JUSTICE

though his face remained without expression, he seemed to be examining her. His manner was one of curiosity, and not menacing—or so she hoped. After a long silence, during which he looked her over carefully, he spoke.

"I am White Bull, Lakota. I have come to warn you. You must leave this place, for you are in danger here. Black Hat searches for you. I think he means to kill you."

Abby could only stare, wide-eyed, as the Sioux warrior talked. Although his tone was not threatening, she could not understand a word he was saying. After he spoke, and stood staring down at her, she continued to stare at him for a long moment. Then she shook her head violently from side to side, indicating she could not understand. White Bull repeated his words, but again she shook her head frantically. Then, trying to use hand gestures and the few words of English he knew, he attempted to make her understand.

"Go." He signed the word "fast," but could see she did not understand. "Go," he repeated and thought for a moment, trying to remember English words. "Bad," he recalled. "Go . . . bad."

She understood "go," and surmised he was telling her to get out of his country. She wanted to tell him that she would gladly leave but she could not make him understand. "I go," she said, nodding her head.

This did not seem to satisfy him. "Go," he repeated over and over. He picked up her rifle and went to her saddle. Sliding it in the boot, he picked up the saddle and carried it to her horse. There he stood motioning at her, then the saddle, then the horse. She understood and got to her feet and moved to take the saddle from him. "Go," he pleaded.

He stepped back and watched her saddle her horse. Still he was not satisfied and she was at a loss as to what he was upset about. "I'm leaving, dammit," she muttered, working as fast she could.

Suddenly he raised his rifle and, pointing it at her, made gunshot sounds. Seeing that this only served to frighten the woman, he searched his memory for words. Finally, he recalled and pointed the rifle at her again. "Pick," he said. "Pick, Pick . . . come. Pick come."

"Pick?" she repeated. "Pick?" Then a terrifying thought struck her. "Pike?"

He nodded vigorously "Pike! Pike!"

She felt as if the blood drained from her body into her feet. "Pike come? . . . Pike come?"

"Pike come." He nodded solemnly, realizing that at last she understood.

There was no need for further coaxing. "Damn . . . damn," she mumbled to herself as she frantically finished tightening the girth strap and ran inside the cabin to gather what supplies she had. White Bull helped her tie her saddlepack on and she was ready to ride. Stepping up to the stirrup, she paused and turned back to face the Lakota warrior. Wanting desperately to thank him, she reached out to touch his arm. He backed away in alarm. She could not know that he was reluctant to touch one who was perhaps touched by a spirit. She tried to smile as warm a smile as she could muster under the dire circumstances and nodded her head up and down. He understood and nodded in return. She climbed on the horse and rode through the stream and out across the narrow meadow toward the pass beyond.

White Bull remained in the little clearing, watching the white crazy woman until she dropped from sight on the far side of the ridge that ran down to the valley floor. He was not sure why he had felt the desire to warn her about Pike. The woman may have been talking with the spirit of the water. She may have been touched by other spirits as well. Who

CHEYENNE JUSTICE

could say? Lodge Smoke was a wise chief and he had felt it best to leave the woman in peace. One thing he was certain of—Black Hat had no business with the woman. That was reason enough to warn her. Black Hat had no respect for the earth or the spirits. He was nothing more than a greedy leech and White Bull was glad that Lodge Smoke had finally had enough of the evil man and had cast him out of the village.

A movement from upstream caught his eye and he turned to search for the cause of it. Nothing more at first, but then, far up the stream, he saw a rider making his way down the rocky stream bed. A moment more and he recognized the familiar black hat, the wide brim flipping down in the front, hiding the upper half of the man's face. *Ahh*, White Bull thought, *the coyote wasted no time*. He felt an immediate rise of bile at the sight of the contemptible man. It was unfortunate that there had been a casual mention of the miners' shack. Otherwise it might have been days before Black Hat looked for the woman here. White Bull would have avoided him but he assumed that Black Hat had already seen him, so he remained where he was, watching the white man approach.

Pike made his way around the boulders and guided his horse out into the clearing. He climbed down from his horse, his eyes constantly on the Lakota warrior standing silently, a cunning smile etched in his dirty whiskers. "Well, now, White Bull. I didn't figure on running into you again so soon." White Bull made no reply. Pike casually looped his horse's reins over a pine bough. "I'm right glad to see you. Yessir, I kinda hoped we could still be friends, you and me." He attempted to broaden his smile. Still there was no reply from the stoic Sioux brave. Pike went on. "I can say for myself, they shore ain't no hard feelings." He glanced over at the cabin.

"What you doing here, anyway? You ain't fixin' to set up housekeeping in that old shack, are you?"

"Why do you come here, Black Hat? You have no business in this land."

His smile still fixed in place, Pike snorted as if amused by White Bull's remark. "I'm on my way outta here but first, like I told ol' Lodge Smoke, I'm lookin' to pick up some of my property." He glanced around him. "I'm figuring that there woman was staying here in this cabin. And I'm figuring that she ain't here no more, since you're standing here." He glanced around again. "Or maybe she is, though I don't see no horse or nothin'."

"The woman is not here," White Bull stated. He kept his eye on Pike, carefully watching his every move, his rifle resting across his forearm.

"No, I reckon she ain't," Pike said, thoughtfully scratching his chin under his whiskers. Then, seeming to suddenly itch all over, he reached up and rubbed the back of his neck, still with the smile permanently drawn across his homely face. "But I bet she ain't been gone long, has she?"

White Bull shrugged his shoulders. "I go now. There is no white woman here." He was only catching bits of Pike's conversation since Pike's Sioux was elementary at best. But he understood the direction it was going in. He was not careless enough to give the grimy white man his back and, seeing that Pike's rifle was secured in his saddle boot, he decided it was safe to mount his horse. In one graceful move, he jumped on the pony's back and prepared to back the horse away.

"Hold on a minute," Pike pleaded. "You could tell me which way she headed. You could at least do that, after all the guns I brought you and your friends."

White Bull had had his fill of the evil man. Even now, as he held on to White Bull's rope halter, the

CHEYENNE JUSTICE   201

dirty coyote could not stop scratching himself with his other hand. "The woman is not here. I have nothing more to say to you."

"Dang, too bad you feel like that. Why, hell, I always kinda liked you. You and me ought to be friends. I shore don't mean no harm to you. Look here, I won't even wear my gun while I'm talking to you, friend." He reached down and quickly unbuckled his belt, letting his pistol fall to the ground. "There, don't that tell you somethin'? Leastways now you won't feel like you gotta back your horse outta here." White Bull still did not trust the man. Seeing that, Pike said, "Hell, you may be right about the woman. Maybe I'll just let her alone."

"That is best."

"All right, then. No hard feelings." He started to move close to White Bull but suddenly stopped and shuddered. "Damn, these bugs is eatin' me up!" He scratched his belly violently with his left hand. With his right, he reached behind his back to scratch.

White Bull shook his head in disbelief at the man's filth. He was not prepared for the next move. Pike's right hand came from behind his back with a long skinning knife that had been strapped there in a leather sheath. Striking quicker than the blink of an eye, he brought the knife up under White Bull's ribs and thrust it all the way to the handle. White Bull screamed with the pain that tore at his innards as Pike hacked away at the wound. He tried to bring his rifle up but Pike grabbed the barrel with his left hand and, with a violent tug, pulled the stunned warrior from his pony.

On his back now, White Bull struggled in vain as Pike ripped the eight-inch blade out and thrust it in again, this time into the middle of his belly. He wrenched the rifle from White Bull's hands and flung it aside. The Lakota warrior could resist no more as his strength ebbed with the flow of his blood on the sandy soil. Pike, his conquest now in hand, taunted his victim as he butchered him.

"Now, you son of a bitch, you never did nuthin' but bad-mouth me. I been wanting to see what your gizzard looked like when it was carved up just right. Now, I'll tell you what I'm gonna do. I'm gonna carve your guts up good then I'm gonna take a piece of that topnotch of yourn. Right now you're a dead man. But it's gonna take a little while. It ain't gonna be quick."

Finished with his gruesome work, Pike took his leisure in preparing to start out again after Abby. He tied White Bull's rifle to the warrior's pony and tied a lead line to his own saddle. Satisfied that he had left nothing that might be useful to him, he climbed in the saddle. Before he rode out, he paused to leave some parting words for the dying warrior.

"Well, Mister White Bull, I have to hand it to you. You ain't making much fuss for the fix you're in. Hurts like hell, don't it? If you feel like it, you could try to get up and walk out of here. 'Course, your innards'll most likely fall out on the ground. Well, I best be going along. I got me a crazy woman to catch."

When Jason found him, White Bull still lay where he had fallen. It was late afternoon when the tall scout first sighted the cabin set back against the slope of the mountain. He had tied the paint out of sight and worked his way down the stream on foot. The wounded man was easily seen, lying near the water's edge, but at first Jason couldn't tell if he was dead or alive. He took the time to carefully scout the rocks and trees around the clearing to be sure there was no one else waiting in ambush. There was no one there. He went back to get his horse and then rode into the clearing.

"Damn," he murmured softly under his breath

CHEYENNE JUSTICE

when he came up to White Bull. The Sioux warrior had been brutally butchered and left to die a slow, agonizing death. No man should have to die that way. It was plain to Jason that there was little he could do for the man but he knelt down beside him to see if he could somehow ease his pain.

White Bull, his eyes open and aware, though wracked with the intense pain he felt, stared helplessly at the white scout bending over him. The look he saw in Jason's eyes was one of compassion and he knew the scout was trying to help him. His hands were covered with his blood as he pressed them close to his abdomen, holding his intestines in. After great effort, he forced one word between his lips. "Water."

Jason nodded and fetched his canteen. He let the water trickle over the Indian's lips, permitting only a little at a time to enter his mouth. White Bull started to retch when the cool water leaked out of his torn stomach and into his bowels. Jason Coles knew there was no hope for the man. He was as good as dead already but it was Jason's guess that the warrior would last for several hours or more before his agony was finally over. When White Bull's spasms from the water subsided enough to permit him to lie still once more, he looked up into Jason's eyes. He seemed to be pleading for relief from his pain.

Jason bent close over him. "The white woman. I must find her. Was she here?" White Bull tried to speak but was too weak. He nodded slightly. "Who did this to you?" White Bull could not speak. "Was it a white man?" White Bull nodded. Jason sat back on his heels. It was the man with the nicked horseshoe—he had suspected as much—and that man was still after Abby. Judging from the way he had slaughtered the Indian, Jason feared for Abby's life. He hoped the butcher was intent on keeping her for a wife and not hunting her for revenge.

Jason looked down at White Bull once more. Their eyes met and held briefly then the warrior took his hand from his stomach and signed that he was dying. Jason nodded understanding. He signed back, "Go in peace," and got to his feet. Moving out of the dying man's eyesight, he went around behind him. He stood there for a moment, looking down at him. He didn't want to do it but he knew the Lakota warrior would thank him for it. He slowly drew his pistol from his belt and as quietly as he could, cocked the hammer back. Hesitating just a moment more, he put a bullet through White Bull's brain, ending his suffering.

He stood over the now-still form for a few moments longer. "I'm sorry I can't give you a proper burying, but I'm afraid I'm running out of time."

Chapter XII

"Come on, damn you!" Abby bent over the little nest of tinder and dead grass she had formed and struck the flint over and over without results. The grass was dry enough. It should have caught a spark but, no matter how hard she labored, it refused to light. "Damn it!" She cursed the grass and blew on it lightly, trying to encourage the reluctant kindling. She paused for a few moments, sitting back on her heels and looking around to reassure herself that no one would be likely to find her in the pine-covered ravine she had chosen for her camp.

She had been at a loss to explain why the Indian warrior had chosen to warn her about Pike. But she was grateful to the man. He had terrified her at first when he suddenly appeared behind her but something in his manner made her know that she had no reason to fear him. Whatever the reason for his warning, she had wasted no time putting some distance between her and the little miners' cabin. She was not skilled in estimating miles, but she was confident that she had bought herself a good head start. She had pushed her horse hard until darkness overtook her and she was forced to stop for the night for fear of breaking the animal's leg. The country was rough and there were too many gullies and holes to step into in the dark ravines.

"Dammit!" she cursed, knowing she had waited too long before trying to get her campfire started.

She could barely see the kindling before her as she set in on the flint and steel again. Over and over she struck the flint. The sparks flew like tiny little stars in the darkness, lived for half an instant and then died. She shivered with the chill of the evening. It was cold down in the ravine when the sun disappeared. Still she worked the steel until finally a tiny red glow appeared in the dead grass and she picked the nest up, cupping it in her hands while gently blowing life into it. A thin wisp of smoke rose from her hands and then a fragile flame followed reluctantly, and she nurtured it with the shavings and twigs she had gathered. *At last*, she thought, *a fire.*

Somehow she had the feeling she could hold everything together as long as she had a fire to keep warm with and to cook her food. Her fire was gaining strength now and she placed some larger sticks on it. Confident that it was past the danger of going out, she put her flint and steel away and watched the flames strengthen to a healthy blaze. She put on more wood and sat back to watch it. Her shivering stopped and she once again regained the confidence she had in her ability to survive in this wild country. Then a sobering thought struck her and she spent an anxious moment wondering if her fire was too big and might be seen. She got to her feet, her rifle clutched tightly in her hand, and walked up the side of the ravine a few yards, looking around in an effort to pierce the dark shroud that covered her retreat. *No one can see*, she decided. *Pike would have to be right on top of me to see my fire.* She went back to her camp.

She took some strips of the meat she had tried to dry and looked at them carefully. She wasn't sure what jerky was supposed to look like. She had eaten jerky that Jason had provided and it didn't look like that which she had prepared. Maybe there was something else you were supposed to do to it other than just drying it in the sun. She decided to roast it over the fire. She was hungry and didn't care what it looked like—it was meat.

She was awakened the next morning by the sound of her horse gnawing the bark of a stunted shrub. She lay there for a little while and watched the first rays of the sun filter through the pines and settle on the rim of the ravine. She knew she could not afford to linger but she wasn't feeling up to snuff for some reason. There was an uneasy feeling down in her stomach and she decided she must be hungry, although she didn't really feel like eating anything.

"I guess I'd better keep my strength up," she announced to the horse and roused herself from her blanket. There were a few of the strips of meat left from the night before so she ate them and washed them down with water from her canteen. As soon as her breakfast was finished, she saddled up and got under way again, striking due east, hoping to find the Missouri.

It was past midmorning when she first began to feel queasy. It was puzzling to her that she felt somewhat under the weather but, assuming she would soon shake it off, she pushed on. She stopped at every high point she crossed that offered a long view of her backtrail, watching the country behind her, fearing the possibility of seeing a rider coming on fast. So far, she had seen no sign of anyone.

Another hour of riding found no improvement in her discomfort and, in fact, she began to feel worse. Soon discomfort gave way to nausea and dizziness and she realized that she was becoming physically ill. *It must have been the meat*, she thought. It had spoiled. She should not have eaten it but it was too late to think of that now. Her stomach began to churn and she feared she was going to vomit. *Good*, she thought in her misery, *maybe I can empty it out of my stomach*. Barely moments later, the contents of her stomach rushed to her throat and she lay on her horse's neck and retched.

Once started, her stomach began to convulse over and over in waves that left her fighting for breath. She could no longer stay upright in the saddle. Feeling a desperate need to be on solid earth, she tumbled from the saddle while trying to dismount and landed on her back. The horse stopped and stood looking at her. At that moment she didn't care what the horse did. She was too sick to care. Finding that she couldn't stay on her back because the earth kept spinning beneath her, she rolled over and got up on her hands and knees as another wave of retching swept over her. There was nothing left for her stomach to give up, but still she heaved uncontrollably. She tried to lie down on her side, but this only started the earth's spinning again. The only position she could tolerate was on her hands and knees.

She stayed in this position for what seemed hours, though it was really only a short time. When at last the world around her seemed to stabilize, she gradually became able to function on a rudimentary level once more. No longer wishing to die, she began to think about her safety again. She told herself that she had to get back on her horse and ride, but she was so weakened by the retching of her insides that she longed to rest for a little while. Giving in to the desire, she pulled herself up beside a tree and lay back against the trunk. Her horse stood patiently watching her. "Good boy," she mumbled, for she had been too violently ill to even think about tying his reins. She closed her eyes.

A clicking sound penetrated her dozing mind and she opened her eyes again, not really focusing. How long had she been there sleeping? Her mind skipped back and forth between waking and sleeping for a brief moment before she became aware of her surroundings and she was once again fully alert. She glanced up, her heart almost skipping a beat as her eyes focused on a pair of dusty black boots. Raising her eyes quickly, she was stunned to discover the dark figure of Jack Pike, his pistol leveled at her head, standing before her. The clicking she had heard had been the sound of the hammer as he cocked it.

There was an immediate feeling of panic and she reacted at once, bolting upright and trying to get to her feet. But she was stopped cold by the roar of the pistol almost in her face and she was stung by the sand kicked up only inches from her head. Terrified, she turned to the other side, only to be stopped again by another shot that splintered the bark of the tree she had been resting against. The shock of it was so sudden that she didn't even hear herself scream involuntarily. Thinking that she was staring death in the face, she froze, her eyes wide with fright, her heart beating against her breastbone.

"Hello there, Miss Sassy Britches." The floppy brim of his wide black hat shaded the deep-set eyes, giving him the appearance of a dark specter, an angel of death. "You know, you've caused me a damn sight of trouble, chasing after your ugly ass."

Regaining some measure of her calm when it appeared he wasn't going to murder her right away, Abby made an attempt to hide her fear. "Why the hell don't you leave me alone, Pike? I've got nothing for you."

Pike snorted a laugh. "Oh you ain't, huh? Well, I say the hell you ain't. The way I figure it, you run up quite a bill with me and I aim to collect on it."

"I don't owe you a damn thing, you son of a bitch."

Her response seemed to delight him and his beard parted in a wide grin. "Well now, I recollect as how you murdered my partner and stole that 'ere horse. And there's a little matter of a poke of gold dust you run off with. I figure you owe me plenty and I'm taking the first payment outta your behind."

Not realizing at first that he meant that literally, she sneered at the vile narrow-faced menace as he leered down at her. When he continued to leer at her, it occurred to her that he intended to have his way with her. She responded in kind. "The hell you are." In spite of her weakened condition, she resolved to defy any attempts on her person from the likes of the dingy and foul-smelling Pike. She reached down to pull her pistol from her belt.

Pike may have looked slow and clumsy but he proved to be deceptively quick, moving to block her attempt before she had drawn the weapon halfway out of the leather holster on her belt. His hand closed on her wrist with the force of a beaver trap, while with the other hand he brought the barrel of his pistol sharply across the side of her face. Stunned by the impact of the cold steel against her jawbone, Abby went limp. Her head spinning, she fought to remain conscious, knowing that if she fainted she would be finished. Her effort proved in vain because Pike, fully aware of the fight in the woman, had no intention of permitting her to recover. He cracked the heavy cavalry pistol across the back of her head and everything went black inside her brain.

When she began to come to, the first sensation that registered in her brain was an intense throbbing in her skull. A few moments more and she remembered where she was and what was happening. In a panic, she tried to get to her feet, although she could not yet seem to focus her eyes. Everything was spinning around her head and she felt the nausea rising in her stomach. Then she became aware of a tugging at her legs, which she tried to resist but could not. Finally her head cleared enough to see what was happening to her and she realized that her trousers were down around her knees and Pike was struggling to take off

CHEYENNE JUSTICE 211

her boots. The sight of the evil man was enough of a shock to jolt her out of her passive stance.

"Oh, no, you don't, you son of a bitch!" She tried to strike him with her fist, realizing only then that her hands were bound together and tied to the tree behind her. "No!" she screamed and tried to kick with her feet.

Pike paused and looked up at her, a grin spread wide across his whiskered face, his eyes reflecting his evil intent. "You might as well relax and enjoy it." She tried to kick out at him but he held her ankles immobile. "I reckon you ain't so high and mighty right now, are you? If I like it, I might keep you alive."

"I'd rather die than be with you." She spat at him.

He easily avoided the saliva hurled at him. It only served to amuse him. "Have it your way, then. You could make it easy on yourself and join in the fun, but I like a horse that bucks a little too."

He tugged at her boot but she hung on with her foot, refusing to straighten it. Soon he tired of the struggle and took out his skinning knife. "All right, dammit, keep your damn boots on!" With the knife, he started hacking away at her trousers until he had cut them apart, freeing her legs. When he had ripped the last shreds of her trousers away, he stood up and leered down at her nakedness. Then he unbuckled his own buckskin pants and dropped them around his boot tops, exposing his dingy gray underwear.

Abby was desperate. She was helpless to defend herself yet determined to die trying before permitting this foul excuse for a human being to violate her body. She wanted to look away when he peeled his underwear off but she forced herself to keep her eyes steady and unflinching. Unable to fight him off physically, she tried to combat him mentally.

"You call yourself a man? Why, you ain't much bigger than a little boy." He was surprised by her comments but they did not dissuade him. She tried again. "I bet you ain't had many women with no more than that to work with—maybe a frog would be more your size."

The smile suddenly disappeared from his face and he looked down at himself, not sure if she really thought him that lacking. Then the anger twisted his eyes into narrow slits and he reached down and hit her with his fist. "Shut up or I'll kill you right now!" Her head rocked back with the blow and, within moments, a trickle of blood ran down from her nose.

Refusing to yield to his brutality, she kicked at him again. "You dirty bastard!" She tried to struggle out of his grasp but he hit her again. Knowing she was fighting a losing battle to save her life, she refused to submit, although he slapped her again and again. She tried to fight with her feet, the only defense left to her, and she fought hard enough to cause him to drop his pistol and use both hands to immobilize her flailing legs.

"By God, I'll take you dead if I have to," he swore as he strained to force her legs apart.

Resigned to her fate now, she spat at him again. "By God, you'll have to!"

Stalemated for the moment, he picked up his pistol again and pointed it at her forehead. She stared him down, her eyes defying him to the end. The fierce rage reflected in his eyes told her that he had made up his mind to end it. He cocked the hammer back and she closed her eyes for an instant, waiting for the blow that would end her life. Then, in one final moment of defiance, she determined to look death square in the face. When she opened her eyes again, she caught a movement over Pike's shoulder and her eyes opened wider. There, on the ridge behind them, she saw him, sitting tall in the saddle, his rifle in one hand, silhouetted against a cloudless sky.

"Jason!" she uttered.

CHEYENNE JUSTICE

Her sudden exclamation startled Pike and he froze for an instant before jumping to his feet. The very name of the scout provoked a sense of panic. He searched the slopes behind him frantically, trying to spot him. She had been staring at the ridge when she saw Coles. He wasn't there now, and Pike knew that if he was already making his way down the slope, he would be here within minutes. He glanced quickly back at the battered woman tied to the tree. He never counted himself as a fool and she wasn't worth risking his life for.

Knowing time was his enemy, he wasted no more of it. Pulling up his pants as he ran for his horse, he was in the saddle within seconds. Once mounted, his fear of the Indian scout gave way for a final moment of anger and he wheeled his horse around to look down at Abby. "Don't think you're gettin' away with this, bitch." He drew his pistol and pumped two shots into the helpless girl's chest. She recoiled with the impact, then lay still. He grinned briefly then kicked his heels into his horse's sides and was off up the ravine at a gallop.

Some two miles away, Jason heard the pistol shots and urged the paint to pick up the pace. This made four shots fired in the last twenty or thirty minutes and all from a pistol. He couldn't even guess what the shots meant—someone was firing at close range, since that was all a pistol was good for. After leaving the miners' cabin by the stream, it was easy enough to pick up the trail. Abby had left tracks that anyone could follow and the man riding the horse with the nicked shoe was right on her trail. Jason knew he was gaining ground even though the tracks showed that Abby was pushing her horse hard. The nicked shoe was not pushing as hard. He didn't speculate on what the pistol shots meant any longer—he would cover the ground as fast as he could without getting careless and find out when he got there. From what he had seen following this man, he was chasing a ruthless murderer and he didn't like the thought of the animal catching up to Abby. She might think she was tough but this was a two-legged critter with the conscience of a coyote.

He covered the two miles in short order and pulled up on the top of a ridge to scout the ravine below before riding down. His eyes picked up the form lying beneath the pine tree. From that distance, he could see that it was a body. He looked the ravine over carefully before descending the slope to the bottom. It was apparent that there was no one else around, so he made his way cautiously toward the body under the tree.

As he approached, his mind was filled with the dread that he was about to find something he didn't want to find. When he got a little closer, he was able to see the form under the tree more clearly. "Ah, damn," he uttered as his heart sank. It was just what he had feared.

She was lying still, her hands tied to the tree behind her, her body naked from the waist down. *Poor darling,* he thought, *the son of a bitch left her all bloodied and naked to the world.* The anger boiled up in his throat and his first desire was to gallop after the bastard and gut him like the pig that he was. Instead, he dismounted and went to Abby's side.

He took the torn trousers lying on the ground and covered her nakedness. Then he cut her hands free. When he did, she groaned. He was startled by the sound, for he had been convinced she was dead. He knelt beside her and propped her head on his knee while he looked at her wounds. One look told him that she was not far from gone. It looked as if all the blood that was in her had drained. His heart went out to her. If only he had been here sooner—if he hadn't taken so much time tracking her to the miners' cabin—if he hadn't taken time with the dying Lakota.

But in his rational mind, he knew he had done the best he could.

Her eyes fluttered briefly, then opened, and she stared into the face of Jason Coles. It was weak, but she managed a smile when she recognized the sunburned face and the deep blue eyes that peered at her so intently with such deep compassion. She started to speak but could not before coughing up blood from her lungs. After a moment she was able to manage a few words.

"Jason," her voice barely above a whisper. "I saw you on the ridge. I knew you would come."

"Abby," he started, not really knowing what to say. "You're gonna be all right. We'll fix you up in no time."

She smiled and shook her head slowly. There was no uncertainty in her voice. "No, I'm dying." She groped for his hand and he took hers and held it. "Pike ran when I saw you on the ridge, but he shot me before he left."

"I know, Abby. I'm sorry I was late getting here."

She coughed up more blood, convulsing in pain when she did. Calm again, she tried to squeeze his hand but her grip was so weak it was barely more than a twitch. "I knew you'd find me. I knew you cared about me. We'd have made a good team."

"That's right, Abby. I care about you." He felt badly that he had held very little emotion for the girl but he wanted to comfort her. "We'd have made a helluva team."

Her smile faded. "Get Pike, Jason. Promise you'll get him."

"I promise. I'll get him." And he knew inside that he would. If he had to chase him to hell and back, he'd get him.

She suddenly stiffened with a sharp painful spasm before her body went limp again. After a moment, she spoke almost in a child's voice. "Hold me, Jason.

It's getting cold." He sat down with his back against the tree and cradled her in his arms. "Don't leave me, Jason. I'm afraid." He pulled her closer.

"I won't leave you. I'll stay right here with you."

She relaxed then, content to be in his arms. She knew she was dying but somehow the thought of dying was not so frightening anymore. She felt safe at last, safe in Jason's arms. He had come for her as she knew he would. And he had come because he cared for her—he had said so. She was at peace.

He stayed with her, holding her in his arms until, when it was almost evening, eternal night settled its misty veil gently over her and Abby passed peacefully into the beyond, a smile on her face. Jason had witnessed Death's call many times, perhaps more times than a man was meant to. But he had never reached the point where he was indifferent to it. With the passing of Abby's last breath, there was an emptiness that settled around him, an emptiness he could feel, like the gentle breeze that stirred the leaves of the tree he sat under. Even though he knew she was gone, he continued to hold Abby close to him, gently rocking back and forth as if calming a baby. All she wanted was for someone to care about her and he felt guilty that she had never found that person, as if he should have cared more. He sat under the tree, holding her cold body long into the night before finally laying her gently on the ground and covering her against the chill night air.

There wasn't much in the way of personal items to collect, but he found a silver locket and a fine comb in her coat pocket. He took those, along with her Colt and a rifle that looked like the one Nathan White Horse had carried. He wondered how she ended up with it. He packed them in her saddlepack to take back to Fort Lincoln for her father. *That is*, he thought, *if I get back to Fort Lincoln*. For he had it in his mind that he was going after Pike, no matter

CHEYENNE JUSTICE

where the murdering dog ran—he owed her that. It didn't sit lightly on his mind that his job had been to find Abby and bring her back safely—and he hadn't done that worth a damn.

He didn't have a shovel to dig her a proper grave but he was determined to lay her to rest somehow. So he found as soft a spot as he could and scratched out a shallow grave with his knife, using a frying pan for a shovel. When he had wrapped Abby up as best he could, using her coat as a shroud, he laid her gently into the grave and filled it in. Then he piled rocks on top of it to keep the critters away. When it was done, he backed up a few steps and sat down on a rock to try to think of some kind words to say over her.

There had not been enough time to get to know the girl, but she seemed spunky enough and she had evidently been a fighter right up to the end. "It's a damn shame," he mumbled. Her last words pointed to the idea that she thought he had some special feelings for her and he had let her think so since it had seemed to ease her passing. He couldn't see any harm in it. When he thought back on her last words, it struck him that she had said something mighty curious. He concentrated hard on just how she had put it. She said she saw him on the ridge before Pike shot her. But that was impossible because he was at least two miles away when he heard the last two shots. Even when he did get to the ridge, he doubted if she would have been able to see him, lying half under that tree like she was. Yet she was dead sure she had seen him. Jason shook his head, bewildered. What, he wondered, did she see? Maybe she saw an Indian . . . or a ghost. He couldn't say, but it did strike him as curious.

He got up from his seat on the rock and stepped closer to Abby's grave. Taking his hat off, he looked up at the sky. "Lord, if you're listening, I reckon you already know about Abby's passing. She was about the homeliest woman I think I've ever seen, but I feel certain that the ugly was mostly on the outside. I hope you'll set her a place at Your table. Amen." He started to put his hat back on then paused and looked back up at the sky. "And Lord, tell her I'm gonna get that son of a bitch that shot her."

Satisfied he had done everything he could do for the girl, he climbed on the paint, and started out after Jack Pike.

Chapter XIII

Pike rode his horse hard until the poor beast foundered. Only then did he stop in his flight from the narrow ravine where he had left Abby. As quickly as he could, he pulled his saddle from the beaten animal and put it on the extra horse he had been leading since leaving Selvey by the river. As an afterthought, he pulled the saddle off Abby's horse and dumped it on the ground. Ordinarily he would not have discarded the saddle, since it would have some trading value, but now he didn't want the extra weight. He couldn't be sure how far back Jason Coles might be and the uppermost thought in his mind was to travel as light and as fast as possible. He packed his supplies on Abby's horse and, with no more than a glance at the discarded saddle and a few other items that he deemed unnecessary, he was off and running again. Coles would find the saddle, and probably the spent horse, but that didn't concern Pike at the moment. Of most importance to him now was the need to gain as much distance as he could. When he felt he had that safety margin, then he would make an effort to disguise his trail.

Pike figured his best prospects for staying alive would be to make his way back deep into Indian territory—or better yet, into the relative safety of a large Indian camp. For reasons he could not fully understand but was well aware of, he had worn out his welcome in the few Sioux and Arapaho bands he had traded with. The one village he could think of that might still tolerate him was the Cheyenne: Two Moon's. He didn't even consider pushing south to Laramie, or north to Fort Lincoln, since he was wanted by the army for desertion.

Two Moon was more than likely still somewhere on the Tongue River. Pike set out in that direction after leaving the South Fork of the Cheyenne River, where he had attempted to lose his trail by following the river downstream for most of an hour. Coles had been good enough to track him through the mountains, so he had taken more pains than usual to cover his trail.

After another full day's ride and still no sign of anyone on his backtrail, he began to feel more comfortable. *Coles may be as good as they say,* he told himself, *but he ain't slick enough to catch Jack Pike.* Feeling in command once again, he began to think of his prospects for financial gain in regard to his dealings with the Cheyennes. Guns, they always wanted guns, and he had nothing to offer them in his present situation. *Something would have to turn up,* he thought, and almost as an answer to his prayers, he spotted a small black object on the distant horizon.

Keeping to the low side of the ridges and tablelands, he rode on a path to intercept the object. He wanted to make sure he was not spotted by whomever it was until he knew what he was stalking—it wasn't healthy for any white man to encounter a hostile hunting party. It took more than an hour to close the angle between himself and the object to a point where he could identify it. "Ain't that sweet?" he sneered, a grin spread wide across his face. "Just what the doctor ordered."

It was a large freight wagon, pulled by six mules. Pike couldn't have been more pleased. He hoped it was prospectors instead of homesteaders who may have strayed from the trail. Homesteaders never had

CHEYENNE JUSTICE 221

much of value, while miners usually equipped themselves with weapons and ammunition for their defense and, sometimes, a supply of whisky. His thoughts of Jason Coles were not entirely forgotten but, with the immediate prospects before him, they faded somewhat. He would be a great deal more welcome in Two Moon's camp with some rifles and bullets to trade.

Harley Dawson craned his neck and squinted his eyes in an effort to make out the figure that appeared at the top of the rise before him. He made it out to be a man, sitting a horse with a pack horse behind. He didn't appear to be an Indian.

"Seth," he called back over his shoulder, "get yourself up here. We got company."

Harley's younger brother roused himself from his blankets, where he had been catching up on some sleep, and climbed over the wagon seat to join his brother. Harley pointed to the rise ahead. "Look like a white man to you?"

Seth studied the figure for a few moments before answering. "Looks like," he finally stated. "I'd better get my rifle." He climbed back in the wagon and retrieved his rifle, then rejoined his brother on the seat.

Both brothers studied the stranger as they approached, keeping a sharp eye for any signs of an ambush. They had not made it this far from the Platte by being careless, and a lone white rider in this part of the territory was cause for suspicion. There had been no occasion to use their rifles to defend themselves other than one halfhearted attempt by a party of half a dozen Pawnees—looking, no doubt, for weapons—who had been easily discouraged by the two brothers, both crack shots with a rifle.

"Look out behind us again," Harley said. "If it's

an ambush, it ain't a likely place for one. I can't see a soul on either side of us."

"I don't see nobody behind us," Seth reported. "I reckon he's alone."

They were within a hundred yards of the stranger now and the man took off his hat and waved. They continued on up the rise until they pulled up beside him. "Keep your eye on him, Seth," Harley warned in a low whisper. "He's got a look about him."

"Howdy, neighbor. Name's Jack Pike." He rode over closer to the wagon. "I'm a wagon guide just took some folks up to Montana territory." He fashioned a grin that was intended to be friendly. "Looks like you boys are a long way off the trail. Where you headed?"

Harley answered. "We're figurin' on heading up to Dakota territory."

"Prospectors, huh?" Harley nodded. "Heading up to the Black Hills, I reckon, looking fer some of that gold." Pike's grin spread wider. "Well, there's plenty of it up there. I've took some folks up there myself." He shook his head to emphasize the wonder of it. "Yessir, folks is gittin' rich up in them hills. Me, I don't have no cravin' fer the stuff. Guiding's my business and I'm glad I happened on you boys. I can save you a powerful load of grief and maybe your scalps to boot."

This caused Harley to raise an eyebrow. "Oh? How's that?"

"Well, fer one thing, the way you're headin they's a heap of hostile Injuns just waiting fer a wagon like this to come along." Both brothers sat up at this. "You boys is lucky I was riding this a'way. You need to strike further to the west to git around 'em. I can show you the way."

"Much obliged, but we wouldn't want to take you out of your way. I figure you were on your way somewhere, same as us." Harley glanced at his

CHEYENNE JUSTICE 223

brother. "We're pretty handy with a rifle, ain't we, Seth?" Harley was a little skeptical about guardian angels that popped up in the middle of this wilderness, especially guardian angels that looked as capable of mischief as this one.

"You're dead right. I'm on my way back to Laramie. I've been hired to lead another train, but they won't be ready for another week or two so it ain't no trouble to see a couple of fellers like yourself to safety. Lord knows them bloodthirsty devils is kilt enough folks out here, and just to keep 'em from having gold that the savages ain't got no use fer anyway." It was becoming a strain for Pike to maintain a kindly facade. This Harley was a suspicious cuss and his little brother kept staring at him with that Henry rifle cradled in his arms. Pike would have preferred to have shot both of them by now and been on his way, but they were watching him so closely that he couldn't risk fighting both of them. He would just have to play along for a while until he got a good shot at their backs. Since it was obvious the two brothers were not keen on the idea of his joining them, he made another attempt. "You're right, though. I reckon I had better get on down to Laramie. Them folks always feel a lot better when I'm around to help 'em get ready fer the trail. I wouldn't feel right though if I didn't at least lead you a few miles and show you a safe trail to take. That's the least I can do."

Harley glanced at his brother. "Well, that's considerate of you, if it wouldn't be no trouble."

While the brothers watched, Pike tied his packhorse onto their wagon and then led them out toward the west, constantly scanning the horizon to both sides as if concerned for their safety. When he was in front of the wagon, and they could no longer see his face, a scowl returned to replace the friendly grin. He was irritated that he had to waste time with the two prospectors. He even wished he had Selvey back with him. It would have been a simple matter for the two of them to get the brothers between them and gun them down. Now he was beginning to fear he would not get an opportunity to take both of them. He might have to bid them farewell and then sneak back after dark and bushwhack them, but he didn't want to wait around that long.

He led them across a long, low ridge, toward the setting sun, looking for a good spot to do his business. He had led them much farther than the few miles he had originally proposed but, he figured, as long as they were willing to follow he might as well lead them in the direction of Two Moon's camp. On the back side of a long, treeless ridge, a series of coulees led down to a sizable creek—Pike had no idea what creek it was. He rode back to the wagon and pulled in alongside.

"That there's Wolf Creek down below. You can turn back toward the Black Hills from there. Shouldn't have no trouble a'tall from there. I know there's a little daylight left but my advice is to make camp here. There ain't no more water after this until you strike the Cheyenne River." He knew they had no idea whether there was water or not.

The brothers talked it over for a minute and decided to take him at his word. He certainly acted as if he knew the territory well. Besides, there was wood here for a fire and grass for the mules. Why risk getting caught in darkness with no water or wood? The decision made, they drove the wagon down beside the creek and Harley unhitched the mules while Seth and Pike gathered wood for a fire. While Seth started the fire, Pike stood across from him, making conversation.

"I need to be gittin' on my way but it's too durn late to start out now. Reckon I'll stay here with you boys tonight and head out first thing in the morning.

CHEYENNE JUSTICE

That is, if you boys don't need me anymore. I can take you further on if you want me too."

"Nah, ain't no point in troubling you further, Mr. Pike," Harley said as he approached the fire. "We'll be just fine and we're obliged to you."

"Fine, then, 'cause I got folks waiting fer me." He cocked his head toward Seth and added, "I notice he don't never put that rifle down. You don't have to be so careful here. Ain't no Injuns nowhere near here."

Harley didn't change his expression. He poked the end of a burning branch, pushing it toward the center of the flames. "Just a habit, I guess. I wouldn't pay it no mind."

Pike didn't comment any more on it but it irritated him to have to continue playing his game. The brothers shared their supper with him and then Pike allowed as how he wanted to get an early start the next morning so he got his blanket and rolled up on the edge of the firelight and pretended to sleep. Harley and Seth moved over toward the creek to talk.

"I don't know. Whaddaya think, Harley? It looks like he ain't got nuthin' on his mind but goin' to sleep."

Harley stared back at the prone form stretched out by the firelight. "He probably don't mean no harm, but I don't trust him as far as I can tote one of them mules. I think one of us had best keep an eye on him all night. He don't have to know we're watching him. We'll roll up in our blankets but won't but one of us'll sleep. We'll split it up. You can take the first watch and when you start to get sleepy, just poke me with your toe. I can watch him the rest of the night. That all right with you?"

"Yeah, that'd be best. You're better at staying awake than I am. I might poke you before too long, though."

Harley nodded. "That's all right. I only need a couple of hours."

They walked back to the fire and, making it obvious they were turning in, both men rolled up in their blankets. But, unlike Pike, who had left his rifle and pistol belt on the ground beside him, Seth and Harley hid their pistols inside the blankets. Harley was soon asleep, as evidenced by the resonant sound of his snoring. Seth stretched out so that he could see any move Pike might make, his eyes half closed to convey the picture of a sleeping man.

The fire began to die down and still there was no sign of stirring from the man on the other side of the fire. Seth had almost decided it was a waste of time to watch him, but he wouldn't take any chances; Harley was usually right about those things. He wondered how long it had been since Harley went to sleep. His eyelids were getting heavy already and he wasn't going to wait much longer before poking his brother. It was warm and comfortable by the fire and he closed his eyes for a moment to rest them. The moment turned into several and he quickly popped his eyelids open. *Uh-oh*, he thought, *that could be dangerous. Better keep 'em open*. That was his last conscious thought.

Undetected by anyone, there was a thin smile on the face of the supposedly sleeping form across from them. *You think you're a right slick young pup*, Pike thought, *but I knew you'd be sleeping like a baby before the fire died down*. Like a serpent sliding from his hole, Pike slowly peeled off his blanket. Silently he moved, placing one foot carefully after the other, ignoring the urge to hurry in spite of the excited beating of his heart. This was as close to passion as Pike ever came—when he knew he was about to kill someone.

He stood over the two sleeping forms for a moment, deciding which one to shoot first, anticipating the pleasure he was about to experience. Then he became angry at the two brothers, angry because they had not trusted him. *You wanted him to poke you*

CHEYENNE JUSTICE

awake, he thought. *I'll poke you*. With that, he drew his boot back and placed a kick squarely in Harley's back. When Harley jerked his head up, it was to meet the barrel of Pike's forty-five a split second before the bullet cracked his forehead. Pike turned immediately and shot Seth in the back of the head before the boy was fully awake. His anger abated, a thin smile returned to his face as he looked down at the work he had done.

"Well, boys, I reckon I saved you from the Injuns, just like I said I would. I reckon I'll go back to bed now and wait for sunup to see what you've got in that there wagon." He tossed a few more branches on the fire and rolled up in his blanket, pleased with his night's work.

The morning sun found Pike unhurriedly moving about his camp, tending the fire and enjoying a breakfast of salt pork and dried apples from the Dawson brothers' wagon. The bodies of the brothers still lay where he had murdered them the night before, undisturbed, save for the stripping of anything valuable Pike found on them. He was in no hurry to leave the scene of his cowardly act, for he had climbed to the ridge above the creek and scanned the horizon all around and seen no sign of a living soul anywhere. He felt confident that he had lost Jason Coles.

An inspection of the wagon revealed some merchandise of value, primarily food stores and ammunition, but there were only a few weapons. There was another rifle, a Winchester, in addition to the one Seth Dawson had constantly held. He also found the pistols they carried on their bodies and an old Sharps buffalo gun wrapped in a woolen blanket. It was disappointing—he had expected a much more valuable inventory. There were some tools for digging and panning but Pike had no use for them.

"Damn fool greenhorns." He spat, and kicked Harley's body in contempt.

When he had sorted out what he could use, he made up a pack saddle for one of the mules and loaded his things on it. Pike had no use for the wagon—It would slow him down too much. Ready to start out for Two Moon's camp, he paused to take one last look at his handiwork. He looked at Harley's balding skull and then back at his younger brother's long blond hair. "That there's a right fine-looking scalp you got there, sonny. It'd look right shiny hanging in a Cheyenne lodge." He drew his long skinning knife and took the boy's scalp and held it up to the sunlight to admire it.

Jason dismounted to look at the saddle lying on the ground. There were a few odds and ends scattered about also, things that Pike had obviously thought expendable. A few hundred yards away a spent pony grazed on the long grass. It was plain to see that the man who murdered Abby knew he was being chased. And from the look of that horse, Jason knew he was riding his horses into the ground in an effort to put distance between them. Pike had a good head start but that fact did not overly concern Jason—he would track him for as long as it took. He would find him and he would kill him—this much he vowed to himself. He would get Pike if he had to walk into the middle of a hostile camp to get him.

Back in the saddle, Jason took up the hunt again. He gave no thought to the consequence of riding alone into a country that was a hotbed of hostile activity. He had one purpose, and that was to hunt down Jack Pike. He stayed doggedly on the trail of the two horses, sometimes losing it temporarily, then doubling back until he found it again, pushing on until he had to remind himself to rest his horse. He himself needed no rest.

After allowing the paint to rest for close to an hour, he resumed the hunt. It was close to sundown when he spotted the five mules grazing in the grass of a shallow ravine. Their traces had been cut and were dragging behind them. Glancing up toward the northwest, he saw the buzzards wheeling overhead and he knew that he could expect to find more of Pike's handiwork. Pulling his Winchester from its sling, he headed for the ring of buzzards.

Poor devils, he thought, looking down at the two bodies still half out of their blankets. *Murdered in their sleep, I reckon.* One of them, the one who had been scalped, was no more than a boy. The sight sickened Jason inside and he knew he had to stop this mad dog. Looking around him at the wagon and strewn articles of clothing and mining tools, he pictured the evil Pike rummaging through the miners' belongings like a coyote plundering a campsite—the story was clear to see. Pike had taken what he wanted and one of the mules to pack it for him and headed out toward the north. Jason figured Pike to be maybe a day and a half ahead of him and he looked to be heading somewhere in the Wolf Mountains or maybe the Big Horns.

The buzzards were swooping right above the two bodies when he climbed aboard the paint once more and continued on, following the obvious trail left by Pike. Now there were two horses and one shod mule to follow, which made tracking that much easier. He made good time until he reached the banks of the Cheyenne River, where he lost the trail. Unfazed, for he expected the man to try to cover his trail at some point, he crossed the river and scouted the other side looking for the point where Pike came out of the water. From the tracks he had been following for two days, Jason knew Pike was running flat out and, since he was, it figured that he would have gone downstream. Going with the current would be easier and faster, so Jason started working the riverbank downstream from the point where Pike entered the water.

Patiently, Jason combed the bank of the river, carefully examining every likely place where rocks or grass were handy to disguise the trail left by the two horses and the shod prints of the mule. He was no longer following the horse with the nicked shoe—that was evidently the spent pony he had seen near the discarded saddle, though Jason had not thought to inspect the animal's hoof. But it didn't matter anyway, unless Pike's trail doubled onto somebody else's trail, because the mule would be hard to disguise.

In spite of the mule, Pike had done well to cover his tracks. Jason spent the better part of three hours working the riverbank without finding a single print. *The man had to come out somewhere*, he thought, and unless he swam two horses and a mule all the way to Pumpkin Buttes, he'd find where he came out. On the thought that Pike might be trying to lead him in the opposite direction, Jason crossed back to the other side of the river and started scouting that bank. He had not worked down a quarter of a mile when he found the tracks where Pike came out of the water. No effort had been made to disguise them—they stood out plain and clear up a sandy gully until they disappeared in the grass of the slope above the river.

Jason was not misled by the trail. Pike wanted him to see those tracks. It wasn't until he reached the grass on the slope that Pike tried once again to hide his real intentions. Jason dismounted and studied the grass carefully. It was not difficult to pick up the trail again and follow it for another half mile until he found the place where Pike had crossed the river again and resumed his original course. Relentlessly, Jason tracked his man from the point where he last left the river. Pike was heading northwest, deep into

CHEYENNE JUSTICE

hostile country. Jason followed him past Pumpkin Buttes on his left, toward the Little Powder. The trail was no longer evasive, for Pike evidently believed he had lost Jason by then and he was traveling in a straight line. Ahead and to the south Jason could see the Wolf Mountains. Pike seemed to feel secure in this country—maybe he had reason to believe he had nothing to fear from the Cheyennes or the Sioux. Jason could well imagine why—he wondered how many troopers had been killed with rifles supplied by men like Pike.

Chapter XIV

Jason sat by a wide stream that had made its way through a little valley where cottonwoods competed with a few skinny willows for the water's nourishment. He watched the paint drink from the stream while he cut up strips of flesh from the pronghorn he had taken with one shot behind the shoulder. He had not realized that he had gone two days without eating until he began to feel weak from hunger—such was his focus on the task he had set for himself, a task that superceded all others. Finally giving in to the incessant cries from his empty stomach, he left the trail he was following and rode off toward the mountains to hunt. In the dangerous country he traveled, he thought it best to ride some distance away from the trail he followed before risking the one shot it took to bring the antelope down.

Now, as he sat before his small fire, waiting for his supper to cook, he reflected on his life since first signing on as a scout at Fort Cobb, an unusual train of thought for Jason Coles, who tried to avoid serious thought on things past and things that might have been. But the recent turn of events that had brought about the wanton killing of Abby Langsforth had struck a melancholy chord in Jason's mind, one he found hard to explain. He had certainly felt no closeness to Abby and yet he felt a deep loss at her death. There was just no sense in it and he felt badly that someone like Abby had had the misfortune to cross paths with vermin like Jack Pike. Jason felt a need—more than that, a driving force—to eliminate the Jack Pikes from the earth. The thought of Abby's horror just before she was shot made Jason's bile rise and he told himself to be patient. At this point, he honestly didn't care what happened afterward, but he wanted to be damn sure nothing kept him from finding Pike. Once that was accomplished, he would deal with whatever came next.

Pike's trail led him across the Little Powder and the Powder, turning more northerly to skirt the Wolf Mountains. It was obvious to Jason now that Pike was heading to the Cheyenne camp of Two Moon's. He was still more than a day ahead of him and Jason was not likely to catch him before he reached the Tongue River, where Two Moon was camped. It would have been more to Jason's liking to catch the renegade before he reached his Indian friends—if indeed they counted Pike as a friend. In earlier days, under different circumstances, Jason would have been more cautious. Knowing Pike would find refuge in a hostile camp, Jason would have had to change his plans and watch the village, waiting for a chance to catch Pike alone. At this point, however, Jason's frame of mind was such that he really didn't give a damn if it was crazy to ride into the Cheyenne camp after Pike or not. He was not especially suicidal—if the choice was between life or death, he would choose life—but at this point he did not dread death that much. He had already made up his mind to go in after Pike, wherever the hell Pike went. And if he caught a bullet in the process, well, that was just something that was bound to happen sooner or later anyway. He pushed on toward his inevitable settlement with Pike.

Jack Pike guided his horse down to the water's edge. His horse had scarcely set foot in the shallow water before he was spotted by some women working skins on the far side. The camp was alerted almost immediately so that, by the time he had made his way across, leading the horse and the mule, there was a reception committee of half a dozen warriors to meet him. They recognized him at once, since he had been to their village several times in the past, the last time with Selvey and a wagonload of ammunition and supplies.

"Friend, friend," Pike called out, making use of his limited vocabulary of Cheyenne words. He signed the peace sign and kept repeating, "Friend, friend," as if afraid Two Moon's warriors might have forgotten that he had brought them guns before. It was unnecessary because the warriors could hardly forget the dark lanky man with the thin face and the broad black hat with the brim that flopped down, hiding his eyes. Like their friends, the Lakotas and Arapahos, they knew him as Black Hat.

"I come to see my friend, Two Moon," Pike said, using sign to help convey his message.

One of the warriors, an older man called Bear Hump, looked Pike over carefully before nodding understanding, then turned his pony toward the camp and beckoned Pike to follow. The small procession trotted up from the river and into the assembly of tipis. They reined up before the chief's lodge and Bear Hump slid off his pony and stood at the flap of the tipi, calling Two Moon.

"Ahh, Black Hat," Two Moon acknowledged as he stepped out of the tipi. "You have come to trade." The greeting was not cordial, but neither was it uncivil. Two Moon had traded for guns with Black Hat in the past. He was not fooled by Pike's insistence that he was a loyal friend of the Cheyenne. He assumed that Pike had stolen the property he brought for trade, but it served Two Moon's purpose to trade with him. He wanted the guns.

CHEYENNE JUSTICE

Pike tried to force a grin. "I got a few things to trade but I really come this time to visit my friends, the Cheyennes, and to bring my friend, Two Moon, a present." He dismounted and went around to the mule and pulled the old Sharps buffalo gun from the pack. "You can set in the door of your tipi and shoot buffalo across the river with this here gun."

Two Moon took the gun and turned it over in his hands, examining the powerful weapon. He smiled and nodded his head to Pike. "It is old and worn, but it is a fine gift. I thank you for it."

"Oh, it's old but it's still a Jim Dandy buffalo gun," Pike quickly replied. "Yessir, that there's a fine enough gun."

"You do not come to trade? Then why do you come?"

"Oh, I got goods to trade, all right. Look at that there mule there. But I got gifts too. I got some flour and some pots and pans. I got some dried apples. I brung 'em to my friends."

Two Moon had never been overly fond of the dark, chisel-faced white man. He had tolerated him because he was useful, but he had never counted him as a friend and he had never known Black Hat to express such friendship for the Cheyenne people. There had to be a reason for this recent flood of goodwill. "What is it you want from me?" he asked bluntly.

"Why, nothin'. I don't want nothin'. I just come to visit for a spell." Pike knew how contemptuous the Cheyennes were of cowardice and he was afraid that if he told Two Moon he just felt safer with a few hundred armed Cheyenne warriors around him, the chief would refuse his hospitality. Pike was pretty sure he had successfully lost Jason Coles but he didn't see any percentage in taking a chance. After all, there were more than a few tales floating around the territory of the tall scout's ability to track. He was determined he could take care of Coles but he wanted it to be on his terms.

When Black Hat maintained that a visit was all he desired, Two Moon shrugged and told him he was welcome to camp with them but he was not invited to share his tipi. This was all right with Pike. He would set up his own camp, smack in the middle of the Cheyenne camp, and stay a few days—a week, maybe—until he felt he wasn't going to get bushwhacked the minute he rode out of the village. If Coles was tracking him, he wasn't likely to risk getting caught by Two Moon's warriors.

Pike set up his lean-to of animal hides and hobbled his horses nearby. To show Two Moon his heart was in the right place, he gave most of the food stores he had stolen from the Dawson brothers to the chief's wife for a celebratory feast. He didn't like to give anything away as a rule, but he deemed it a necessary thing to do to try to sweeten his image with the Cheyennes. He was gratified to note a lessening of the cold and sometimes hostile glances he received from many of the warriors in the village, and he even noticed an isolated smile or two. That set Pike's mind to turning. Maybe he could get real friendly with some of the warriors and convince them that Two Moon should spend more time driving the miners out of the Black Hills. He could use some more gold dust—a man never had enough gold to do him and it was Pike's plan to acquire enough to ensure him a life of luxury in the California territory, or maybe Oregon. His unique method of "mining" had been quite lucrative when he was still on a friendly basis with Crooked Leg and his Arapahos—that is, when he could convince the ignorant savages to give him the yellow dust they found in the miners' shacks. Even after he passionately pleaded the importance of the seemingly worthless dirt, half of the time the savages emptied the pouches out in the streams. Pike

CHEYENNE JUSTICE

liked it best when he rode with the Indians and served as a decoy to bring the unsuspecting miners out in the open, where they could be set upon and slaughtered. He enjoyed the killing but, more important, he was there to search for the precious dust himself. He knew where to look for it, beneath the floorboards of the cabin—if there was a floor—or buried beneath the bank of the streams, or, sometimes, close to the place the miners had designated as their toilet area. Wherever it was hidden, if it was there, Pike usually found it. As valuable as gold was, it was even more coveted when it had been someone else's labor that produced it. When he reflected on his relationship with the various bands of Sioux, Cheyenne, and Arapaho, he was puzzled by the fact that he was no longer welcome in many of their camps. *The damn savages*, he thought, *they get to thinking they's better than white men. Well, to hell with 'em. A few more pouches the size of the two I've already got and I'll shake the dust of this territory off my feet for good.*

Jason took his glass from his saddlebag and steadied it on his forearm as he trained it on the Indian camp on the far side of the river. *Cheyenne*, he thought. *It's Two Moon's camp, all right.* The camp had been moved about seven miles upriver since he had first visited it when returning the sacred arrows. It didn't take long to determine the location of the man he had tracked over the past several days. Pike had set up a rough lean-to, using skins as a shelter, and he had positioned it as close to the center of the village as he could. In fact, if Jason's memory served him, the tipi closest to the lean-to was that of Two Moon's. *Looks like he intends to set up a permanent camp*, he thought. After another minute or two, scanning the village from north to south, he replaced the glass in its case and eased back down from the ridge he had been lying on.

When he reached the bottom of the coulee where his horse was waiting, he sat down to think things over. *The bastard is settled in the middle of all those Cheyennes like a tick on a shaggy dog,* he told himself. He could only speculate on what influence Pike had on his Cheyenne hosts. He might be in real tight with them and, if that was the case, he could have Jason shot on sight. Jason thought about the location of Pike's lean-to, close to Two Moon's lodge. Even at night it would be short odds for a man, even one of Jason's skills, to make his way into that camp without being detected. *Yeah, Pike was as safe as if he was in jail.*

Although he gave thought to these considerations, there was never any concession to his own safety. He had long since decided that this promise he had made to himself and Abby would more than likely be the end of him. His concern was that he must keep that promise and stay alive until he saw Pike dead. From the look of it, Pike had decided his life might be in danger so he intended to stay within the safety of the Cheyenne village. He gave it more thought but could not come up with any plan that would ferret Pike away from the protection of his hosts. He would have to take his chances on the disposition of the Cheyenne camp and ride in as boldly as you please, hoping he could count on Two Moon's sense of honor. It might work, if some trigger-happy buck didn't take a shot at him as soon as he crossed the river.

Big Turtle squinted his eyes against the glare of the early-rising sun. He shaded his forehead with his hand as he stared at the river. A moment earlier, when he had glanced that way, there was nothing on the far bank. Now, a solitary figure seemed to have materialized from nothing. At first he thought his eyes were playing tricks on him but, after staring

CHEYENNE JUSTICE

as well as he could into the sun, he could see that it was a man on a horse and he was almost across to the near bank now. A lone rider entering the camp was nothing out of the ordinary, but Big Turtle was curious to see who might be visiting at this early hour. A minute more and he was startled to discover the visitor to be a white man. This was unusual—first Black Hat and then this man only a day later. He went to Two Moon's lodge to alert his chief.

Two Moon studied the rider now walking his pony past the outer ring of tipis. Something looked familiar about the tall scout on the paint pony. He had visited his camp before, but that time he had ridden a spotted horse like the mounts bred by the Nez Perces. By this time, the visitor had been spotted by a few more of the early risers in the camp and a small gathering of women and warriors joined Two Moon and Big Turtle. Some of the men ran back to their lodges and returned with their weapons.

As Jason neared the center of the village, more and more of the people became aware of the white man in their midst and soon shouts of alarm rang out and the gathering around Two Moon increased to a crowd of many curious and some angry Indians. A solitary warwhoop split the morning air and a young warrior raised his war axe. Two Moon stayed him with a motion of his hand and the rider was permitted to approach unmolested.

Aroused from his sleep by the noise from the rapidly building crowd, Jack Pike stuck his nose out of his blankets to see what had caused the fuss. What he saw froze the blood in his veins. He had never had the misfortune to meet Jason Coles face to face but he knew instantly who the tall scout was, sitting easy and without display of emotion in the saddle. His next reaction was without conscious thought, born out of a natural instinct to survive. He snatched up his rifle and lurched, almost stumbling as he did, into the crowd, pushing and shoving his way through in an effort to get a clear view of the rider. The crack of the rifle split the early-morning air like a bolt of lightning, sending the crowd of people into a frantic scramble of confusion. The bullet whistled harmlessly by Jason's head, Pike having been jostled by a woman as he tried to aim. Jason leaped from the paint, his rifle in hand, and was almost at Pike's throat before Two Moon shouted for him to stop and three warriors set upon him. Pike, at first terrified by the spectre of an enraged Jason Coles charging him, fell back a few steps, his eyes wide with fright. When Jason was forcibly subdued by the three Cheyenne warriors, Pike recovered his courage and raised his rifle again to complete the assassination. Before he could pull the trigger, Big Turtle grabbed the barrel of his rifle and the second shot was spent in the air. Two Moon immediately ordered Pike held and his rifle taken away.

After Two Moon ordered Jason disarmed and brought before him, he directed two warriors to watch Pike. Two Moon looked long and hard at the white scout before speaking. "This is the second time you have risked your scalp by riding into my camp alone."

"I came in peace the first time, to bring the arrows back for my blood brother, Talking Owl. I was glad to bring the sacred arrows back where they belonged. This time I come on a different matter, to right a wrong that has been done."

"I see. And what is this wrong that is so important that you risk your scalp to come here?" Two Moon was favorably impressed by the white scout the first time he had come to the village. He believed him to be a man of courage and integrity. He had seen it in his eyes and now, listening to Jason conversing with him easily and fluently in the Cheyenne tongue, he was even more inclined to believe the scout did not deal in deceit.

"I came here to rid your camp of a murdering coward." He nodded toward Pike. "He is a backstabbing butcher of women and he dishonors the name of Two Moon, and all Cheyennes, by hiding away in your village."

Two Moon did not answer right away but looked first at one white man and then the other. He did not doubt that Jason might be telling the truth. One look at Black Hat's scowling face told him Jason's charges were most likely true. "Are you asking that I permit you to kill this man? He has done no wrong to my people that I am aware of. He has traded with us, brought us guns and bullets. It would not be right to let you kill him."

Pike could hold his tongue no longer. "He's the one needs killing, Chief. You're right, I'm a friend of your people. Jason Coles has kilt more Cheyennes and Sioux than a regiment of cavalry. I say kill him right now! Tell your boys to turn me loose and I'll kill him for you!"

Two Moon fixed his gaze on Black Hat for what seemed a long time, considering the accusations just made. He decided at that moment that he did not like Black Hat. The man had the look of a coyote about him. He was about to speak when a warrior stepped up behind him and whispered something in his ear. His expression immediately changed from one of patience to one of grave concern. He turned back to Jason.

"This pony you ride, with the dark mask around his eyes, this was Yellow Hawk's pony. Yellow Hawk's body was found to the north of here on this very river. His was not the only body. There were two more of my warriors found dead also—Hungry Wolf and Walks With Limp. They rode with nine other warriors, all brave fighters. Eight of them were found a little farther up the river. Lame Otter was never heard from again." Two Moon's normally bland features were now alive with the anger he felt. "How do you come by Yellow Hawk's pony? You must have been with the men who killed my warriors." His unblinking stare demanded an answer.

Pike's face lit up with this twist of events. "See, Two Moon! I told you he's your enemy! Let me kill him."

Jason had remained calm while Two Moon spoke. He did not strain against the hands that held his arms. He looked at Pike with cool, hard contempt for a moment before turning back to Two Moon. "If a man shoots your horse, is it not fair to take his horse? If a man ambushes you and tries to kill you, do you not defend yourself?" Jason spoke calmly and with a softness that captured the attention of the people gathered around him. "I do not deny killing those warriors who attacked me as I was peacefully leaving Sitting Bull's camp. I and two others—one the innocent woman this dog murdered," he said as he motioned toward Pike again, "were merely on our way to Fort Lincoln." He shook his head from side to side. "We meant no harm to your people. The scar-faced warrior—the one who tried to kill me when I left your camp before—he ambushed us. I had no choice but to kill him. You would have done the same." He glared at Pike again. "I killed only to defend myself, not like a skulking coyote like this filth does."

Two Moon had to consider Jason's words. It was true that Hungry Wolf had kindled a hot hatred for the white scout and had talked a great deal about his intent to have Coles's scalp on his lance. But there were others who rode with Hungry Wolf, good men, brave warriors. If what the white scout said was true, and he was inclined to believe that it was, then Coles himself had killed a dozen of his fighting men. This

CHEYENNE JUSTICE 243

was not something that could be forgiven, even if he was the one who was set upon. He decided the matter important enough to discuss in council with the elders of the village.

"Tie them both, hands and feet; I will talk with the elders on this matter." He turned and walked to his lodge, followed by eight of the older men of the village. Jason and Pike were led off to a clump of trees by the river and bound securely to separate cottonwoods. Jason did not resist. It would have been to little avail amidst the throng of Cheyenne braves. There was a calm about him that was almost peaceful. He had determined before entering the hostile camp that his fate was already decided, and it was his choice to walk this path. So he awaited the decision of the council without fear and, if the chance came to free himself, he would not attempt to escape. To kill Pike would be his only thought. He gazed over at the murdering coward as two warriors bound him to the tree. Pike did not go quietly to await his fate. He complained and argued, protesting that he was the Cheyennes' friend. When his complaining was ignored, his tone changed to a whine of protest. It was plain to see he was not happy with the sudden change in his status from guest to prisoner.

Chapter XV

Two Moon sat in the circle of elders and principal warriors of his village, patiently listening to the advice of those whom he always listened to in matters of importance. Bull Hump expressed his bewilderment over calling a council to discuss the issue—he argued that there was nothing to discuss. The white scout, Coles, was an enemy and had violated a treaty by coming into Indian territory. He had spilled the blood of Cheyenne warriors and he should be killed, the same as any other enemy of the people. As for the evil-looking little trader, Black Hat, he was like the fleas that tunnel into the fur of the camp dogs. He should be driven out or killed too—it was unimportant which. Having said his piece, Bull Hump sat down and another warrior rose to be heard. Though not an elder, he was an important member of the village and the council gave him their attention.

"I, Red Hawk, am Keeper of the Sacred Arrows only because this white man showed the courage and strength of heart to return them to the village. You have honored me by allowing me to accept the responsibility of guarding the sacred arrows, just as my father before me. Now I say that my father looked into this man's heart and saw the strength there. When he returned the arrows, he proved my father to be right. I say he has earned the right to leave this camp unharmed. He did not bring war; he did not come to steal horses or to trade whisky. He came looking for another white man. Why do we protect this man, this Black Hat? Is there any among us who would place any value on this man's word?" He paused and gazed around the circle. No one spoke to defend Pike's name. "I say let the two white men settle their trouble between them."

Big Turtle got to his feet. "I do not argue with what Red Hawk says. I understand his feelings for the white scout who tended Talking Owl's wounds and then returned the arrows. I think it is plain to see that Coles has the steel of a warrior in his soul, while Black Hat is little more than a thieving coyote. But the coyote brings weapons and bullets, which we sorely need. That is all I have to say."

Two Moon listened, giving his attention to everything that was said as he went around the circle. Each man either had something to say on the matter, or nodded approval or disapproval of someone else's comment. It appeared that the council was almost equally divided upon the issue. Some were for permitting Jason to leave the village freely, as he had come. But still, half the warriors could not forgive the killing of Hungry Wolf and his followers. Some pointed out that Coles worked for the soldiers and, consequently, there might be retaliation if they killed one of their scouts. This, they said, might not be a wise thing to do, since they still maintained that they were not at war with the army at the present time. Others rebuked this attitude, saying the army would not be foolish enough to send soldiers this deep into Indian territory.

Two Moon listened patiently until all had had an opportunity to speak. They had been talking for more than an hour on the matter when he finally rose to render his decision. "I have given consideration to all the words spoken here and I think there is steel in each man's opinion. I agree with Red Hawk and others who say Coles is an honorable man and a brave warrior. He knows the ways of the Cheyenne and respects our beliefs." Here he paused, looking solemnly around the gathering of elders. "But he has killed twelve of our young warriors and, for that, he must be punished. And the punishment is death. But because his medicine is strong and he is a brave warrior, his death shall be quick, and there will be no mutilation of his body.

"As for Black Hat, I am sickened by the sight of this man. Before Coles is killed, he shall have his chance to face Black Hat in combat. We will see which man's medicine is strongest. If Coles survives, then he will be killed. If the little coyote survives, he shall be permitted to leave but he will be killed if he shows his face here again. That is my decision."

The members of the council nodded to each other, all accepting the decision of their chief. After a few minutes of individual discussion among them, they rose and filed out of Two Moon's tipi.

Jason sat passively, his feet and arms tied together and bound to a tree behind him. He appeared not to even notice the dark figure bound likewise to another tree some fifteen yards away. Knowing it was useless to struggle against rawhide, he waited patiently for whatever fate had in store for him. So unlike the treacherous murderer of Abby, he showed no emotion as Two Moon and his warriors emerged from the lodge.

Pike started pleading immediately when Two Moon stood before him, but the chief silenced him with the raising of one hand. "Untie them," he ordered. When the two men were untied, several warriors grabbed each man and brought them to the center of the camp, where a circle of men, women, and children had formed to make an arena. Jason was not sure if it was to be a fight or an execution until Two Moon spoke.

"Now you both will have what you have asked

CHEYENNE JUSTICE

for," he said. Looking directly at Pike, he continued. "You begged me to let you kill this man. Now I will let you do it." Looking back at Jason, he said, "You have asked only to be given the chance to face this man in combat. You will be given that chance."

Pike, whose face broke into a smile when he heard Two Moon's first statement, now turned ashen with the chief's last remark. He looked quickly from side to side as if searching for an avenue of escape. If what he was hearing was what he thought he was hearing, the chief meant for the two of them to fight. And he had no desire to fight Jason Coles in face-on combat. His reaction did not go unnoticed by Two Moon. The chief spoke again.

"Coles is bigger and stronger than you are and I think he would kill you quickly. You will be given a knife and a war axe and Coles will have no weapons. This will make it fair."

This brought some measure of reassurance to Pike's face. It was still not his style of fighting, facing his opponent, but he fancied himself as being handy with a knife. He would run if he had any chance of getting away, but since he didn't, he felt confident that he could cut Jason to ribbons before he could get close enough to him to use his advantage in strength.

Two Moon's decision was what Jason had hoped to hear. Since finding Abby back in the Black Hills, the only thought that had driven him was to settle the score with Pike—nothing else mattered and nothing was too great a risk if it accomplished that. He felt no excitement and no elation at the knowledge that he was to be permitted to meet Pike face to face. Instead, there came a grim satisfaction that justice was to be served. The rules that Two Moon laid down—that Pike was to have the weapons—was of no great concern to him. He would do what he had to do, whatever it took.

Several knives and axes were brought before Pike

and he looked them over carefully, finally making his choice of a long skinning knife with a bone handle. He held it in his hand, testing the balance deftly. It was obvious he had done a lot of work with a knife. Thinking to intimidate his opponent, he made a few slashing passes through the air, an evil smirk spread across his face as he stared at Jason. Jason gave no visual evidence that he noticed but remained calm, waiting patiently for his captors to release his arms and give the signal to fight. A few more slashes in the air and Pike nodded his acceptance of the weapon. He then picked up a war axe with a steel hatchet blade that had been sharpened to a fine edge. He laid the blade on his forearm and, with a couple of short strokes, shaved a patch of hair off. Looking up at Jason, he grinned. Two Moon did not wait for Pike to signal his readiness. With a wave of his hand, he motioned for the other knives and axes to be removed. When this was done, he signaled the combat to begin. "Now you may kill each other, white men."

The warriors holding the two men released them and shoved them toward each other in the middle of the circle of people. They stood motionless for a minute or two, each man evaluating the strengths and possible vulnerabilities of the other. Pike had a smaller frame than Jason, but he was wiry and tough and he had dispatched men bigger than Jason, though not usually in a fair fight. He was confident, however, as long as he had the knife and axe, and he was determined to slash the scout's arms and face at long range, never allowing Jason to get close enough to get his hands on him.

Jason pulled his buckskin shirt off and wrapped it around his left arm to help shield him from the razor-sharp skinning knife. As if on signal, the two adversaries began to slowly circle each other, Jason slowly and patiently, Pike constantly feigning with his knife while he held his axe ready to strike. It became obvious to Jason that Pike was not inclined to push the attack, even though he held the weapons. Pike's plan, instead, was to hold back and fend off Jason's attacks by slashing at his arms and torso, making the scout pay severely when he attacked.

Pike continued to feign with thrusts with his knife hand but he failed to get any reaction from Jason beyond a penetrating, unblinking stare. He mistook Jason's patience for a lack of confidence and it served to encourage him. His uncertainty replaced by a feeling of dominance, he sneered at the white scout and, waving the war axe in slow circles, he taunted Jason.

"You ain't so brave without a gun, are you? Why don't you come on?" he taunted. "I'm gonna cut you in little pieces."

Outwardly, Jason did not respond to the taunts. But his eyes never left Pike's. Staring at the dark, deep-set eyes underneath the flopping brim of the dingy hat, Jason's mind's eye held an image of Abby. Poor, helpless, homely Abby, her face must have been a mask of terror as she fought off this vile excuse for a human being. Still he was patient, slowly circling, waiting for an opening.

The longer Jason waited, the more confident Pike grew and the more bold his feints and thrusts became until, finally, he abandoned his defensive stance and made a move. It was quick and it caught Jason by surprise. Reacting as quickly as any man could have, Jason managed to dodge the axe as it whistled by his face, and he almost evaded the knife, aimed at his midsection. As it was, he was quick enough to avoid a deep wound, but the point of the sharp skinning knife opened a long slash across his belly. Pike exclaimed in triumph when he saw the blood running down Jason's bare stomach. But Jason did not acknowledge the wound. He continued to circle Pike slowly. Pike, convinced now that it was a matter of merely butchering his unarmed adversary, became bolder and bolder. He feinted with his knife hand and struck out with the axe. Jason avoided the blade but the blow landed against his shoulder and caused him to stagger a step to the side. Pike exclaimed again as he positioned himself to go in for the kill. Poised to strike, he looked into the eyes of the tall scout and immediately felt the sensation of the hunted and realized at that instant that he was not merely in a brawl, he was being stalked, for the look he saw in Jason's eyes was the same a lamb sees in the eyes of a wolf. The smirk disappeared from his face and he began to back away, for it struck him at that moment that no matter what wounds he inflicted upon him, Jason was going to keep coming until they were both dead.

A feeling of panic suddenly overtook him and he realized he was staring death in the face. In an effort to stop Jason's advance, Pike lunged at him, slashing at his face. Jason parried the attack, catching the thrust with his arm, the knife blade glancing harmlessly off the buckskin-wrapped forearm. Pike struck out at him with the axe but Jason easily avoided the steel blade as it whistled by his head. Jason stepped back as if retreating and Pike, in a genuine panic now, charged after him. Jason ducked into a half-crouch and came up under the charging man, catching Pike's wrists in each hand. The force of Jason's counterattack drove the lighter man over backward and he landed on the ground with a grunt as the air was forced from his lungs, Jason on top of him. Pike struggled briefly but he knew the brief battle was over for him. He was helpless to move in Jason's grip as the powerful hands tightened on his wrists until he could not longer feel anything in his hands. All the while, Jason's eyes held him captive with the same relentless lethal stare. Finally, Pike's hands went completely numb and Jason easily knocked the weapons from their powerless grip. Jason's words were low and filled with a deadly emotion.

"Now you have the same advantage that girl had when you killed her."

Pike was paralyzed with fear. "Please! Don't kill me! I didn't mean to kill her. I swear! It was an accident!"

The look in Jason's eyes almost burned through Pike's skull. "You cowardly son of a bitch, you accidentally beat the hell out of her and then accidentally shot her twice in the stomach. Well, this ain't gonna be no accident and I promise you, it's gonna hurt.

He got up, dragging Pike up with him until they were on their feet again. He released one of Pike's hands and landed his fist flush on the smaller man's nose, smashing it and stunning Pike. Then, in a lightning-like move, he spun him around and picked him up in the air. Dropping to one knee at the same time, he came down with all the force he could muster, slamming Pike's body across his knee. There was a dull crack as Pike's back was broken as easily as he might have snapped a dry limb.

There was a brief moment of consciousness in the dying man's brain before he slid into death's abyss. During that moment, Jason bent down close to his face and said, "That was for the girl." Pike's eyes fluttered briefly before they stared, wide and frightened, into the next world. Jason got to his feet and stood staring down at the man he had hunted for so long, lying before him, his body bent at a sickening angle.

There was not a sound within the circle of people who had witnessed the horrifying display of power. After what seemed several minutes, Two Moon ordered his warriors to seize Jason. Jason, weakened by the tremendous release of his own pent-up anger, did not resist. He had done what he had promised Abby and himself he would do, and at that moment, he did not care what happened next. Pike was dead, that was all that mattered.

Two Moon was clearly stunned by the raw, animal-like execution he had just witnessed. Black Hat's killing seemed more closely related to the natural act of a cougar's attack on a rabbit. It had been quick and brutal, yet efficient and final. He looked with newfound respect at this white scout standing tall and silent, yet defiant in his serenity. This was a warrior, this Jason Coles. There must have been some grave mistake for this man to have been born with white skin. It was a shame to kill such a warrior, but his decision had been made. There was still the matter of twelve Cheyenne warriors sent to the spirit world at the hand of Jason Coles. Two Moon had planned to execute Coles as soon as the two white men had fought, but now he decided to wait until the next day. Without emotion, Jason shook his arms free of the grasps of his captors and calmly unrolled the shirt from his arm. No one moved for a few moments while Jason pulled the buckskin shirt back over his head, ignoring the knife wound across his belly. His guards looked bewildered at their chief before again taking Jason's arms. Again, the scout made no move to resist, standing passively, waiting for his judgement, whatever it might be. Two Moon was amazed by the apparent dominance of the scout, even though a prisoner and massively outnumbered. What he had heard was true—Jason Coles was big medicine. He shook his head sadly. It was late in the day and, in truth, he was reluctant to have him killed.

Jason's hands were tied behind his back once again and he was taken to an empty tipi. Once inside, his ankles were tied together and then tied to his hands, leaving him trussed up and helpless to move. When the warriors who had tied him up left the tipi, one young brave entered the tipi and sat down near the entrance to guard the prisoner.

Struggling to work his arms and legs back and forth, Jason managed to shift his body around so that he faced the brave sitting by the entrance. The young man watched Jason's efforts with interest, never offering to help but not threatening him in any way either. Jason knew that Two Moon had instructed his warriors not to abuse their prisoner. He was to be killed but, as a tribute to his courage, he was not to be tortured.

Jason glanced around at the inside of the tipi. It had been hastily erected just to hold him; he was sure of that. There was no evidence that anyone had occupied it—the grass on which he lay was still green and there was no fire circle in the center. It was obvious to him that he was being afforded special treatment. It did not make dying any more attractive, however, and Jason's natural instincts to fight until finished were once again foremost in his mind. Up until Pike's death, Jason had developed a fatalistic, almost morbid, attitude about living. He had decided it worthwhile to forfeit his life for a chance to end Pike's. Now that Pike was dead and he still lived, although perhaps for hours only, the game had changed. He would not be led willingly to the stake to be roasted alive. He would fight with any means available to him—kicking, biting, using whatever weapons he could find. He would die just the same, he knew, but he would die fighting. He glanced at the young warrior guarding him. The young Cheyenne was watching him closely. Jason relaxed. There was nothing he could do now, so he would wait and hope for an opportunity.

The hours passed slowly as darkness descended on the Cheyenne camp. Jason's arms and legs began to ache after an hour or so. By the time the fire outside the tipi had begun to die down, the aching had eased and his limbs became numb and he dozed from time to time for short periods. He was not aware of the changing of his guards until his eyes fluttered open and he saw a different warrior seated by the entrance. He had no idea of the time but he judged it to be quite late, for there were no sounds of any activity in the camp outside. He slid into sleep once again.

When he woke up again, he lay there for a moment before trying to shift his body around in an effort to keep the blood circulating in his cramped limbs. His efforts did not seem to cause any reaction from his guard. Jason looked up at the man's face and realized he was asleep. In almost the same instant, he felt the tugging at his hands behind him as a knife blade sawed away at his bonds.

"Do not make a sound," was the whispered warning. "We must not wake White Bird."

Jason glanced up at White Bird. The warrior was deep in sleep. The voice behind him again warned him to make no sound as he continued to work away at the rawhide thongs. It seemed like minutes but it was actually only seconds before his hands and feet were free and he turned to see his liberator. It was Red Hawk, the son of Talking Owl, Jason's blood brother.

There was no hesitation on either man's part as Jason sprang to his feet, helped by Red Hawk, only to stumble and almost fall if the young Cheyenne had not caught him. He staggered toward the slit in the back of the tipi where Red Hawk had entered, rubbing his leg muscles vigorously to force circulation. He glanced back briefly at the still-sleeping White Bird before slipping through the back of the tipi and out into the cool night air.

It was a dark, moonless night. Jason could barely make out the features of the Cheyenne Keeper of the Sacred Arrows as he motioned for Jason to follow him, and then turned and was gone. Jason was quick to follow after the fleeting shadow, past the outermost tipis to the edge of the camp. Red Hawk waited until Jason dropped down beside him. They both were silent for a few moments while they listened to make sure there was no alarm in the camp.

"I am Red Hawk, son of Talking Owl," he started.

"I know," Jason quickly replied.

"This thing I do is wrong. Two Moon is wise and he believes his decision to be just. But you were friend to my father, and you showed your friendship to my people by returning the arrows. I feel that I must return that friendship in my father's name. I mourn the loss of some of the warriors you killed, but I know that Hungry Wolf was a bloodthirsty man and I believe you when you say you had no choice but to defend yourself."

"I thank you, Red Hawk. I know how dangerous this is for you and you have my eternal friendship in return. If I can ever help you, I will." He grasped the young Cheyenne's arm in gratitude.

"Now you must hurry. I tied your horse down by the river. I am sorry that I could not risk taking your saddle or your weapons. This is all I can do for you."

Jason clasped Red Hawk's arm once more before disappearing into the darkness. "You have done more than enough for me. I thank you again."

"Go fast, Jason Coles. Two Moon will send warriors after you as soon as he finds you gone." Red Hawk looked into the darkness after him for a few minutes before making his way back through the sleeping village to his lodge.

Chapter XVI

Jason rode hard, making his way as fast as he possibly could over the uneven ground. The night was dark and there were many holes and gullies hidden in the coulees that extended down toward the river. It would start to get light in a few hours and daylight would bring a horde of angry Cheyennes after him. He knew exactly where he must go first and, for that reason, he was sticking close to the river instead of striking straight for Fort Lincoln. He needed a weapon and he knew where weapons and ammunition were waiting for him if no one had found the cache he had left. If the cache was still there, providing he could find it again, he could arm himself and then strike out for Lincoln. He should have all the head start necessary to outrun his pursuers.

It was hard to calculate, but he figured the small gully he had buried the Winchester 74 in should not be more than a few more hours up the river. He was making good time in spite of the darkness. That was the last thought he remembered for several minutes before going sprawling over the paint's head into the darkness. When his head stopped spinning and he was able to regain his senses, he found himself sitting on the ground. It took a moment more to realize he had been thrown.

He quickly checked himself over to make sure he had no broken bones. Although a pain in his hip told him he had landed pretty hard, he discovered no real damage. Behind him, he heard his horse grunting as he struggled to his feet. Jason got up immediately and went to him. "You all right, boy?" He took the reins and led him a few yards. "Dammit!" he uttered. The paint was limping badly, unable to put any weight on his left front leg. "Dammit," he repeated. "I'm sorry, boy. I shouldn't have pushed you so hard." This changed things drastically. The horse could not carry any weight. Jason started again, this time on foot, leading the paint. Now it became imperative to find the cache, and as soon as possible.

Soon after he started walking, the night began to lose its intensity and the black turned gradually to a deep gray. Before he had covered another mile, the trees along the riverbank began to take shape in the gray mist. *Sunup in another hour*, he thought, breaking into a dogtrot now that he could see his footing a little better. When the sun first looked over the distant hills, Jason stopped to study the riverbank. He decided he was still some distance downstream from the site of the attack by the dozen Cheyenne warriors. Kneeling at the water's edge, he pulled up his shirt and examined his wound. It was not serious—it was superficial and had already scabbed over—but it would annoy him for some time, because the scab cracked whenever he moved. He paused briefly to examine the horse's leg. It did not appear to be broken, but the horse recoiled whenever Jason lifted it. He looked at the hoof, which appeared okay but would not bear weight. Maybe the pony had suffered a bad bruise. He would just have to keep leading him and hope he mended. Being practical, Jason knew the horse had other uses beyond that of transportation. He might have to use him as a breastworks, and he could always eat him if it came to that.

Another half mile and he came to the spot where he had first found the paint. It wasn't far now. He led the horse down closer to the water's edge and continued on, passing the ravine where he had waited for the four Cheyennes while Abby and Nathan White Horse had hidden above him. Less than a quarter mile from the ravine, he came to the narrow gully where he had found Nathan White Horse's body. He stopped and turned around. "I missed it," he announced, and he began to retrace his steps.

Examining the shallow gullies carefully, he walked slowly back the way he had just come, stopping and closing his eyes, trying to recreate the picture of the river he had sought to burn into his memory. When he opened them and started walking again, his gaze caught the sight of a small, odd-shaped gully. He smiled—that was it. He had not recognized it at first because there was a dead cottonwood lying across it. The tree had not been there when he buried the rifles.

There was no indication that the cache had been disturbed. Having no tool of any kind, not even his knife, he looked around until he found a stout stick to dig with. It was not a very efficient digging tool but he worked feverishly with it until the dirt became softened enough for him to help with his hands. Working steadily, he finally uncovered the corner of the hide that contained the Winchester. With renewed energy, he set to his task with a vengeance and soon he was able to pull the bundle from the dirt.

He unwrapped the rifle and inspected it. It seemed to be in perfect condition, with no more than a hint of rust on the underside of the barrel, and Jason was not sure that hadn't been there when he buried it. He cocked the lever back, ejecting a round. "Damn," he laughed, "I buried it with a cartridge in the chamber." If there had been any serious rust, he might not have been able to eject the cartridge. *That would have been a helluva note,* he thought.

Satisfied that the rifle was in good working order, he examined the two belts of cartridges he had wrapped up with it. Content that he was once again armed and ready for whatever came his way, he also took a knife but left the other rifles in the hole, covering them up again. No need to leave them for the Indians to find, but he could see no sense in carrying a load of rifles and knives when he was on foot. He put the hide that had contained the Winchester on the paint's back and hung a cartridge belt on his neck. "I reckon you can carry that much."

He looked up into the morning sky. The sun was well up on its way toward noon. *They'll be coming on soon,* he thought. *My trail won't be very hard to follow, but it'll be a sight more difficult from here on in.* He took the paint's reins and led him off into the river.

He left the river a half-mile upstream and made his way carefully up the bluffs, taking great pains to place each foot so as not to leave footprints. There was no way to disguise the horse's hoofprints in the hard dirt, but Jason attempted to make it look like a wild horse had gone up from the river. Any reasonably competent tracker could tell that the horse was not carrying a rider. A better than average tracker could see that the horse was lame. If they found no man's footprints, they might assume a stray horse had wandered that way, a lame horse that couldn't keep up with the herd.

All afternoon he kept up a steady pace, walking for a while, then trotting for a while, the paint limping along behind him. Since he was on foot and unable to make decent time, he decided it best to try to make his way to Camp Carson at the mouth of the Tongue, that being the closest army post. He knew there were several bands of hostiles camped between him and the fort, but it was his best chance of surviving. He didn't think much of the idea of walking all the way back to Fort Lincoln.

Late in the afternoon, just before the sun was ready to set behind the Big Horns, Jason lay flat on his belly watching a Sioux hunting party that was crossing a low ridge some three miles away. He observed them until they dropped out of sight beyond the ridge, then went back down the side of the hill to get the paint. The sight of the hunting party reminded him that he had not eaten in some time and the thought of some roasted antelope made his stomach growl. But he could not risk a shot, even if he came up on a pronghorn. He couldn't even shoot one and then take it somewhere else to butcher it. On foot he couldn't get far enough away from the site of the kill before a curious Sioux found him.

It wasn't to his liking at this point, but he found it necessary to travel at a much slower pace due to the many fresh trails he crossed. There were hunting parties riding through in every direction. Nightfall found him back close to the river again and he led the paint down to the water to drink. Then he tied him in a stand of willows that provided plenty of tender bark, as well as some sparse grass near the river. Once his horse was taken care of, he took the antelope hide off the paint's back and laid it down near him to use for his bed. Then he gathered up as much dead wood as he could find and, using dead grass as kindling, made a fire beneath the bank of the river. He was grateful that Two Moon's warriors had not emptied his pockets while he was a captive in their camp. Consequently, he still had his flint. He had attempted, at one time in his life, to make a fire using a bow drill like the Indians used, but he was not successful with it.

By this time, his belly was constantly reminding him that it had been painfully neglected, but he had nothing to appease it. He looked over at his horse, contentedly stripping the bark from a willow branch, and he wondered how that lame leg of the paint's would look turning on a spit over the fire. *Tomorrow*, he promised himself, *I'm going to find something to eat, hostiles or no hostiles.*

To get his mind off his stomach, he decided to take a look around his camp before trying to sleep. Full darkness had set in now and he had to watch his step when he climbed up from the riverbank to the top of the bluff. Long before he reached the top, he saw the rosy glow in the sky. He knew full well what it was—the glow of a large Indian village, maybe two hundred lodges or more. Of even greater concern was the fact that the village lay between him and Camp Carson. Who could it be? With that many lodges, Sitting Bull? Crazy Horse, maybe? But Sitting Bull was supposed to be somewhere in the Little Big Horn valley and Crazy Horse was on the Rosebud. Well, whoever it was, he would have to give them a wide berth and, even then, it would be difficult to avoid their hunting parties. "Ain't much I can do about it now," he stated softly and scrambled back down the bluff and turned in.

He set out early the next morning, before the sun was up, striking out to the east, toward the Powder. His thought was to avoid the huge Indian camp. He was in no shape to outrun a band of Indians. His only chance of survival was to remain undiscovered by those between him and the fort and hope that the Cheyennes chasing him would lose his trail. It was not encouraging to know that, with every step he took, the Cheyenne ponies closed the distance by several yards.

As he walked and trotted, the ache in the pit of his stomach never let him forget his hunger, so he reminded himself to keep a sharp eye out for any food source. But there was nothing. Had he been able to continue along the river, there might have been some wild berries on the bank, but on the hills and ravines there was little to eat but grass. Along about midmorning, he made up his mind that he would risk a shot if he happened upon any game. So when he started over a steep rise that bordered a small stream, he stopped dead still. There, by the water, two black-tail deer stood drinking. Jason looked around him at a vast expanse of seemingly empty land and decided it was worth the risk.

He had never fired the Winchester before so he hoped the weapon's aim was true, for he did not want to chance more than one shot. There was no wind to amount to anything, so he laid the front sight behind the closest animal's left shoulder. He hesitated half a moment, then squeezed the trigger. The report of the rifle sounded as loud as a cannon in the morning stillness, although he knew it was exaggerated in his mind. The deer fell to his knees, then sprang up once and landed still in the stream.

Jason did not move for a few seconds, listening. Then he stood up and scanned the country around him, searching for any sign that his shot had been heard. When he could see no riders in any direction, he descended the slope down to the stream and pulled the carcass out of the water.

Several miles away, south of the little stream, in a wide ravine, Wild Pony, a Lakota warrior, stopped and listened. He turned to his companion, Small Bear, and saw that he too had heard the single rifle shot. There were eight of them in the hunting party. All eight had heard the shot.

"What do you think?" Wild Pony asked. "Do you know if anyone rode out to the north of us?"

Small Bear shook his head and said, "No." He looked at the others for comment. They all shrugged. One of them, Walks Big, said, "Only one shot—maybe it is Gray Wolf. He sometimes hunts alone."

"Maybe," Wild Pony replied. "Maybe it is some Arapahos from Crooked Leg's camp."

They listened for a few minutes longer, then decided it was nothing of importance and continued on their way.

Before butchering the deer, Jason carefully noted

the location of the bullethole behind the shoulder. The wound was a little high, but not enough to concern him. A variance that small could well be his fault. He decided he could trust the sights on the Winchester without making allowances.

He could not afford to take the time to cut up the whole animal, so he would take what he could carry with him. As soon as he gutted the deer, he cut out the liver and ate a chunk of it. His empty stomach almost rejected the warm, raw mouthful he gulped down, but he waited for a few moments until it settled down. Then he swallowed more of it. The Sioux considered the raw liver a delicacy but Jason never cared for any meat that wasn't cooked and, as a rule, he never ate the internal organs of anything. Nevertheless, he needed the nourishment the liver would provide, and he was hungry enough to eat a prairie dog raw at this stage. Already feeling stronger, he cut up several slabs of the fresh meat and wrapped them in a square of the hide. These he would take with him to roast for his dinner.

Tying his horse's reins to the back of his belt so that he had both hands free to carry his possibles, he started on his way again, leaving the half-butchered carcass to the buzzards.

They had ridden hard, not resting until the horses were almost foundering. Even then they were mounted and riding again as soon as the horses could go. Two Moon had decided to lead the war party himself, such was his desire to be a witness to the end of the white scout. Coles had escaped and Two Moon was not really surprised. The man's medicine was strong, perhaps strong enough to make White Bird's eyes heavy and sleepy, as White Bird had insisted. These things were possible. How he had escaped didn't matter—the thing that mattered was that he must be overtaken and punished for the lives he took that day on the Tongue.

Two Moon was certain Coles could not be far ahead of them now. It was plain that the white scout was on foot, leading a lame horse. They should have caught up with him already, but he had managed to lose them back at the river and his scouts had to search the banks several times before finding a single print from the horse.

"Ki-ya, Ki-ya," Big Turtle called out, racing back to meet Two Moon and the rest of the war party. He pulled his pony up to a stop and reported. "We see riders up ahead, on the ridge beyond this valley!"

Two Moon was concerned but not alarmed. "How many? Can you tell who they are?"

"Only eight or nine," Big Turtle replied. "They are not soldiers—I think maybe a hunting party."

Two Moon nodded and rode out ahead of the war party with Big Turtle to get a look for himself. They whipped their ponies to run hard in an effort to climb up the slope before the riders were out of their view. At the top of the ridge, Broken Foot waited. When Two Moon and Big Turtle pulled up beside him, he turned and pointed toward a long ridge, shaped like a buffalo's hump. He simply stated, "Lakota."

Two Moon studied the riders for a moment before confirming Broken Foot's statement. "Yes, they are Lakotas." He raised his rifle in the air and fired two shots. The Lakota hunting party stopped immediately. Though over a mile away, Two Moon could see their heads turn as one toward the sound of his rifle. He raised his rifle again and waved it back and forth. The leader of the Lakotas waved in return and then turned to ride toward the Cheyennes.

Wild Pony and his party rode down to meet their friends and allies and words of greeting were exchanged between the Lakotas and the Cheyennes.

CHEYENNE JUSTICE

When Wild Pony wondered why Two Moon led such a large party of warriors through this territory. Two Moon explained that they were searching for a lone white man who had been responsible for the deaths of many Cheyenne warriors. Wild Pony glanced at his friend, Small Bear. They both immediately thought of the single rifle shot they had heard no more than an hour before.

"Where did the shot come from?" Two Moon asked.

Wild Pony indicated a low range of hills to the north. "It sounded like it came from beyond those hills. How far is hard to tell—maybe three or four miles from here."

The two men discussed the probability of the white man's intended route. They agreed that Jason was more than likely trying to make his way to Camp Carson, since he was on foot and the fort was the closest army post. They considered where the Lakotas had heard the rifle shot and surmised that Jason had no doubt seen the Lakota village and was making a wide circle around it, but would probably cut back to his original path to the fort.

"We will help you catch this white man," Wild Pony said. "My friends and I will ride back to our camp and get more warriors to help. If this man is trying to go to the soldier fort, he will be following the river. It will take a man on foot a long time to reach the Yellowstone. We should be able to get around in front of him and cut him off before he reaches the fork where the Pumpkin leaves the Tongue. If you and your warriors continue to follow him, we will trap him between us."

The plan seemed a good one to Two Moon so he thanked Wild Pony for his offer. Soon the two bands were off again, the Lakotas to their camp and the Cheyennes after Jason.

* * *

Jason knelt by the small fire he had made in a hollowed-out basin beside a small stream. He had walked at least four miles from the spot where he had killed the deer until he found a place that afforded enough concealment to suit him. The raw liver he had eaten seemed reluctant to leave his stomach and he was anxious to put some cooked meat in to help it along.

When he had satisfied his hunger and felt strong again, he took up the paint's reins and started out once more, working his way around the hostile village and then cutting back toward the river. His muscles began to remind him that it had been a long time since he had walked that far. He felt a nagging stiffness in his thighs that made his steps feel heavy, but he continued to push himself, knowing that, if he paced himself properly, he could go on indefinitely. Glancing behind him, he noticed that the paint's condition did not improve. If anything, the limp seemed more pronounced. It was bad luck, but there was no need to spend thought lamenting the way things had fallen.

Paralleling the line of trees that traced the river's course, Jason kept to the low country as much as possible. Once, just when he was about to cross over a ridge, he had to stop and lay hidden for a few minutes. A band of forty or fifty Sioux warriors suddenly appeared on the other side of the river, traveling in roughly the same direction he was. He lay still and watched them until they rode out of sight. They did not cross over to his side of the river, so he had to assume they would not cross his path. They had seemed in a hurry to get wherever they were going and, wherever that was, he figured it didn't concern him. There was no reason for the Lakotas to hold him as an enemy. Still, they wouldn't be thrilled to find any white man this deep in their hunting grounds.

It was well past noon when he decided to rest for a few minutes near the base of a high hill. For the past several miles, he had been aware of a pain in his right heel. He had a pretty good idea that his boot had rubbed his heel raw, but he was reluctant to remove the boot to examine the extent of the damage—once if was off, he was afraid it would be too hard to put back on. So he decided to ignore it. Sitting on the ground, he stretched his legs out before him and massaged his thighs. He glanced up at the paint. "I sure as hell ain't used to this. What did you have to step in a damn hole for?"

After only a few minutes' rest, he made himself get up again to avoid getting stiff. Before continuing, he climbed to the top of the hill to check his backtrail. The sight that greeted him was what he had hoped to avoid seeing altogether. They were maybe two miles back, a long, single file of riders, moving exactly along the way he had come. There was no need to wait until they were close enough to identify. He knew it was Two Moon. "Well, shit," he uttered. Feeling concern but no fear, he lingered but a few moments longer watching the progress of the war party before descending the hill. They were gaining fast. He had hoped he had lost them but evidently he hadn't. Well, he thought, no use fretting over that now. The valley he was now in was open and treeless offering no place to hide. He looked hard at his horse, wondering just how bad the paint's leg actually was. "Let's just see," he murmured and, grabbing a handful of mane, pulled himself up on horse's back. The paint squealed with pain, took a few staggering steps and went to his knees. Jason jumped off. "Well, I reckon we can forget about that option." He cradled the horse's head in his arm and stroked his neck. "Come on, then. We'll make for the river. There ain't no cover out here."

On second thought, he pulled the extra cartridge

belt from the horse's neck and threw it over his shoulder. "I reckon this is where you and me part company. Maybe your leg will heal directly. You ain't no use to me like you are." He dropped the paint's reins and started trotting toward the river, a distance of about a half mile. He did not concern himself with trying to hide from the Cheyenne war party. His only thought now was to find a place to stand them off, and the banks of the river offered the best protection. Another point of consideration was, if he was in for a long period being pinned down by Indians, at least he wouldn't die of thirst. For now, the important thing was to make it to the river before Two Moon got there. He picked up his pace a little. The paint, accustomed to being part of the team at this point, followed along at his heels.

There was a wide level tableland between him and the bluffs of the river, crisscrossed with cuts and gullies. It made for difficult running and the heavy ammunition belts beat against his shoulders and back with each step. He had just about reached the halfway point across the flat when a bullet kicked up dirt a couple of yards in front of him. He was already diving into a narrow gully when he heard the report of the rifle. The shot might have been a signal, for it was followed by a barrage of rifle shots that peppered the dirt around the rim of the gully. Suddenly the valley exploded with the war cries of a band of angry Sioux on the attack as they rushed up from the bluffs and raced toward the lone white scout.

"Well, the fat's in the fire now," Jason stated aloud. He calmly removed his ammunition belts and laid them beside him. Hot lead was popping about him like hailstones. The paint screamed in pain and dropped to his side as several bullets hit the unfortunate animal simultaneously. He was dead almost immediately, his head hung over the side of the gully, the eyes wide with fright. Jason didn't have time to notice, thinking only that he wished the horse had fallen on the other side of the gully, between him and the Sioux.

Jason crawled along the gully, dragging his cartridge belts along with him, until he found a spot to quickly scratch out a place to lay his rifle. The foremost Sioux were within a hundred yards of him now and he figured it was time to join the dance. He calmly sighted down on the first warrior and knocked him from his horse. Shifting slightly, he brought the Winchester to bear on the warrior immediately behind the now-riderless pony. He squeezed off another round and now there were two horses without riders. This broke up the charge and the warriors dispersed somewhat but still pressed the attack. Jason picked off two more of their number, but there were more than forty warriors in the war party. *The same mob I saw on the other side of the river*, he thought.

Seeing that they were suffering heavy losses, the Sioux drew back out of range to regroup. Several individual warriors rode back and forth before their comrades, waving their rifles in the air and hurling insults and threats toward the man trapped in the gully. Jason looked quickly around him to assess his situation. It wasn't good. If he had been given the opportunity to select a place to stand off a mob of Sioux warriors, it sure as hell wouldn't have been this shallow gully in the middle of an open flat. While there was a short lull in the shooting, he considered his chances of scrambling out of the gully and sprinting back toward the hill he had just come from. The tableland was scarred and cracked with many gullies—maybe he could retreat from gully to gully until he reached better cover. He knew, even if he was successful in reaching the hills, without a horse he would be run down in no time at all by the swift Sioux ponies. Then, too, he had to consider the Cheyennes somewhere behind him. It wouldn't do to run into them. But he couldn't see that he had any other option, except to surrender, and he was damned if he was going to do that.

A barrage of renewed war whoops told him that the Sioux were preparing to try another assault on his flimsy breastworks. He watched their leaders as they spread their line of warriors in an effort to minimize the lone rifleman's effective firepower. He levered a cartridge into the chamber and steadied his aim, waiting for the charge. When it came, it met the same deadly fire that the first assault had felt, causing the Lakotas to lose three more warriors. Wild Pony again signaled his braves back, calling for them to shower the little gully with lead and arrows. Jason kept as low as he could, hugging the side of the gully for protection against the hailstorm of bullets. Crawling back and forth to new positions to fire from, he tried to keep them from zeroing in on him. He managed to knock one more warrior from his pony before Wild Pony pulled his men back further. He started to crawl to a new position when he felt a hammerlike blow on the back of his thigh. He knew without looking that he had caught an arrow. It was inevitable that he would be hit by a lucky shot, what with the hundreds of arrows that had been showered down on his gully.

"Damn!" he uttered. The arrow was not imbedded too deeply in the muscle but it was already painful. He tried to dislodge it but, though not deep, it refused to be withdrawn. He decided to deal with it later and broke the shaft off and returned his attention to the fix he was in.

He peered over the edge of the gully. The war party had pulled back to a safe distance from his rifle to discuss their next plan of attack. Jason knew that any responsible war chief was very concerned about losing too many warriors. Cavalry charges were not the Indians' way of doing battle—they favored am-

CHEYENNE JUSTICE

bushes and quick-striking hit-and-run tactics. He also knew that there were fanatics, like Hungry Wolf, who would sacrifice all their men if they were driven enough. Jason hoped this war chief was one of the former group. He had taken some heavy losses already and had to be considering whether the price was too high to continue frontal assaults. If he was smart, he would wait Jason out until dark and then surround him. By the same token, this option gave Jason his best chance of escape because as soon as it was dark Jason would be long gone from the gully. It became apparent that this was the plan the Sioux war chief had decided on, for he fanned his warriors out in a half circle, out of rifle range. Then they waited.

Knowing now what to expect, Jason crossed his cartridge belts across his shoulders so he would be ready to make his escape. It would be dark in about an hour, so he tried again to dislodge the arrowhead in his thigh. It was stubborn and the more he worked at it, the more it bled. *Maybe I ought to leave the damn thing in there*, he told himself; *at least it's plugging up the hole.* His concern now was the fact that his leg had begun to stiffen up and he needed to be able to move fast when the time came.

His attention was called back to the threat before him when a lone warrior decided to display his bravery and suddenly charged his pony toward the gully, screaming war cries at the top of his voice. Jason waited until the Indian was within fifty yards, where the warrior pulled up short and raised his rifle in defiance. "See! I do not fear you!" the warrior screamed out just before Jason raised up and calmly put a bullet through his brain.

"Now, that's more like it," he uttered to himself. "I wish they'd all ride up one by one." He sat back to wait for darkness. For the time being, he was in no more threat of attack. The Sioux were biding their time with war chants and some loud threats but Jason knew they would be coming as soon as it was dark. His chances were not good, but at least there was a chance.

While he waited, his mind wandered back to the circumstances that brought him to this dusty, shallow rip in the ground. A mental image of Abby formed in his brain and he again felt the sorrow of her death. Poor Abby, he thought. She didn't have much of a life, and what there was of if didn't last very long. The son of a bitch—it was worth the price he was now paying to settle Pike's hash. Jason had always tried to do the sensible thing when it came to dealing with hostiles, but he didn't regret what he had done to avenge Abby. Maybe it was suicidal to go into Two Moon's camp after Pike, but he wasn't dead yet. He might luck his way out of this yet. And if he didn't—what the hell, there wasn't anybody waiting for him back home. That thought brought old memories to mind that he had sought to bury in the deep recesses of his mind. It had not always been this way. Most of his life had been spent alone, but there was a brief period when there was someone waiting at home for him. Home then was a little valley in the Colorado territory. He was surprised to find that thoughts of Lark no longer brought the pain of remembering the last time he had seen her, with her skull smashed by a Cheyenne war axe. When he thought of her now, he visualized her sweet face when she greeted him in the evening. She had been given to him for only a short while, but he was thankful for that time and counted himself a fortunate man to have known her at all.

His thoughts were suddenly interrupted by a chorus of shouts from the band of Sioux. When he raised up to see what the fuss was about, he could see that they were waving their arms wildly, some jumping on their ponies and riding about in circles.

CHEYENNE JUSTICE 273

Jason looked behind him and immediately discovered the cause. Two Moon had found him.

Well, I reckon this changes things some, he thought. All his prior speculation on how successful he might be in escaping into the night was now no more than mental exercise. For Jason knew there would be an immediate attack from both sides. Two Moon was bound to press an attack with his Cheyenne warriors, and the Sioux, not wanting to appear timid, would launch another attack of their own. Jason knew at that moment that he was a dead man.

The gully was too shallow to afford him protection from both directions—he might as well be standing out in the middle of the flat, facing the entire horde of hostiles. He had seen the aftermath of several battles in which cavalry troops had been overwhelmed by superior numbers of hostiles, and it had not been a pretty sight. Some of the soldiers had obviously saved their last bullet for themselves, choosing not to be tortured by the Indians. Jason never considered that option. He knew he had no chance of survival but he would make his death an expensive proposition for them. He checked his rifle and waited for the worst to come. He did not have to wait long.

On a signal from their chief, Two Moon's warriors sprang to the attack. Jason turned to meet it. Behind him Wild Pony's Sioux responded with another assault. Jason did the best he could, which was better than any other man could have done. Seeking to slow the Cheyenne's attack, he fired as rapidly as he could pull the trigger and crank the lever-action Winchester. His fire was deadly, knocking down the first four warriors in line. Their tumbling horses caused further chaos in the charge, causing the Cheyennes to wheel about and circle back to regroup. While this was happening, Jason had already turned around and cut down two more of Wild Pony's Lakotas.

He had halted the first combined assault from the

two bands, but it had not been without cost to himself. For now he was bleeding from a shoulder wound that had spun him around in his tracks. The fire from the bullet wound caused him to grimace in pain as he quickly reloaded his rifle. Jason knew that Two Moon now knew how vulnerable his position was and that the next attack would finish the white scout.

Jason had always known that this time might come. There was a strange quiet that settled over the river valley as if all the Cheyenne and Lakota warriors knew that the white scout was finished. Jason accepted the inevitable. He had always known that if there was nowhere to run, and nowhere to hide, then there was nothing left to do but fight. He crawled back to the body of his horse and pulled the bridle and reins off of the paint's head. Then he climbed up out of the gully and stood before the hostiles, unprotected. One shot was fired from the band of Sioux but it glanced harmlessly by his feet. No other shot was fired as the Indians watched the actions of the white scout, anticipating his surrender.

He reached down and picked up a lance that had been hurled during one of the attacks. Very deliberately, he broke it over his knee and drove it into the ground, using his rifle butt as a hammer. Then, while they watched, he tied one end of the reins around his ankle. The other he tied to the lance in the ground. Then he stood up and, holding his rifle over his head, he fired one shot into the air. "All right, now come on, you son of a bitches," he said softly.

His actions were understood by the hostiles. It was symbolic and it told them that he would not run, as demonstrated by staking his leg to the ground. It told them that he would fight to the death.

There arose an almost simultaneous explosion of savage war whoops as both bands of hostiles acknowledged his challenge. Those Sioux warriors who

CHEYENNE JUSTICE

were already mounted did not wait for a command, but galloped full speed toward the solitary scout, staked to the ground. Two Moon acted quickly to hold his warriors back while he watched the Sioux attack.

Jason turned to meet the charge, standing erect and defiant. He seemed in no hurry as he coolly picked off one after another of the disorganized hostiles, oblivious to the rain of hot lead flying about him. Two Moon rode back and forth before his warriors, admonishing them to remain passive. A few of the younger braves could not stand by and watch the Sioux kill the white scout. They broke by their chief and galloped to join in the slaughter. Their reward was a bullet from the deadly Winchester in the hands of the tall scout.

As Two Moon watched, Jason was hit and staggered, the bullet entering his thigh a few inches below the broken shaft of the still-imbedded arrow. Yet he did not go down. Now he was forced to reload. The Sioux, seeing this, charged in closer to make the kill. Jason was hit in the side and fell to the ground. There was a low rumble of voices when the scout went down, but Jason, refusing to quit, rolled over on his stomach and completed reloading. An arrow found its mark in his lower back. Still he fought. His rifle reloaded, he cut down two warriors who had ridden within a few yards of the him, hoping to count coup. He rose to one knee and continued firing; each time he pulled the trigger, there was one less hostile. Those who had ridden too close frantically whipped their ponies to escape the deadly fire. As they fled, Jason stood up and knocked two more warriors from their ponies.

Wild Pony called his warriors back and there was a lull in the fighting as the Sioux leader realized that this scorpion, though badly wounded, still had a stinger. He had already lost too many of his warriors to this one man. He would wait now and let the Cheyennes go in for the kill. Jason, though unsteady and bleeding from several wounds, stood tall, his feet spread wide, waiting for the next attack.

Through the smoke and dust that swirled around the tiny fissure in the treeless flat, Two Moon saw that the man was still standing. A veil of fascination seemed to have descended on the valley like a shroud as Sioux and Cheyenne alike looked on the man, amazed. Torn and bleeding, it was unbelievable that the white scout was still standing, tall, defiant, and poised for battle. There was a grudging admiration forced on them for the man they were killing that day. And more than one of the warriors who stood silently watching knew in their hearts that this was the way a warrior should die—and the glory that was Jason's they could only wish for themselves when it was their turn to face death.

It was a shame to kill such a man.

Two Moon held up his arm, directing his warriors to stay. He nudged his pony softly and the animal began walking slowly toward the gully. Jason, who had been facing the line of Sioux warriors, turned to see the Cheyenne chief slowly advancing toward him. He cocked his rifle once more and raised it to his shoulder, but he hesitated. Two Moon's rifle lay across his thighs. He made no move toward it, but continued to walk his pony slowly toward Jason. Jason lowered his rifle and waited. A gentle breeze carried the murmur of astonished voices from the band of Sioux warriors across the valley to the two men now facing each other. Two Moon dismounted and walked up to stand in front of the wounded scout. He placed his hand on Jason's shoulder.

"No man here is a braver warrior than you, Jason Coles. You have earned the right to walk this land in peace." He turned away to face the warriors who were now quietly closing in around the two men. "I,

CHEYENNE JUSTICE 277

Two Moon of the Cheyennes, say that this man has earned the respect of all fighting men. I say that he will go in peace, but I can only speak for the Cheyennes." He turned to look directly at Wild Pony.

Wild Pony did not respond at once. Finally he nodded and said, "Go in peace, Jason Coles." His words were punctuated by a loud spontaneous shout from the gathering of warriors.

Jason was dumbfounded. He said nothing but his eyes told of his amazement. His legs were numb and he longed to drop to the ground but he feared that, if he sat down, he would be unable to rise again. So he stood there, feet widespread, his rifle hanging down at his side as, one by one, Cheyenne and Lakota warriors passed by him and touched him lightly. He understood that this was an honor to each man to count coup on him and it was not an insult to him. He was almost in a daze, not really seeing each man who touched him until one dismounted and stood before him. He looked into his face and recognized Red Hawk. The Cheyenne Keeper of the Sacred Arrows smiled and clasped his arm. Jason nodded and returned his smile.

Two Moon studied the tall scout, standing firm while the warriors passed by him. This Coles was an unusual white man, worthy of being a Cheyenne. He looked at the many wounds and the carcass of the paint, the empty cartridge belt draped across his shoulders. "We will take you to our camp and tend to your wounds. Maybe you will not die." He shook his head, wondering. "I don't know, maybe you cannot die at all. Your medicine is strong."

Chapter XVII

Lieutenant Page Jeffers pulled his horse up to a halt and signaled the patrol behind him. Sergeant Roy Ryman rode up beside the lieutenant and waited for the scout approaching at a gallop, riding hard to meet the column.

"He shore seems in a helluva hurry," Ryman offered in his usual dry monotone.

Jeffers did not reply but continued to watch the rider intently, looking past the scout, half expecting to see a horde of savages chasing the man. The scout, a half-breed Crow named John Bramble, did not usually spook very easily, so Jeffers could only guess what he had seen that caused such excitement. In a few minutes' time, Bramble was beside him. He pulled his horse up so suddenly that the animal's hooves slid to a stop.

"Lieutenant!" he almost yelled, though no more than two yards separated them. "They's about two hundred Injuns on t'other side of that rise! And they're heading this a'way!"

Jeffers's reaction was one of confusion. What could it mean? A concentration of hostiles that large within this distance of the fort? Bramble didn't stick around to do much scouting after first discovering them, so he wasn't sure if it was a war party or not. He just knew there were a helluva lot of them. Jeffers thought for a moment. His troop numbered thirty-five men, and he didn't have any intention of con fronting two hundred Cheyennes with thirty-five troopers. But he had to attempt to find out what their intentions were.

"All right," he finally said, "let's ride up there until we can get a look at them." In the back of his mind, he was considering the possibility of gross exaggeration by the half-breed scout. There was also the possibility that it was a band coming in to the reservation now that winter wasn't too far away.

A fifteen-minute march to the top of the rise brought more questions than answers to the lieutenant. Spread out across the valley, a great throng of Indians approached at a walk. Bramble had not exaggerated. "Damn!" Jeffers uttered. "Sergeant, better pull back before they see us."

"They done seen us, sir." He pointed to a lone Indian scout about a half mile off to the side and parallel to the column. "There's another'n on the other side."

"Damn. Well, in that case. I guess we'd better stand fast and act like we aren't afraid of them." He glanced over at Ryman. "But when I give the order, you better have the men ready to ride like hell." Ryman nodded.

"Cheyenne," Bramble stated as the band continued their unhurried approach. "Them's Two Moon's bunch." He hesitated a moment more before adding, "And they ain't painted for war."

Jeffers decided to wait a little longer before ordering his troop back to the fort. By the time the Cheyennes reached the foot of the long rise, Jeffers could see that there was a horse pulling a travois in the middle of the throng. It was flanked by two warriors on ponies, one of whom Bramble identified as Two Moon. Jeffers was uncertain what he should do, but there seemed to be no aggressive intent on the part of the Indians. They vastly outnumbered his troop of cavalry, but they showed no signs of mounting an attack.

The Indians stopped at the foot of the slope and Two Moon and the warrior on the other side of the travois rode on to the front of the band. Two Moon led the horse with the travois on a line behind his horse. He held up a white flag and continued up the rise toward the waiting soldiers.

"Everybody just sit easy," Jeffers said as he watched the Indians approach. He prodded his horse forward a few yards to meet the Cheyenne chief. His curiosity at a peak, he craned his neck in an effort to see what or who was on the travois. It wasn't until the Indians were right before him that he could see what appeared to be the body of a man, covered by a blanket.

Two Moon raised his hand to the cavalry commander and, in his broken English, he stated, "You take. Big warrior, big medicine." After his simple speech, he did not wait for a response, but dropped the lead line on the horse and abruptly turned and rode back to his warriors. He did not stop when he reached the ranks of braves waiting for him, but rode straight through and the warriors silently wheeled their ponies and followed in behind him.

Lieutenant Jeffers sat, astonished by the curious episode with the Cheyenne chief. He looked at Ryman and saw that he was just as mystified as he was. They made no move toward the body on the travois until the band of Cheyennes had almost disappeared back over the rise. Once Jeffers was sure Two Moon was not going to reassemble on the far side of the rise and mount an attack, he stepped down from his horse and went to the travois. Sergeant Ryman was a step behind him.

Jeffers reached down and pulled the blanket away to discover the prone figure of the white scout who had routed the Arapahos that had ambushed his pa trol on the Tongue River. He lay still, his eyes closed, his rifle by his side. It appeared that the Cheyennes had attempted to treat several wounds on his body, for they were bound with cloth.

Ryman remembered the name. "Jason Coles," he said. "They musta thought he was something special." He pointed to a solitary eagle feather tied in his hair.

"Jason Coles," Jeffers repeated, shaking his head in disbelief. "Every time I see that man, he looks like a ghost."

"They shore shot him full of holes," Ryman said. "I reckon we can take him back to the fort to bury him."

The body on the travois stirred and his eyelids fluttered open. "I'd be obliged if you didn't bury me quite yet. I may be pretty much stove up, but I ain't gone under yet."

"Jesus Christ!" Ryman blurted and stepped back startled. Then he laughed at himself. "Hell, man, we thought you was dead. You shore as hell *look* dead."

"There was a time, a few days back, when I thought I was. But I reckon I'll make it."

Lieutenant Jeffers ordered the patrol to turn around and return to Camp Carson, detailing one of the troopers to take charge of the travois carrying Jason. Even though they had been ordered to make a sweep that extended fifty miles farther, he could think of no more important task than transporting Jason Coles back for medical care. The man had damn sure earned that.

Don't miss the first book
in Charles West's new western
adventure series,
coming to you soon
from Signet:
Wind River Country

Chapter I

"Now what the hell's ailing you, Sadie?" Squint Peterson dug his heels into the belly of his balky old mule. "You been cranky all morning."

The mule had been restless all morning, more so than usual. She was naturally bad-tempered anyway, so much so that Squint had named her after an ill-tempered prostitute who had accommodated him at the rendezvous in the summer of '39. He grinned as the thought of that particular union came to mind. It was his first and last rendezvous. He hadn't been much more than a kid, fifteen years old. He had spent the winter trapping on the Yellowstone with his Uncle Bris. In fact, it was his Uncle Bris who introduced him to Sadie with instructions to "Rub the peach fuzz offen him." He laughed when he recalled his introduction to "the sins of the flesh." She rubbed it off all right, but not without a gracious plenty moaning. The poor woman had whined and complained the whole time he was trying to satisfy his needs.

"You'da thought she was the Queen of Sheba," he announced aloud. When he concentrated on it, he could still see her screwed-up expression when he removed his buckskin britches, revealing long underwear that had not seen the light of day for at least two months before that night. The abrupt biological release that followed cost him two prime beaver pelts. She had wanted two more, since he hadn't washed before coming to her tent, but he lied that two were all he had left. He might have been green as a willow switch and rutty as a springtime buck, but he wasn't about to let go of his hard-earned plews for one go-round on a puffy-faced old whore. She reluctantly admitted him to what she referred to as her paradise, the memory of which lingered with him long after he had journeyed back down the south fork of the Powder. As a matter of fact, he had not been able to rid himself of the last of those memories until that winter's first freeze, when he submerged his buckskins, with him still in them, in an icy mountain stream. He almost froze himself to death, but it got rid of the stubborn body lice.

"Matter of fact," he told the mule, "that was about the last real rendezvous they had." He shook his head in amazement when he thought about it. "Twenty-four . . . no, twenty-six years ago. . . . Damn! Has it been that long?" It was hard to imagine he had spent that many years roaming around these mountains, and still had his hair. There had been a couple of times when the threat of Indian trouble had influenced him to head back to civilization for a while, but it never lasted. The longest was a period when he had tried his hand at being a lawman. Two years of that was enough to drive any man back to the mountains.

He shifted in the saddle a little to ease the ache in his back. It caused him to ponder his chosen way of life and the future it offered. He liked it best in the mountains, but he wondered if he wasn't approaching the age where his senses might start to lose their keen edge. And he knew that when you lost that edge, you usually lost your scalp along with it. The thought of his hair decorating the lance of some Sioux warrior didn't serve to overly frighten him. He just didn't like the idea of being bested by anyone when it came to surviving by one's wits.

Excerpt from *Wind River Country*

There were a few gray hairs showing up in his beard already, but he could still cut sign quick as most Indians and shoot better than any man he'd met so far. He had to admit, however, that it was getting easier to thread a needle if he held it at arm's length, a fact that accounted for several briar rips in his buckskins that needed repair. Maybe he should give more thought to moving out of hostile country. Maybe it was time to move on to Oregon, a big territory. Squint needed a big country. He was a big man and he needed room to stretch out. *Well*, he decided, *I reckon I got a few years yet before I'm ready to turn toes-up.*

"Sadie, git!" he admonished and stuck his heels in her again. She seemed reluctant to step across the narrow gully that had been formed by the recent snow and runoff. Had he not been thinking of a prostitute at rendezvous, he might have been more alert to the mule's skittishness. As it was, he was taken completely by surprise.

He found himself in midair before he had time to realize what had happened. At first he thought he had been attacked by a mountain lion or a bear. He landed on his back, his assailant on top of him. The force of his contact with the hard ground knocked the wind out of him. By then he realized his attacker was a man and, in spite of the pain in his lungs, he struggled to defend himself from the thrust of the knife as it sought a vulnerable spot. There was no time for conscious thought. He fought totally by reflex, sparring with the arm that held the knife, while pushing against the man's neck with his other hand. He could hear the man grunt as he strained to gain advantage. Finally his assailant tore himself from Squint's grasp on his neck and raised his knife hand for one desperate thrust. Squint managed to catch his wrist in his hand and block the assault. There was one final attempt to free himself and then the strength seemed to suddenly drain from the man's arm like water from a busted water bag and Squint realized that he was in complete control. His assailant had given up the fight.

Squint quickly rolled over on top of the man, pinning him to the ground while he fought to regain his breath. His initial thought, as soon as he could breathe again, was to dispatch the red-skinned son of a bitch—for he could now identify him as an Indian—straight to hell. As furious as he was at having been attacked, he was almost equally angry for letting himself be taken like that, like a damn green tenderfoot.

There seemed to be little resistance from his adversary as he shook the knife loose from the Indian's hand. When he stuck the point against his throat, the man made no effort to defend himself. This lack of resistance caused him to hesitate and, since the man no longer seemed an immediate threat, Squint paused to consider what manner of being he was about to send to the great beyond.

"Why, hell, you ain't no more than a boy." He sat back on his heels, still astradle the Indian. "And a pretty damn scrawny one at that."

There was no response from the boy. His eyes, dull and lifeless, appeared to focus on some faraway object. It was obvious to Squint that he was prepared to die. In fact, he looked like he was two-thirds gone already. It was evident that he had mustered all his strength for that one desperate attack, and when it failed, it had drained him. Moments before, when they had struggled for possession of the knife, Squint could have killed him without thinking twice about it. Now, as the boy lay helpless beneath him, he was reluctant to dispatch him.

"What the hell did you jump me for?" Squint demanded, not expecting an answer for he spoke in English, even though he could converse a little in

Excerpt from *Wind River Country*

several Indian dialects. It was a little late for caution but he stood up and looked around to make sure the boy had acted alone. At the same time he kept an eye on his assailant, still lying there. Satisfied that he was in no danger of attack from another quarter, he turned his full attention to his captive. It occurred to him that the boy wasn't dressed too well for the chilly weather that had descended upon the valley for the past few weeks, wearing only a buckskin shirt and leggings. It was then that he noticed the dark crusted spot in the shoulder of the shirt.

"Damn, boy, looks like you been shot or something." This might explain the boy's apparent weakness. "Better let me take a look at that."

When he started to open the shirt over the wound, the boy recoiled in pain and made one feeble effort to resist.

"If I was gonna hurt you, I'da done kilt you," Squint grunted as he brushed the boy's hand aside.

The wound was bad. From the look of it, Squint guessed it was a bullet wound, and from the way it was all inflamed and swollen, the bullet was still in it.

"I tell you what," Squint decided, "that thing looks like it's festering and I'm gonna have to dig it out of there."

If he had any objection, the boy didn't register it. He didn't have any fight left in him and offered no resistance when Squint took his arms and pulled him up so he could heft him onto his shoulder.

"Boy, you ain't got no weight to you a'tall." He marveled that the lad had been able to summon enough force to knock him off his mule. When he realized how light he was, Squint couldn't help but feel a little sheepish that he had allowed himself to be taken so easily.

"Whoa, Sadie. Hold still." He spoke softly in an effort to calm the mule. Sadie still seemed a mite skittish, what with the smell of Indian still in her nostrils. Rolling back her eyes in an effort to keep the man and his burden in view, she attempted to sidestep her hindquarters away from him. He began to wish he had ridden one of his horses and left the mule back in his tiny corral. "Hold still!" A tiny bit of impatience crept into his tone as he grew tired of following the retreating beast around in a circle, the wounded Indian boy on his shoulder and the mule's reins in his free hand. Finally he gave the reins a hard jerk to show the reluctant mule who was boss and she kicked her hind legs once in response. But, after registering that one complaint, she settled down and accepted the load Squint slid off his shoulder onto the saddle. She grunted once more in protest when Squint stepped up behind the boy. He gave her a couple of hard kicks with his heels and she broke into a trot for a few yards, then settled down to a slow walk. Squint knew he could kick her till her slats caved in and she would still give him no more than a few yards at a trot before falling back into a walk. She would run, but only when she was with the horses and they ran. So he resigned himself to a leisurely ride back to his camp. "I hope you don't bleed to death before we git back." The boy drooped over Squint's arm, unconscious or dead, Squint wasn't sure.

As he settled his body into the rhythm of the mule's walk, he wondered what manner of creature he was bringing home with him. He wasn't accustomed to running into anyone this far up in the hills and he didn't particularly care to have anyone know he was even there, let alone take them to his camp. This was not the first time he had decided to winter in the mountains, instead of going down to one of the settlements until spring. He knew it wasn't a real good idea to winter in the same camp two years in a row. Somebody might discover it and lie in ambush

Excerpt from *Wind River Country*

for you the next year. But this one was so well hidden he figured the odds were good that he was still the only man who had set foot in the small ravine he had stumbled on while tracking a wounded deer, two years ago this spring.

His mind returned briefly to that chilly spring morning. He had jumped the deer accidentally while making his way down through a stand of lodgepole pine, on his way to the river to water his horses. When the buck suddenly sprang from a thicket, he took Squint completely by surprise. He reacted quickly enough to grab his rifle and get off a shot, even though the animal was running directly away from him and didn't offer much of a target. Squint only had time for one shot. He hit him, but he didn't kill him. The shot caught the deer in the shoulder. The impact was enough to knock the deer down and roll him over, but he was back on his feet immediately and off again. Squint hated it when he didn't get a clean kill shot at an animal. That meant tracking him till he bled himself out and died.

He must have followed that deer for a mile or more before he lost the trail just on the other side of an outcropping of rock overlooking a stream swollen with winter's runoff. There was no sign of the wounded animal anywhere. Beyond the stream, a clearing stretched for a quarter of a mile. If the deer had crossed the stream, Squint would have been able to see him long before he reached the other side of the clearing. He was sure he had not lost the trail up until he had reached the rock outcropping. There was no other place for the buck to go, unless he went straight up the side of a cliff. If it had been a bighorn, that would have been a possibility, but a deer? Squint didn't think so. Still, there was no deer.

Feeling as though he had been totally bamboozled by a dumb animal, Squint dismounted, for his horse was having difficulty maintaining sure footing on the rock. As he led him back the way they had come, he stumbled and would have fallen had he not caught himself with one hand. As he was about to straighten up, he glanced to his side at what he had thought was a little stand of pines in front of a solid rock wall. From his position, close to the ground, he was surprised to find that he could see daylight between the tree trunks. Instead of standing in front of a wall, the trees were in fact standing in front of an opening in the wall. The fact that there was a solid bridge of rock spanning the opening made if appear there was a solid wall behind them. Leading his horse through the trees, Squint found an opening big enough for two horses to pass through side by side. Once through the opening, he had found himself in a clearing, maybe half an acre in size. It was walled in by the mountain on three sides, with a small stream trickling through the northernmost point. The floor was carpeted with grass, and under a clump of low growing laurel, the deer lay dying.

A sudden groan from the Indian boy, as Sadie almost stumbled, brought Squint's mind back to the business at hand. Now, two years later, he was bringing another human being into his secret camp, although the wounded boy might be closer kin to the wounded deer he had originally followed here. He had to admit that he had some doubts about giving away the location of this place. If there ever was a perfect camp, this place had to be it. What with the trouble that was brewing all over between the army and the Indians, a man needed a good secure camp to hole up in.

Another groan from the Indian boy caused him to wonder if he wasn't just toting a body a helluva long way to bury it. *Probably should have just cut his throat back there and been done with it*, he thought. It was a useless thought because Squint couldn't bring him-

Excerpt from *Wind River Country*

self to kill a defenseless boy and that was what irritated him. "Too damn softhearted for my own good," he mumbled.

A low snort from one of the horses, probably Joe, told him that they smelled the mule approaching. He carefully guided Sadie over the rock and onto the thick floor of pine needles so as not to leave a track leading up to the entrance of his camp. As a matter of habit, he stopped at the opening in the rock and waited, listening. Joe snorted again and the mule answered. All seemed in order in his camp. Even so, Squint entered the clearing cautiously, looking first to the ledges over the opening and then toward the clump of laurel, behind which the horses were tethered. He always did this. Long ago he had inspected his little hideout from the perspective of someone who might have a notion to ambush him. He decided these two positions would be the most likely places to hide, so he always checked them first. Content that his camp was safe, he entered the camp.

Squint didn't know a helluva lot about doctoring but he knew enough to recognize an infected bullet wound when he saw one. Usually, if the victim didn't die right away, and the wound bled freely, it healed well enough if left alone. Sometimes, however, the bullet would be close to the surface and the wound would fester if it hadn't bled clean, like this Indian boy's, and it would be necessary to dig the lead out and cauterize the wound. It wasn't much fun for the person with the wound, but Squint didn't know any other way to stop the festering. He had seen it go untreated before and the result was usually the loss of a limb or worse.

After he had checked on the horses and unsaddled the mule, he went about building a fire and readying himself to take care of the boy. His patient didn't appear to be faring any too well and Squint wondered anew if he was just wasting his time. Maybe it would be more humane to simply leave the poor kid in peace and not complicate his dying. Still, he thought, the boy was obviously unconscious. The only sign of life was an occasional babble of some kind that Squint was unable to make out. It sounded like Cheyenne—he couldn't say for sure. At any rate, the boy was out of his head so it didn't figure to make much difference whether Squint dug the bullet out or not. The boy wouldn't feel it anyway, so he might just as well operate on him.

He took his skinning knife and cut the boy's shirt away, leaving the wound exposed for him to work on. It looked bad, swollen to the point that it looked like it was ready to bust open on its own accord, like a huge boil. He could see a dark blue spot in the center that had to be the bullet. It appeared to be just beneath the surface. Squint's experience with bullet wounds told him that it would be a lot deeper than it looked. He watched the boy's face as he stoned a keen edge on the already sharp skinning knife. There was still no sign of consciousness.

"Let's get it done," he sighed and wiped the blade of the knife on his leggings. "You're damned lucky you ain't awake for this."

Once resigned to the task, Squint didn't waste any time on gentleness. Human hide was tough and he sank the knife deep into the boy's shoulder at the top of the wound and then cut straight down across the entire swollen area. The boy stiffened perceptibly, but made no sound. Almost at once, thick, yellow pus oozed from the incision and Squint recoiled when the acrid smell of rotting flesh assaulted his nostrils.

"Damn!" he exclaimed and backed away for a moment before continuing. He cleaned the wound as best he could with a square of cloth. Squeezing the cloth out in a pan of water he had placed near the

Excerpt from *Wind River Country*

fire to warm, he wiped away the rest of the pus. The wound was still weeping, but now it was mostly blood. He probed in the wound for the bullet, but found that he had to cut deeper to expose it. The wound was becoming a bloody, pulpy mess and it was difficult to see the piece of lead he was groping for. Still, he was determined to dig it out. After inflicting this amount of damage on the boy's shoulder, he couldn't quit without retrieving the bullet. Finally, he felt the blade tick the piece of metal and, with the knife point, he worked at it until he had gotten it free of the surrounding flesh. After rinsing it with water, he held it up to examine it.

"That shore ain't no musket ball," he announced. It was a slug from a breech-loading rifle. "Army Spencer, more likely." Squint's interest was one of idle speculation. He wasn't really concerned with how the boy had come to get himself shot. Now that he had extracted the bullet, he concerned himself with the wound.

From the look of it, and certainly from the smell of it, there was a great deal of rotten flesh around the edges of the wound. *Little wonder the boy's so sick,* he thought. *It can't do him much good to have all that rot around that open wound.* He pondered his next move for a moment or two before deciding to proceed with the cauterization. He remembered seeing a medicine man in Wounded Elk's camp treat a lance wound that had festered about as bad as this one. He had stuck a handful of maggots right on the wound and let them eat away the rotten flesh. Squint didn't have any maggots. Even if he did, he figured that burning it away with a hot knife was better than maggots anyway.

Again, there was little response from the wounded boy when Squint applied the red-hot skinning knife—just a mild convulsive tremor before falling limp again. Since the response was so slight, Squint took his time and thoroughly seared the flesh over the entire wound, the smell of infection now masked by the odor of burning flesh. The surgery complete, he sat back on his haunches to examine his work. The boy was breathing steadily. The thought crossed Squint's mind that the boy might fool him and pull through. It was, after all, a shoulder wound. If he had been gut shot, his chances wouldn't be worth much. It would probably depend on the boy's constitution, and how badly he wanted to live. Time would tell. Squint had done all he knew to do for him.

He decided it best to leave the wound open to the air that night. He could put some grease on it and bandage it in the morning. The night air would probably do it some good, and this time of year, there wasn't any problem with flies getting into it. He rigged up a bed for the boy and covered him with a deer hide. Night was settling in over the mountains by then and Squint decided he had taken care of the boy as best he could for one day. If his patient woke up in the morning, he would see about feeding him. If he didn't, he would bury him.

The boy was strong. He was still among the living when the sun rose high enough for the first rays to filter over the mountain and illuminate the delicate crystals of frost that had formed on the grass floor of Squint's camp. Squint yawned and shivered involuntarily as he stood at the edge of the clearing and emptied his bladder, absentmindedly watching the stream formed by his warm urine on the frost.

Cold, he thought. *I hate being cold.*

He glanced back over his shoulder at the still form of the Indian boy. He had checked on him as soon as he was awake and, although the boy still seemed to be asleep, he appeared to be breathing easily. His fever might even be broken. Squint couldn't tell for sure. "I reckon I better put some wood on the fire and see about getting us something to eat."

As he picked a few sticks of wood from his pile, he pondered his options now that he had taken on an invalid. He was still not sure the boy was going to make it. If he did, then Squint would have some decisions to make as to what he should do with him. He wasn't even sure the boy wouldn't attack him again when he got strong enough. "Hell," he muttered as he balanced a stick of firewood across the load already on his arm, "I might have to nurse him back to health just so I can cut his throat."

He stirred up the coals, all that was left of the fire, until he worked up a flame. Then he laid some small sticks on it until they caught well enough to start up the larger pieces. He had a pretty good-size wood pile and, if the winter was not too severe, it should probably last him through. He didn't like to go out looking for firewood in the deep snow. As he stared into the growing flame, feeling its warmth on his face, he couldn't help but remember how he had sweated when he had cut the wood last summer. It had been a chore and Squint was not one to appreciate chores. "But, when you got yourself a year-round camp," he muttered, "you have to do things like cutting firewood and drying jerky." It was almost like homesteading. And the wood had to be hauled in by mule from the other side of the mountain because Squint was afraid he might give away the location of his camp by cutting wood close by.

A groan from the boy pulled his attention from the fire and he turned to look at his patient. The boy, still asleep apparently, muttered several words that Squint couldn't make out. But they were words. Squint was sure of that. They weren't just grunts. He still thought it sounded like Cheyenne. He bent low over the boy in an effort to hear what he was mumbling. As he did, the boy opened his eyes and he and

Squint stared at each other for a long second. There was a strangeness in the boy's gaze that confounded Squint. Finally he sat back and announced, "Dang if you ain't the first blue-eyed Cheyenne I ever saw."

The boy answered, his voice weak but clear, "I ain't Cheyenne. I'm Arapaho."

This served to startle Squint more than a little, not because of the boy's apparent lucidity, but because he had answered in English.

"Well, I'll be . . ." Squint gazed at the wounded boy in disbelief. "Well, I'll be . . ." he repeated, never finishing the statement. He simply stared at the boy for a long while. Finally he blurted, "Well, what the hell did you try to bushwhack me for?"

There followed a long pause, during which the boy gazed intently at the grizzled mountain man hovering over him like some great bear about to devour him. There had been a moment of alarm when he first opened his eyes to find the man staring down at him, a moment when he wasn't sure what was in store for him. But he quickly decided the bear intended no harm and he answered, "I thought you was a soldier."

Squint considered this for a moment before replying, "Well, any fool can see I ain't." He was trying to make up his mind about the boy. Based on his remark, he wasn't sure whether he was a good Indian or a bad one. He didn't know many Indians who did like soldiers, so he couldn't blame him for that. He had to admit that, since living in the mountains for most of the last twenty years, he wasn't sure he liked soldiers himself, and that went for settlers and prospectors, and railroads, and everybody else who was so damn hell-bent on civilizing the territory. He couldn't help but get riled up whenever he thought about it. If the damn government would just live up to their own treaties and leave the Indians alone, then there wouldn't be all this trouble that had

Excerpt from *Wind River Country*

been heating up over the last two summers. Now it had gotten so the Sioux were out to get any white man they saw, no matter whether he'd done them harm or not. It didn't take a genius to figure out that the Cheyenne, the Arapaho . . . in fact, all the tribes on the plains were pushed about as far as they were going to be pushed. There was going to be all-out war and he was likely to be caught in the middle of it. Realizing his mind was wandering from the situation at hand, Squint brought his attention back to his patient.

"Can you eat somethin' now?"

The boy nodded. His eyes betrayed the fact that the offer was met with some enthusiasm. It was not lost on Squint.

"I bet you ain't et for a spell," he said, "from the look of you."

Squint sat back and watched as the boy devoured half of a cold snow hare that he had cooked the day before. The other half had been Squint's supper. He had planned to eat it for breakfast himself but it was disappearing fast. It was apparent to him that the boy had not eaten for quite some time, small wonder he was so weak. Since one half of a rabbit wasn't much nourishment for a healthy young buck, much less one that was half dead, Squint dipped into his precious supply of baking soda and mixed up a little batter for pan bread. His pan bread wasn't the best in the territory but, by Squint's standards, it was passable. He poured the batter into a frying pan and set it on some coals at the edge of the fire to let it rise. When he thought it was ready, he pushed it closer to the fire to let it bake. The boy's eyes followed his every move. When the bread was done, he flipped it out and tore it in half. The boy didn't hesitate to accept the half extended toward him.

"You don't waste a lot of time chewing, do you? Just sort of choke it down like a dog."

The boy did not answer, but continued to stare at his benefactor. When he was finished, he indicated that he needed to relieve himself and Squint helped him to his feet. He almost fell when the sudden movement sent a stab of pain through his shoulder and Squint had to grab him to keep him upright. He seemed none too steady and Squint offered to help him over to the edge of the clearing, but the boy refused. He made it clear that he needed no help when taking care of nature's demands.

"You a might modest, ain't you?" Squint teased. He stood back and watched the boy stagger toward the woodpile. "Hold on to the woodpile for support. If you fall in your business, holler and I'll come pick you up." The boy made no response. Squint's attempt at humor was lost on him.

While the boy went about his toilet, Squint busied himself getting some jerky from a knapsack. Since the boy had done away with the rabbit, he would have to satisfy his hunger with cold jerky. Busying himself with the knapsack, he pretended to take no notice of the boy but, in fact, he was studying him intently out of the corner of his eye. The kid looked Arapaho right enough but, when he dropped his leggings, he sure had a pale behind. And pale behind and blue eyes sure as hell didn't add up to any Arapaho he'd ever seen. Squint returned to the fire and made himself comfortable. He watched the boy as he slowly made his way back to the fire and gingerly lowered himself to a sitting position. Once settled, he pulled his shirt away to examine his wound.

"It don't look too pretty, but it ought to heal up right proper," Squint offered in the way of explanation. The boy continued to stare at the fair-sized hole in his shoulder, already beginning to form a thin film of scab.

"Did you have to use an axe?"

He blurted it out so suddenly that it startled Squint

and he couldn't help but laugh at the boy's tone. He fished around in the pocket of his shirt and came up with a small lead ball. "Well, first I had to dig this out of you." He threw the bullet to the boy. "Then I had to burn the wound to keep it from going rotten. Like I said, it ain't pretty, but it'll be all right."

"You damn sure made a mess of it."

"If I had'na, you'da been a one-armed Arapaho and that's a fact."

The boy stared at Squint for a long minute while he evaluated the huge man's statement. Deciding that Squint had done what was best for him, he said, "I reckon I ought to thank you."

"You don't have to if it causes you pain," Squint replied sarcastically. The boy didn't reply, but shrugged his shoulders, wincing with the pain the movement caused.

They sat in silence for a long while, the boy obviously uncomfortable with the situation he found himself in, until Squint decided it was long past time for some introductions, as well as a general understanding as to what their relationship was going to be. He broke the silence.

"My name's Squint Peterson. What's yours?"

"Little Wolf."

Squint considered this momentarily. "Little Wolf," he repeated and paused again. "I mean, what's your real name? Your Christian name? Do you remember it?"

The boy hesitated, obviously reluctant to admit to owning one. The intense expression on Squint's face told him that he knew he wasn't a blood Arapaho. A frown creased his face as he replied. "I remember," he said softly. "It was Robert . . . Robert Allred."

"Well, Robert, or Little Wolf, whatever you want to call yourself, where are your folks?" He didn't wait for an answer before adding, "How long you been Arapaho?"

Excerpt from *Wind River Country*

The boy thought for a moment before answering. "I don't know. I lost track. I think this is the fourth winter, maybe the fifth, I ain't sure."

"Boy, where are your folks? You been living with the Arapaho for four or five years?"

"I been living with the Cheyenne. My father is Arapaho."

That would explain why Squint was certain the boy had been mumbling in Cheyenne when he was delirious the night before. The Cheyenne and Arapaho were longtime allies and quite often lived together. Squint continued to prod him for information. "Tell me how you come to get shot."

"Soldiers," the boy replied in Cheyenne, his eyes narrowed as he spit the word out.

"Soldiers?" Squint echoed. He knew that Cheyenne word well enough. He waited for further explanation, but the boy offered no more.

It was apparent that his guest had no use for the military, but Squint still had no way of knowing what he might have done to get himself shot. In his years in the mountains, Squint had occasionally run into white men who had taken up with a tribe of Indians. Most of them were a pretty sorry lot, as far as he was concerned. Some were hiding out from the law back east. Some were just living with an Indian woman temporarily. A few simply preferred the Indian way of life. Squint himself had considered wintering with the Shoshones, but decided he'd rather go it alone. He looked long and hard at the boy, trying to see inside his heart. He could see no meanness in the blue eyes that now gazed absently into the fire. For the third time, he asked, "Where are your folks? I don't mean your Injun folks. I mean your white folks."

"Dead."

Squint studied the boy's expressionless face for a moment. "How? How long?" It was obvious the boy wasn't much of a talker, but Squint was determined to get the whole story out of him so he kept prodding him with questions until finally he wore him down and he began to talk. It was difficult at first and slow in coming but, once he started, the whole story came out.

SIGNET BOOKS

☐ Black Eagle   0-451-19491-8/$5.99

When old-timer scout Jason Coles ended the rampage of renegade Cheyenne Stone Hand, he quit for good tracking outlaws for the army. Settling down with his wife and newborn baby, Coles plans to spend the rest of his days raising horses on his ranch. But that dream is savagely torn from him as his ranch is burned to the ground, and his family is abducted by the bloodthirsty Cheyenne Little Claw, out to avenge the death of Stone Hand! With the lives of his family at stake, Coles must once again strap on his revolvers to hunt a merciless killer!

Find out how the saga began with
☐ **Stone Hand**   0-451-19489-6/$5.99

CHARLES WEST

Prices slightly higher in Canada

Payable in U.S. funds only. No cash/COD accepted. Postage & handling: U.S./CAN. $2.75 for one book, $1.00 for each additional, not to exceed $6.75; Int'l $5.00 for one book, $1.00 each additional. We accept Visa, Amex, MC ($10.00 min.), checks ($15.00 fee for returned checks) and money orders. Call 800-788-6262 or 201-933-9292, fax 201-896-8569; refer to ad #SHFIC3

Penguin Putnam Inc. Bill my: ☐Visa ☐MasterCard ☐Amex _____ (expires)
P.O. Box 12289, Dept. B Card#_____
Newark, NJ 07101-5289
Please allow 4-6 weeks for delivery. Signature_____
Foreign and Canadian delivery 6-8 weeks.

Bill to:
Name_____
Address_____City_____
State/ZIP_____
Daytime Phone #_____

Ship to:
Name_____ Book Total $_____
Address_____ Applicable Sales Tax $_____
City_____ Postage & Handling $_____
State/ZIP_____ Total Amount Due $_____

This offer subject to change without notice.